W9-BLA-765

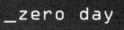

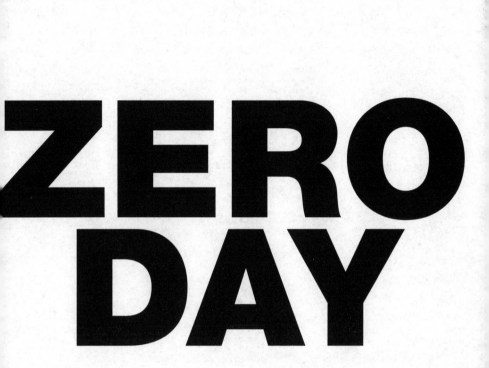

ZERO
DAY

JAN GANGSEI

HYPERION

LOS ANGELES   NEW YORK

First Edition, January 2016
1 3 5 7 9 10 8 6 4 2
FAC-020093-15288

Printed in the United States of America
This book is set in Calisto
Designed by Tyler Nevins

Library of Congress Cataloging-in-Publication Data
Gangsei, Jan.
    Zero day / Jan Gangsei—First edition.
        pages cm
    Summary: Eight years after being kidnapped, Addie Webster, now six-teen, resurfaces under mysterious circumstances, significantly changed, and her childhood best friend, Darrow Fergusson, is asked by a national security advisor to spy on her to uncover whether she is a threat to her father's presidency or the nation.
    ISBN 978-1-4847-2226-8 (hardback)
    [1. Presidents—Family—Fiction. 2. White House (Washington, D.C.)—Fiction. 3. Kidnapping—Fiction. 4. Spies—Fiction. 5. Adventure and adventurers—Fiction.] I. Title.
    PZ7.1.G357Zer 2016
    [Fic]—dc23   2015016310

Reinforced binding
Visit www.hyperionteens.com

SUSTAINABLE FORESTRY INITIATIVE   Certified Sourcing
www.sfiprogram.org
SFI-00993

THIS LABEL APPLIES TO TEXT STOCK

For Sven and Ava,
my heart and soul

PROLOGUE

Governor's Mansion
Richmond, Virginia

Darrow had her. He *finally* had her.

Addie Webster was so going down.

The two sat cross-legged on the floor of the playroom, a game of Connect Four perched between their almost-touching knees. This spot was one of Darrow and Addie's favorite hangouts. Once a generic meeting space, the room had been transformed the day Addie's father was sworn in as governor, and he'd ordered the law books, journals, and conference tables removed. Now it was packed with board games, Play-Doh, Legos, an easel stocked with paints and brushes, and big colorful carpets to sit on. Addie's cheerful drawings decorated the walls. The sound of her laughter echoed through the corridors.

Except . . . she wasn't going to be laughing in a minute. Darrow grinned and lifted his checker above the yellow plastic grid.

"Gotcha," he said, dropping it in theatrically. The red checker fell with a satisfying clink through the open slots and landed on top of Addie's black. One more turn and the game was his. He could hardly contain his excitement. Addie beat him at everything. *Every. Single. Thing.* Monopoly. Mario Kart. The fifty-yard dash. She could even burp louder. Darrow and Addie were best friends, but no nine-year-old boy wants to get schooled—over and over again—by an eight-year-old girl. Even one as cool as Addie. *Especially* one as cool as Addie.

Addie's mouth twisted to the side. She grabbed a black checker and twirled it between her fingers, inspecting the grid like some magical solution would present itself if she concentrated super hard. Typical. Addie always believed she could think her way out of anything.

"C'mon, you know it's over," Darrow said. "You've got no move."

"There's always a move," Addie said. She leaned forward, checker in hand. As she peered down the grid, her knee grazed the latch at the bottom.

Just like that, a dozen red and black checkers spilled out and tumbled across the floor.

"Oops!" Addie said, jolting back, a barely concealed smirk on her face.

"Oops?" Darrow scowled, incredulous. "I can't believe you just did that!"

"Sorry, Dare. Guess we'll have to start over." Addie shrugged.

"Start over? No way," he said. "I was about to kick your butt. You cheated!"

"Did not!" Addie protested. "It was an accident."

"Yeah right, Ad." Darrow rolled his eyes. "An *accident.*"

Darrow had known Addie forever, since her dad's first bid for office, when they'd ridden side by side in strollers along the campaign trail, dripping ice cream everywhere and poking each other with sticky fingers. And now, after playing more games together than he could count, Darrow knew one thing about Addie: she was just like Governor Mark Webster. Always had to win.

"Cheater," Darrow said.

Addie's face turned bright red. She stood up, planted her hands on her hips, and flipped her black hair. "I *don't cheat!*" she shouted. "And I was done playing this boring game anyway." She kicked the grid over and stomped out the door.

"Good! So was I." Darrow stayed on the floor for a moment, tossing checkers back into the box and grumbling to himself. Addie could be so annoying. Stubborn, impulsive, always wanting her own way. And she was constantly getting him into trouble. Like that time she'd decided they should hide in the back of the governor's limo, only to end up ninety-five miles away at a formal dinner for top campaign donors in Old Town Alexandria. Darrow's mom, who just so happened to be Governor Webster's chief of staff, was furious with him. *Furious.* He'd lost his Xbox privileges for a whole month because of that stunt.

But... Addie was funny. And smart. And could climb a tree better than any girl—or boy—Darrow had ever known. Not to mention, she always had his back. There was that time Parker Carrington had stolen—and broken—the brand-new remote-control helicopter their teacher had brought to class, and blamed it on Darrow. No one had believed he was innocent, except Addie. And she'd gotten revenge. When Parker wasn't looking during lunch, she'd loosened the top of his chocolate milk. One big shake and he'd gotten himself a faceful, along with a taste of what it felt like to have everyone snickering at him. The secret smile Addie gave Darrow afterward had entirely made up for being called a thief.

That was Darrow's Addie. Not afraid to stand up for what was right. Even if it landed her in a time-out. Although it hardly ever did—Addie was too smart to ever get caught. Darrow sprang to his feet. He couldn't stay mad at her. Not for more than five seconds, tops.

"Addie, hold up!" He ran into the empty hallway and searched left and right, but she was already gone. Darrow could hear his mother's lilting voice coming from the governor's office. He considered poking his head in and asking if they'd seen Addie, but he knew better than to interrupt his mom while she was working.

Besides, Darrow had a pretty good idea where she'd gone. Same place she always went when she got mad. Or frustrated. Or just wanted a break from the spotlight of being the governor's kid.

The tree house.

Yeah, right now she was probably flopped in a beanbag chair, polishing off their secret stash of M&Ms. He knew he'd better hurry or she'd finish all the blues, his favorite, just to spite him.

Darrow raced down the hallway, running straight into Addie's little sister, Elinor, who was coming up the stairs that led to the back door. She smiled shyly at him. "Hi, Darrow, wanna—"

"Not now," Darrow interrupted a little too quickly. "Have you seen Addie?"

Ellie was a year behind Darrow and Addie in school, and she was always trying to play with them. She usually couldn't keep up, though. Ellie was never as fast, never as smart, never—well, she just wasn't Addie.

Elinor shook her head. Darrow noticed something shiny and silver dangling from her hand. The butterfly locket Darrow had bought for Addie, with his own money, for her seventh birthday. It had broken just days after, and had to be glued shut. But it was still Addie's favorite necklace. She never took it off.

"Give me that," Darrow said, snatching it from Elinor's hand. "You know Addie doesn't like you touching her stuff!"

"But I just found it out here on the floor," Elinor said, looking wounded.

Darrow felt a twinge of guilt for yelling at her. He always forgot that Elinor was much more sensitive than her sister. "Sorry," he said. "We'll play later, okay? I've got to find Addie right now."

He left Elinor there, and ran down the stairs and outside to the giant sycamore that towered at the edge of the lawn. He stuck one foot in the second rung of the ladder and looked up. The sunlight bursting through the leaves blinded him momentarily. He rubbed his eyes and started climbing.

"Hey, Addie!" he said. "I'm coming up. I've got your necklace. There'd better be some blue ones left in there for me!"

No answer.

"Addie, c'mon," he said, pulling himself up rung by rung. "I'm sorry, okay? I don't think you're a cheater."

Still no response.

Darrow made his way to the top of the ladder, poked his head through the trapdoor, and blinked. The six-by-six room was empty, except for the stack of coloring books in the corner and the set of matching green beanbag chairs pushed against the wall.

No Addie. Weird.

Darrow clambered back down and ran through the yard.

No Addie on the swing set, trying to touch the clouds with her toes.

No Addie sneaking through the kitchen, getting bowls of popcorn and root beers so they could watch movies together in the theater room.

No Addie in her bedroom, playing on her computer. Or in the garden, collecting flowers. Or even hiding in the governor's limousine.

No Addie. Anywhere.

It took a good hour before it became clear she was actually missing. Not just off on an impromptu adventure, but *missing*. A crucial hour, police would later say. Long enough for the trail to go cold.

After that, time took on a strange shape, marked not by minutes, but blaring sirens, probing searchlights, candlelight vigils. As the hours turned to days, the gaunt faces of Addie's parents filled television screens across the country, begging for her return. It was a drama just built for cable news: the young, charismatic Governor Webster; his beautiful entrepreneur wife, Elizabeth Chan; the missing golden child. The speculation was breathless. Was it for money? Political revenge? Something more sinister? The Webster case became the most notorious celebrity disappearance since the kidnapping of the Lindbergh baby.

Except this time, there was no note. No ransom. No body.

Nothing.

All that remained for Addie's family and friends was a half-finished drawing on an easel. A swing creaking lifelessly in the breeze. A single moment when time had stopped, now circled forever in their memories with permanent ink, framing the *what ifs*:

What if I'd stopped reviewing the speech and checked on my daughter?

What if I'd delayed the meeting about the new software rollout?

What if I'd just let Addie win that stupid game?

Maybe she'd still be here.

From that day on, Darrow kept a red checker in his pocket. A chipped plastic talisman pressing against his leg, rough and cool beneath his fingers. Even as he grew older, he carried the thing, endlessly clinging to a child's hope that someday—maybe someday, if he was good enough, strong enough, honorable enough—he'd get a do-over.

One last chance to make his final move.

CHAPTER 1

The room was cold. The girl sat alone, shivering on a stiff wooden chair; the blanket draped around her shoulders did little to ward off the chill. Her green eyes were smudged with shadows, and her long, black hair hung listlessly around her pale face. She was maybe sixteen, but with a frame so slight that at the wrong angle she could be mistaken for a child.

Until she looked at you. Then for a moment she'd seem much, much older.

The wind howled outside and rattled the drafty windows. She wrapped her fingers around the Styrofoam cup in her hands, raised it to her lips, and took a sip. The coffee tasted like crap, but at least it was hot. It might have been spring somewhere, but here a light snow still dusted the streets and sidewalks, clinging to barren tree branches and the wrought-iron lampposts that lit the deserted town.

She shivered again, and her eyes darted to the old analog clock on the wall ticking away the time. The second hand twitched forward. Ten minutes past seven. She'd been here for almost three hours now in this lonely little police station, just off I-80 in the middle of nowhere, Pennsylvania. Her shoulders began to droop as her exhausted body got the better of her, until a door slammed in the other room. Voices echoed down the hallway outside.

"You picked her up on the highway?"

"Yes, sir. Flying J Travel Plaza. Clerk found her hiding in a bathroom stall at the end of her shift. Never saw her go in. Freaked her out. And the kid was totally spooked, too. Wouldn't come out, or even talk at first."

"How was she when you picked her up?"

"Still shaky, but talking. And, you know, telling us that story. . . ."

"Right. Where is she now?"

"Chief's office. Follow me."

Footsteps creaked on the old hardwood floors, stopping just outside the door. The girl sat up straight as a young police officer entered, the one who had picked her up earlier that day. He was flanked by a pair of men in dark suits, coiled earpieces tucked discreetly in place, the bulges of service revolvers just visible beneath their jackets. The girl pulled the blanket tighter around her shoulders, but didn't look away.

"Excuse me, miss," the officer said in his Pennsylvania Dutch drawl. "These folks have come up from D.C. to speak with you." He paused for a moment and positioned himself between her and the men, like he felt the sudden need to protect her from the tough guys in suits.

"You okay to go with them?" he asked.

The girl just nodded and stood, dropping the blanket from her shoulders, and followed the agents quietly out the door.

CHAPTER 2

A half-complete undergrad degree in computer science, $150,000 of student-loan debt, and this was all he had to show for it: a tray covered with lipstick-smeared wineglasses, dirty silverware, and plates dotted with shrimp tails and remnants of cocktail sauce.

The busboy weaved his way through the crowd. About two hundred guests were milling about beneath the glass rotunda of the Ronald Reagan Building's pavilion room, clinking glasses and giving each other congratulatory slaps on the back. The room was a huge circle, framed by tall windows and glass double doors, and filled with cocktail tables draped in red-and-white linen. Up front, a podium had been erected. There was a large screen suspended above with the familiar red-and-blue elephant logo and the words PATHWAY TO VICTORY! projected onto it.

The thing was some sort of fund-raiser, a cool thousand dollars a pop to share a few glasses of cheap wine and sweaty handshakes. The busboy shook his head as he cleared a messy table.

These guys threw money around just like they did crumpled-up cocktail napkins.

He balanced the heavy tray on his arm and scanned the room, recognizing several attendees—the Speaker of the House, the Senate majority leader, a couple anchors from right-wing talk shows. They didn't recognize him, of course. But why would they? He was a nobody. Just a nineteen-year-old kid named "Taylor." Well, not really. In his rush to get here, he'd left his own name tag at home. And instead of being written up by HR for a fifth time, he'd borrowed one from some girl who was ending her shift when he'd arrived. Curvy little blonde with a cute smile. He kind of wished he'd gotten her number. Because after tonight, he wasn't sure he'd be coming back to this dead-end job.

He kept clearing tables, eyes turned down, sleeves buttoned tightly over his wrists. These one-percenters might not acknowledge his presence, but they'd certainly notice—and disapprove of—the tattoo that snaked up his forearm.

A man in a black tuxedo with slicked-back gray hair walked to the podium. Christopher Burke, chairman of the Republican National Committee. He stood in front of the microphone and smiled, white teeth flashing against his faux-tanned skin. The crowd moved from the edges of the room and assembled in front of him.

"Thank you for being here tonight," he said. "There's never been a more critical time to come together and take a stand against the deeply misguided—and frankly, dangerous—direction this country is headed in. Within just two short years, the Webster administration has attempted to undo the work of generations of American men and women committed to protecting the country we love. Time and again, this administration has refused point-blank to take threats to our security seriously, even when our citizens at home and abroad—and our very way of life—are under attack. These policies appease terrorists and put Americans at risk."

Burke paused, eyes scanning the crowd.

"But all this is changing," he said. "Because the people have spoken. For the first time in eight years, we have control of the Senate. We have control of Congress." He paused again. "And in two more years, we will regain control of the White House!"

A huge cheer rose up from the audience. Burke let the applause ripple through the crowd, then raised his hands and motioned for silence as he began to speak again.

The microphone crackled. Without warning, the sound cut out. Burke's voice faded to a dull shout. He tapped the mic. It didn't respond. Burke tapped the microphone again, a confused look on his face.

The busboy, who was on the other side of the room now, smirked and set his tray on an empty table. His hand dug into his pocket, fingers gripping the pack of cigarettes tucked inside. It was time. If anyone asked, he was just going on a smoke break. He headed toward the exit.

But before he got there, the sound system suddenly crackled back to life.

"Good evening." The male voice emanating from the speaker was computer-generated and toneless. *"And thank you for your attendance tonight."*

The busboy jumped as the exit doors slammed shut, the locks clicked, and the overhead lights flickered. The room was abruptly pitched into darkness, save for a slant of moonlight that filtered through the skylight. A strange hush fell over the crowd, who were unsure whether this was part of the presentation or not. They began to mumble to each other. The man's voice returned.

"We have control of this room. Remain where you are and you will not be harmed."

There was utter silence, followed by several screams and a mass shuffle as people raced toward the doors. Every exit was locked. Panicked guests took out their cell phones, only to discover that there was no signal. They were trapped.

The voice returned.

"We said to remain where you are. *A bomb containing enough C4 to kill everyone in this room will detonate if you do not follow our instructions."*

A child's high wail rose above the sobs of several guests. A man corralled the people around him and began to strategize the best way to storm the doors. The voice screeched back over the loudspeaker.

"And if any of you are thinking of playing hero, think again." At that, the PATHWAY TO VICTORY image on the screen behind the podium disappeared. A live feed of the Pavilion Room streaming from the security cameras overhead took its place. *"We are watching your every move."*

A woman shrieked. More muffled sobs. The busboy glanced back at his discarded tray, wobbling precariously on the edge of the table.

He had to get out of here.

He crouched low, hiding beneath an empty table, then crawled on his hands and knees to the next. The service entrance was straight ahead, a narrow shaft of light filtering through beneath the steel door. The busboy palmed the card in his pocket and moved closer. All he had to do was make it there and he'd have a shot. . . .

He shimmied out from under the table, making sure to stay low until he reached the door. He held the card up, hand trembling so hard he was afraid it might not work. *C'mon, c'mon!* He waved it again, finally hearing the telltale click of the lock. Relief washed over him as he stood up and twisted the knob.

But before he could slip out, a large hand grabbed him by the shoulder. The busboy spun around to see a pair of wild eyes staring him down.

"What do you think you're doing?" It was Christopher Burke, slick hair disheveled, yellow sweat dampening the edges of his crisp white collar. "They said not to move. Are you trying to get us killed?" He gripped the front of the busboy's shirt, crumpling it in his fist.

"No sir," the busboy said. "I just need to get out of here."

Burke glanced over his shoulder, eyes still crazed, and said in a loud whisper, "Then take me with you."

The busboy shook his head. And with more force than he intended, he pushed the man away and dodged out the door. He heard it click shut automatically behind him as he ran down the hall, sweat trickling down the back of his neck.

On the other side of the door, Burke staggered backward, fury and disbelief mingling on his face—replaced by terror, as a loud boom sounded and the room filled with smoke.

CHAPTER 3

Special Agent Billy Murawczyk couldn't believe it.

He stood outside the interrogation room's one-way glass, observing the girl on the other side. She sat behind a steel table in the windowless room—a cold, clinical place hidden deep inside the Secret Service's D.C. headquarters. She shifted uncomfortably in her chair, picked at her nails, and took a sip from her nearly empty water cup. She glanced intermittently at the door, squinting.

Murawczyk felt a pang of sympathy for the kid. She'd clearly been through hell, regardless of whether her story was true. Murawczyk couldn't be sure of that yet. Sure, she looked the part—slight, with black hair, and eyes that showed some Asian heritage. But he'd seen enough leads go south in this case to approach every development with a healthy dose of skepticism.

He pushed open the door. The girl at the table looked up, momentarily blinded by the bright light streaming in from the hallway. She rubbed her eyes.

"Sorry. Hope I didn't alarm you, miss," Agent Murawczyk said.

"I'm fine," she answered, placing her trembling hands in her lap.

She didn't exactly look fine. But Murawczyk couldn't quite put a finger on how she looked. It was a strange cross between scared, determined, and—something else he couldn't identify. But he would. It was his job.

Murawczyk pulled out a chair and sat opposite her.

"Sorry to keep you waiting," he said. "I know you've had a long day, and we're going to get you out of here as soon as possible." She nodded and Murawczyk slid a tape recorder on the table between them. It scraped against the cool metal, making her flinch.

"I know you've already gone over this before," he said. "But I just need to get your story again. For the record. Okay?"

"Okay," she said.

Murawczyk pushed the *record* button. "This is Special Agent William Murawczyk, U.S. Secret Service." He tilted his head toward the girl. "Could you please state your name, miss?"

"Addie Webster," she said.

"Addie Webster," Murawczyk repeated. Eight years. Eight freaking years with no sign of Adele Webster, and now this. Murawczyk sucked in a breath and ran his eyes over the wisp of a girl seated in front of him. He knew he had to choose his words carefully. If she truly was the president's kidnapped daughter and he pushed *too* hard, adding trauma on top of trauma, they'd be serving Murawczyk's head on a platter at the next state dinner. But if he let an imposter gain access to the most powerful man in the world, Murawczyk would spend the rest of his career guarding doddering former First Ladies.

"Thank you, Miss Webster. Or do you prefer Addie?"

"Addie's fine," she said. "Thanks."

"Okay, Addie. I'd like to ask you a few questions today," Murawczyk said.

"Sure, okay," she said with a small sigh. "But I've already told you guys everything I know. I'm not sure what else I could possibly say."

"Understood," Agent Murawczyk said. "I know you've been here a long time, and I apologize for that. But I'm sure you also understand that we need to take every precaution when it comes to safeguarding the president. And his family, of course."

"Where do you want me to start?" the girl said.

"Let's start with the present and work our way back," he said. "First, tell me how you ended up at the Flying J this afternoon."

She nodded. "David and Helene needed to go into town for supplies," she began.

Murawczyk interrupted. "Those are the names of the people who took you?"

"Yes," the girl said. "Those may not be their real names, though. I'm not sure. They always made us call them Mother and Father."

"Made who call them Mother and Father?" Murawczyk said.

"Me," she said. "And the other kids in the house."

"There were other children? How many?"

"Three," the girl said.

"And were these David and Helene's own children?" Murawczyk said.

"I think so," she replied. "They treated them that way. At least, I was the only one they kept isolated." She shuddered.

"Okay, let's continue," Murawczyk said. "So you went into town for supplies. When was that?"

"Early this morning," the girl said. "They only go in once or twice a year, and usually don't bring us along. But something had gotten them all freaked-out today and they didn't want to leave us home. Something about the government coming to get them, and take us all away. They get like that a lot. Paranoid about stuff. When we got into town, they went into this big feed and grain store and told us to stay in the car. They told the oldest kid to watch us and not open the door for anyone."

She paused and took a shuddering breath.

"Are you okay to continue?"

She nodded. "So we were sitting there when this big blue car pulled up in front of the store. Real official-looking. Then two men in suits stepped out and went inside. I realized this was my chance. I convinced the kids that Mother and Father were right—the government had shown up, and they were in the store to arrest them, and they'd be coming for us next. I told them we had to run. They believed me. But when we got out, I ran the other way. I spotted an eighteen-wheeler in the store's delivery area. The back was open, so I hid inside. When it stopped again, I was in Pennsylvania."

"Where the police found you," Murawczyk said.

"Yes."

"Okay. Tell me a little more about David and Helene. Any idea where they were holding you? Or why?"

She shrugged. "I'm not sure where we started out—we were only there for a couple of months. But later we were on a big compound, somewhere in West Virginia, I think. It was in the middle of nowhere, lots of mountains around it. They didn't get any mail. And they didn't keep license plates on their cars—said it was an illegal tax. Mother and Father—I mean, David and Helene—they, like, never went anywhere. They homeschooled us, raised their own food, used solar panels for electricity. Lived totally off the grid. They said the government was evil and they had to be prepared when society collapsed. We weren't even allowed to watch television. Just some old VHS tapes."

Murawczyk shook his head. There were some real nut jobs in the world, everywhere you turned. Like a damn hydra's head. Chop one off, and two more popped up in its place.

"So do you have any idea what they wanted with you?" Murawczyk said. This is where the story seemed weak. What the hell would these people be doing with Adele Webster, and why hadn't they tried to ransom her, or *something*, after all this time?

"They were part of some group," she said. "Something called Judgment Day? I don't know what their plans were, but once they had me, apparently they realized they were in over their heads. I overheard them..." The girl paused, her voice cracking.

"We can take a break if you like," Murawczyk said.

"No," she said. She took a sip of water. "They had me locked by myself in a room for probably two months in the beginning. I kind of lost track of time. But one day, I overheard them talking to someone else. The other person told them they had to kill me. I was a liability. So..." She took another sip, then coughed a little, like the water had gone down the wrong way. "So when they came to my room later, I was sure I was going to die." The girl looked at the floor, a closed expression on her face. "But they didn't do it. I don't know why. Later, I heard them tell whoever they'd talked to that I was dead. After that, we moved to the compound. They never seemed to communicate with anyone else again."

Agent Murawczyk flipped through his notepad. Everything she said was exactly on point with what she'd already told the other investigators. Which either meant she was telling the truth, or she was the one of the most skilled liars Murawczyk had ever met. And he'd met his share.

"Are we done?" she asked.

"Just a couple more questions," Murawczyk said. "Can you tell me a little more about the day you were taken from the governor's residence?"

She nodded, her eyes roving around the room as she thought back. "I was playing with my friend Darrow," the girl said. "And I went to go outside."

"Alone?"

"Yes, I was alone."

"And then what happened?"

"I never made it," she said. "Someone grabbed me before I got to the door and put something over my mouth. That's all I remember. I think I must have been drugged. When I woke up, I was in a small house somewhere, locked in a bedroom."

Just then, Agent Murawczyk's earpiece buzzed.

"He's here," a voice on the other end said.

Murawczyk spoke into his headset.

"Okay, thanks. Send him right in."

"Send who in?" she said. "My father? Am I finally going home?"

"No," Murawczyk began. "It's . . ."

Suddenly the door banged open. A man in a white lab coat strode inside, black case tucked under his arm. He nodded at Agent Murawczyk and pulled up a chair right next to the girl, scraping the metal legs loudly across the cement floor. A bead of sweat sprang up on her forehead and rolled down her cheek. She didn't even bother to wipe it away.

It was the first time Murawczyk had seen her truly unsettled. It was a risk, but he decided to let her just stay that way for a minute. If she was hiding something, now was his chance to get her to crack.

"Dr. Oliver," the man next to her said, extending a hand.

"Adele Webster," the girl answered, voice breaking.

"Yes, *Adele Webster.* That's what I hear."

Dr. Oliver set the case on the table and flipped it open, exposing a row of syringes, vials, and blue rubber tourniquets. He pulled out a long needle and held it directly in front of his face. The girl recoiled, folding her knees under her chin and wrapping her arms tightly around her legs. She started to shake uncontrollably.

"What are you doing?" she said, voice quivering. "Please— no. I'll tell you anything, you don't have to—" She looked pleadingly at Agent Murawczyk. "Please, stop him," she begged.

"It's okay," Murawczyk said, placing his hand on her arm. "He's not going to hurt you."

The girl unwrapped her arms and slowly slid her feet back to the floor. But her legs still trembled, and her eyelids fluttered a bit too quickly. "What is that? Truth serum? I swear I'm telling you the truth."

Murawczyk didn't answer. He just let the girl's words hang

there for a moment. Most people couldn't resist the urge to fill the silence. He'd caught more people in lies by just saying nothing.

But this girl was different. She simply stared at Murawczyk with big, unflinching eyes.

"It's not truth serum," Murawczyk said, and watched the girl's shoulders relax. "We just need to draw some blood. It's for a DNA test."

Dr. Oliver nodded. "Right arm, please."

Without speaking, she stretched her arm across the table, palm up. In one quick motion, Dr. Oliver tied a tourniquet around her bicep, tore open an alcohol pad, and swabbed her inner elbow.

"Make a fist," he said.

The girl did as instructed and the blue vein bulged. As Dr. Oliver leaned forward with the needle, she looked across the room at her reflection in the two-way mirror. Agent Murawczyk watched carefully as the two girls regarded each other. Con artist versus victim. Truth-teller versus gifted liar. But which was it?

On the other side of the glass, President Mark Webster was watching, too. He leaned forward, flanked by a pair of Secret Service agents, and searched the girl's green eyes. She blinked a few times and bit her lip. For a moment, the president could have sworn she was staring right at him, silently pleading for his help. Just like Addie had used to at the dinner table when she was a little girl and didn't want to eat her peas.

The agent to President Webster's left reached a hand to his

earpiece. His eyebrows pushed together. He tapped the president's shoulder.

"Mr. President, sir," he said urgently. "You're needed in the Situation Room. There's been an attack on the Reagan Building."

"An attack?" The agent nodded, and President Webster quickly gathered his things. As he left the room, he turned one last time to look at the girl. She quickly looked away and pinched her eyes shut as the needle penetrated her pale skin, sucking out a stream of thick, crimson blood.

And with it, the truth.

CHAPTER 4

The busboy heard the explosion, but didn't stop running. There was nothing he could do. He barreled down a set of stairs to the main level of the building and raced out the back exit on 14th Street. He could hear the wail of sirens getting closer. Police. Firefighters. Probably FBI and Secret Service. The busboy didn't want to be anywhere nearby when they showed up. He could still see the horrified look on that guy's face when he'd closed the door on him, and he wasn't exactly proud of his actions. He hadn't expected something to actually blow up.

He sucked in a breath and hurried out onto the sidewalk. A dark sedan was parked on the street nearby. As the busboy started walking, its headlights flicked on, startling him. The car pulled out. The busboy turned down a side street and the sedan turned, too, moving slowly and deliberately behind him. The cool night air stabbed at his lungs as he struggled to breathe. Was it following him?

He could see Pennsylvania Avenue up ahead. If he could make it there, he could get to the Metro. He started to regret leaving the event room the way he had. Their instructions had been clear. *Remain where you are.*

The busboy broke into a sprint, dodging down Pennsylvania Avenue, the car still on his tail. Sweat trickled down the side of his face and into his eyes. He needed somewhere to hide. A pedestrian walkway led to the Woodrow Wilson Plaza. He ran down it and tucked himself behind a huge archway, breathing heavily, and counted to a hundred. He peeked back at the street and watched as the car rolled slowly past and disappeared into traffic.

Not waiting a beat, the busboy threw his name tag to the ground and ran straight to the Federal Triangle Metro station. He didn't slow down until he'd collapsed into a seat on the Orange Line headed east. Catching his breath, he leaned back and rolled up his sleeves, exposing the tattoo on his forearm he'd worked so hard to keep hidden all night—the three heads, fangs bared; the jagged tail snaking all the way to his elbow.

The phone in his back pocket buzzed. He pulled it out. It was a message. From them. He hoped they were satisfied. He'd left the tray with the device right where they'd told him to. Maybe now, he'd move from the ranks of a foot soldier to a more important role. . . . With trembling hands, he read:

Nice work tonight. Did anyone witness you leaving?

The busboy hesitated. He'd carried out his mission. He'd acted for the sake of the greater good. The rest of what happened was his business.

No, he typed. *Clean escape.* And letting out a deep breath, he hit *send.*

Christopher Burke banged at the door the boy had just escaped through. How the hell had he gotten it to open? He coughed as smoke filled his lungs and tears stung the corners of his eyes. Hand over his mouth, he turned to face the chaotic scene. In the dim, smoky light he could see several people on the ground, hands clasped tightly over their heads. Several more were yanking at the balcony doors, frantically clawing at the glass that separated them from fresh air outside.

A woman lay sprawled on the floor in front of him, stockings torn, blonde hair fanned out around her head. Burke lifted his shirt over his mouth and made his way toward her. He reached out a hand and helped her to her feet. She had a small gash on her leg, but didn't appear to be hurt otherwise. Just suffering from shock. She fell against him, crying.

"What's going on?" she sputtered.

Burke shook his head. He had no idea. He could barely process it himself.

Just then, the overhead lights came back on, so bright the party guests had to shield their eyes. The robotic voice on the loudspeaker returned. The woman next to Burke shuddered.

"Consider yourselves lucky," the voice said. *"The bomb that just detonated wasn't real. A harmless prop. But had we wanted you dead, you would be. Never forget."*

With that, the doors surrounding the room swung open at once. As partygoers raced for the exits, screaming and pushing, tripping over each other in their rush to escape, the screen above the podium changed one more time. A message appeared, written in bold black letters against a white background:

YOU HAVE BEEN WARNED.

CHAPTER 5

"*Addie!* I'm Addie Webster, I—"

She bolted straight up in bed, drenched in sweat, heart pounding, completely disoriented. She could tell it was late. The room was dark and strangely quiet. But she had no idea where she was—or even worse, if she'd just shouted out loud.

There was a loud rap on the closed door.

A bead of sweat rolled down her cheek. Shit. She had. She gathered the covers to her chest and swallowed a scream.

"Are you okay in there, miss?" a voice said. The door opened a crack. In the dim light, she could see the outline of a crew cut, crisp white shirt, the telltale earpiece. Secret Service. In a rush, it all came back to her. She was in a small house, somewhere off the Capital Beltway in suburban Virginia. They'd taken her here last night after hours of questioning at Secret Service headquarters.

Since then it had been more questions, along with visits from sketch artists, doctors, psychiatrists. She knew they were just trying to collect information, put together things that would help their investigation. But she couldn't help but feel like they were trying to confuse her. Trip her up. Get her to admit she was something she wasn't. Crazy. An imposter. A fraud.

"Do you need anything?" the agent asked, face earnest. All of these Secret Service types looked the same to Addie. Smooth cheeks, clipped hair: clean-cut all-American.

Addie took a deep breath. "I'm fine," she said. But her hands trembled, despite her attempts to hold them still. "Just a bad dream."

"You sure?" the agent said.

"I'm sure," she answered.

"Okay. You know where to find us if you need anything." The door clicked shut. She blinked and took in her dimly lit surroundings. Paneled walls, one bed, one dresser. No television. No computer. No windows.

Trapped. She was still trapped.

She sucked in another deep breath, wiped her palms on the sheets, and reminded herself she was okay. She was safe. She could get through this.

She'd been through far worse.

She put her head back down on the pillow and tried to go back to sleep. Pointless. Once she was awake, her mind started racing a million miles an hour. She wished she could shut it off, but it ran in an endless loop. All zeros and ones. Keystrokes and codes. Always going back to that voice. The familiar whisper in her ear that made her spine straighten automatically, her body primed for action—or punishment.

Don't run.

Or there'd be a price to pay.

There was no way she'd get any sleep now. So she climbed

from the bed and stretched out, back pressed to the floor, knees tucked up, arms at her side. Exhaling, she counted out crunches.

One, two, three, four...

Exercise always made her feel better. Her own secret strength. Something no one could steal. She moved quietly and efficiently, with the grace and speed of a natural athlete. As she curled into herself, every muscle contracted with perfect precision.

Forty-seven, forty-eight, forty-nine, fifty...

She flipped onto her elbows, popped up on her toes and stretched into a rigid plank. *Breathe in through the nose, out through the mouth. In. Out. In. Out.* She closed her eyes.

As her core tightened, her mind relaxed.

Strength is power. Power is strength.

She exhaled and transitioned to mountain climbers, drawing her knees one at a time to her chest and back. Her quads burned and her breath stuttered. But she didn't stop. She kept going, harder now. She dropped into a set of push-ups. Sweat dripped from her biceps. With each rep, she felt herself growing stronger. Faster. Unstoppable.

Because the next time she had to run, there was no way she'd get caught.

CHAPTER 6

Darrow Fergusson stood in his bedroom directly in front of his desk, squeezing the red checker in his hand so hard it left groove marks along his fingers. Eight years—eight years, and now this. He could barely wrap his mind around the possibility of it.

He stared at the Georgetown Hoyas poster hanging in front of him. He'd tacked it up at the beginning of junior year, when he'd started his early admission application process. Only his mother, and Elinor, knew what was hiding underneath the cartoon bulldog. His stomach knotted as he thought of the last time Elinor had been in this room; the taste of her sour-apple lip balm, the feel of her silky golden-brown hair between his fingers. The look on her face when she said it was over. Was there anything in his life he hadn't managed to screw up?

With one swift motion Darrow ripped the poster away. As it fluttered to the carpet, the past he'd tried so hard to leave behind was exposed. Darrow scanned the faded map of the world, curling at the edges, that hung in front of him. He'd tacked it above his desk when he was only nine. He still remembered when it had been crisp and new, back when he'd woken up every morning thinking: *Maybe today. Maybe today they'll find Addie.* Over the years, he'd carefully marked it with red Xs—one for every place his childhood best friend had allegedly been seen. Prague. Milan. Stockholm. London. San Francisco. Even upstate New York, a small town in Texas, and the remote Caribbean island of Bequia, where someone resembling Addie had been spotted by a half-dozen witnesses running through the J. F. Mitchell Airport.

But just like every other lead, it had been a dead end. Another X on a trail of dots that led nowhere. One day when he was thirteen, he had ripped the map off the wall and torn it in half, only to clumsily tape it back together and put it back up, tears streaming down his face. There hadn't been a lead on the Addie Webster case in four years.

Until now.

Darrow's heart pounded inside his chest. He grabbed a pen and marked another X—right in the center of the nation's capital. Right *here.* He couldn't believe Addie might actually be mere miles from his P Street row house in Georgetown. He wondered if he'd recognize her. He liked to think he would know those green eyes anywhere.

But time changed people. He doubted she would recognize him. He was seventeen now, tall and lean, with a muscular build that came from rowing crew in the spring and playing lacrosse in the fall. He was too big for tree houses and backyard swings. Too big for board games and freeze tag. His voice was deep, and he didn't make wishes on shooting stars anymore. He had grown from a lanky kid into a darker version of his blue-eyed, blond-haired father, the minor-league baseball player who had walked out on Darrow and his mother to chase his big-league dreams when Darrow was only four.

Darrow stood there a moment longer, then pulled his backpack from his chair and started stuffing books inside. He was running late and had a history test first period. Of course, he could probably give some bullshit excuse and Mr. Polanco would eat it up. Teachers loved him; trusted him. They had no idea how close he'd come to blowing everything. And all because of Addie Webster. Well, he wasn't going to flunk AP Euro and lose his early acceptance to Georgetown over her, too.

He slung the backpack over his shoulders and turned to look one more time at the wall. *Addie.* He was about to leave when his mother appeared in his doorway dressed in her D.C.-gray suit, briefcase slung over one shoulder, her thick, dark hair straightened and knotted at the nape of her neck.

"Hey, Mom," he said. "Thought you'd left for work already."

"On my way," she said. "Just wondered if you had a minute?"

"Yeah, sure." Darrow said. His mom walked in and gave him a quick hug, before pulling back and giving him a long, searching look.

"What?" he asked, uncomfortably aware of the time.

"I think you grew another couple inches overnight," she said with a sigh.

Darrow groaned, even though ironically enough, his mother was probably the only adult in the world who didn't completely annoy him. When he'd filled out his college application, he'd written his personal statement about her: Cheryl Fergusson, his hero, the first African American and first female chief of staff for a U.S. president, all of which she'd accomplished while raising Darrow alone. He'd meant it, but at the same time he knew it was exactly the sort of thing college admissions boards ate up.

His mom set her case down on Darrow's desk. Her eyes flicked straight to the map above it. Darrow knew Addie's disappearance had probably hit his mother nearly as hard as it had him. Her relationship with the Websters went way back to their undergraduate studies at UVA. And Cheryl Fergusson had worked with Mark Webster since his early days as state senator, right on through to his meteoric rise to the presidency. She was both a friend and advisor, and had pulled Mark Webster's career from the ashes on more than one occasion, including six months ago when a cybersecurity scandal had threatened to derail his presidency.

"What do you think, Mom?" Darrow said. "Is it her?"

His mother's hand went to the thick silver chain around her neck. She rubbed it between her thumb and forefinger, as she always did when she was anxious.

"That's what I wanted to talk to you about," Cheryl Fergusson said.

"Oh?"

His mother dropped the chain and reached out for Darrow's hand. Suddenly, he felt as though the air had been sucked out of the room. Like a tornado was about to strike. The same feeling that had hit Darrow the day they realized Addie was gone. Only now . . .

"The president just called," his mother said. "The lab in Quantico completed the DNA analysis. Sweetie . . . it's Addie. I can't believe it. They finally found her."

CHAPTER 7

Special Agent Christina Alvarez drove up the tree-lined driveway and parked to the right of the single-car garage. As far as the neighbors were concerned, this simple 1960s brick ranch with its stone walkway and tidy garden was nothing more than the home of a reclusive old woman, who just so happened to winter in Florida and was regularly looked after by her government-employed grandson.

In reality, the Falls Church rambler was a Secret Service safe house, sometimes used to hide a witness. Sometimes used to keep a suspect quiet. Sometimes both.

But right now, it housed what was probably its most famous resident ever.

Agent Alvarez grabbed her bag and stepped from the car. She knocked twice on the front door. An agent she didn't recognize answered. But as soon as she walked into the narrow foyer she heard the familiar call.

"Hey look, guys—it's Big Al!"

Agent Alvarez rolled her eyes. "If it isn't Billy Boy," she

said to Agent Murawczyk, who was seated at the kitchen table with two other members of the president's detail, a deck of cards spread between them. Alvarez and Murawczyk had gone through qualifications together, where she'd earned her ridiculous nickname courtesy of the fact that she was barely five feet tall, and at one hundred pounds didn't even weigh enough to donate blood.

"So they finally moved you off those bogus Gucci purse dealers, hey?" Murawczyk said.

"That would be ATM wire fraud, actually," Alvarez answered.

"See? Something to do with purses."

Alvarez ignored him. "Where's the girl?" she said.

"Secure bedroom," one of the other agents said, jutting his thumb over his shoulder. "Doesn't come out much."

"Yeah?" Alvarez said. "Can you blame her? Look at you three. It's like a bad frat party in here. All you're missing are some cans of Budweiser to smash on your foreheads."

"And a stripper. You ordered the stripper, right, Billy?" another agent said, elbowing Murawczyk.

"Shhh!" Murawczyk said with a snort. "Weren't you paying attention at the last sensitivity seminar? Hostile work environment. Right, Big Al?"

Alvarez flipped them off.

"You here to see if she'll open up to a girl?" another agent chimed in. "Have a little heart-to-heart on fake purses, see if you can bring things around to fake First Kids?"

"Hey, shouldn't you boys be out there looking for whoever fake-bombed that fund-raiser, not holed up in here playing

Go Fish?" Alvarez retorted. She knew it had to be driving them nuts. A terrorist attack right in the nation's capital, and here they were, sitting on the sidelines babysitting.

The boys went silent and Alvarez allowed herself a small smile. She could play the game as well as the rest of them. After all, she'd grown up with four brothers in a Marine Corps family. Knowing how to shoot, curse, and run fast were the keys to survival in the Alvarez house. All were traits that had served Agent Alvarez well since she joined the Secret Service. She'd been number one in her class—a better shot, quicker on the driving course, and just as fast as Billy Boy out there.

Which was why it burned Alvarez a little to get this assignment now—not due to her skills, but because she was a woman. And a young one at that. But the president had been very specific. After his daughter had been grilled by more than a dozen tough guys in suits, he wanted to send in someone who would come across as less threatening. Easier to relate to. Someone Addie could trust.

And Agent Alvarez wasn't stupid. She knew an opportunity when it came along. She'd show them Big Al belonged in this boy's club, along with the rest of those jokers at the card table who had no idea she'd just gotten the kind of assignment that would make any of their careers.

She stopped in front of the bedroom door, knocked, and waited. A small voice answered.

"Yes?"

"It's Special Agent Christina Alvarez, U.S. Secret Service. Do you mind if I come in?"

There was a brief pause. "Okay. That's fine."

Alvarez slowly opened the door. A girl sat on the bed, a magazine open next to her. She looked surprisingly small, legs folded beneath her, hands in her lap. But Alvarez detected a hint of something... strong in the girl's unflinching gaze. Like she might just challenge Alvarez to an arm-wrestling match. And win.

"Are you here to question me, too?" the girl asked.

Agent Alvarez shook her head. "No, I'm not."

"Oh. So did you bring me something to do? It's getting kind of boring in here. The wood paneling is attractive and all, but we're running out of conversation topics."

Agent Alvarez laughed. "Not surprised. I did actually bring you some fresh clothes," she said. "I'm sure you're sick of hanging out in Secret Service sweats."

"Eh, they're okay. Thank you, though. Is that it?"

"No, it's not," Agent Alvarez said. "I'm here because we got your DNA results back."

"What?" The girl sat up straight.

"Yes, Miss Webster," Agent Alvarez said with a smile. "Or do you prefer Addie?"

The girl gasped and jumped off the bed. "So you believe me now?" she said. "Am I going home?"

"Yes," Agent Alvarez said. "I'm here to take you to the White House. I mean, home. I'm here to take you home."

CHAPTER 8

For Addie Webster, life had always been divided into two distinct parts.

First the *before*: Addie, the eight-year-old daughter of the governor and the brilliant software developer. The little girl with the world at her fingertips, lollipops in her pockets, and songs in her head. Blissfully ignorant, innocent Addie.

And then the *after*: Stolen Addie. Terrified Addie. No—survivor Addie. The one who learned to see things for what they really were. Smarter, wiser Addie.

Only problem was, she'd never really considered there could be another "after." The thing she was living. The *now*.

Addie peered out the back window of the presidential limousine as it drove along Pennsylvania Avenue. The road was an eerie stretch of empty black pavement, devoid of any vehicles besides the advance car up front and the two that trailed her limo. The streets had been closed to traffic, a common and annoying occurrence for D.C. drivers whenever the president or some dignitary rolled through town.

But on the sidewalks and pathways, tourists stopped and

gawked, pointing at the motorcade. Addie slunk lower in her seat as the cameras clicked outside, even though she knew they couldn't see her through the heavily tinted glass. She reminded herself she'd better get used to the glare of the flashes. The spotlight was going to be on her now.

Agent Alvarez sat next to her. After giving Addie time to shower and change, the fleet had arrived to pick them up. Alvarez didn't say much. She was busy watching the scene outside as well. But with a different purpose, Addie knew. Alvarez's job was to make sure nobody got to Addie ever again.

Like protecting her now would somehow erase the past eight years. It was too late. They had failed.

And they would fail again. That was one thing Addie knew beyond a shadow of a doubt. The knowledge had been bone-deep for half of her life now: no amount of security in the world would ever keep her safe.

Addie crossed her arms over her chest and hugged herself. The motorcade approached the White House gates and rolled inside. As the huge columned building rose above her, looming larger the closer they got, Addie's palms began to sweat. She wiped them on her legs.

Agent Alvarez spoke into her mouthpiece.

"This is Alvarez," she said. "Songbird has landed."

"Songbird?" Addie said.

"That's your Secret Service nickname," Alvarez explained. "You know, like Adele, the singer."

"Oh. I don't know her," Addie said, even as "Rolling in the Deep" started looping through her mind. "What do you call the president?"

"He's Spider," Alvarez said.

Addie nodded. "I get it. Webster. That's good."

"No, it's not," Alvarez said with a grin. "Luckily he has other guys to write his jokes. All we have to do is keep him safe."

Addie smiled. She kind of liked Alvarez. She wasn't like the other agents. Addie took a deep breath as the limousine pulled into the secure garage.

"Okay, it's time to go inside," Agent Alvarez said. "I'll escort you to the elevator, and the agent on duty will bring you up to the residence. I'll be with the rest of the detail monitoring the situation if you need me. Got it?"

Addie nodded. But her breath caught in her chest. Every noise was amplified: the sound of the limo rolling to a stop, the driver's door opening and banging shut. Still, nothing could drown out the thump of her own heart pounding in her ears. Her car door was flung open and Addie recoiled from the hand that was reaching in to help her out.

"You going to be okay?" Alvarez asked, looking at her closely. "I can go up with you if you'd like."

"No," Addie said. "I'll be fine." She pinched her eyes shut for a moment before steeling her resolve and swinging her legs from the limo, feet hitting the smooth concrete of the garage floor.

I'll be fine. I'll be fine.

She had to be fine. There was no other choice.

There was before. There was after.

And this was now.

Songbird had landed.

CHAPTER 9

As the wood-paneled elevator rose inside the official residence, so did Addie's pulse. Ground floor, first floor, second floor. *Ding.* The elevator stopped and the door slid open.

A vestibule was straight ahead. In it were the president, the first lady, and a little girl with pigtails wedged between them. Addie froze momentarily as they all stared at each other. She couldn't quite believe they were real. A memory suddenly overwhelmed her: eleven years old, in the dark of her bedroom. The moment she realized she couldn't conjure up her mother's face in her head, couldn't recall the sound of her voice. Addie hadn't cried. *Good,* she remembered thinking. *She belongs in the past.* Addie had given up on looking up any photos or videos of them and Elinor—or her new sister—by then. *He* had a browser-history recorder that even Addie couldn't bypass. He always knew. And always made her regret it. Over the years, Liz and Mark Webster had faded into ghosts.

But there they were, huddled together with her replacement—Ellie conspicuously absent—looking at her like *she* was the ghost. Addie noticed the president's hair had grown gray around the temples, making him look . . . not exactly older, just more presidential. And while her mother's jet-black hair hadn't turned gray, there were a few more lines around her mouth, and faint creases by her eyes. Remnants of a million smiles, laughs, and tears that Addie had missed.

Addie's legs shook. She suddenly felt like she was eight years old again, crying for her mother in the darkness, trying to claw her way from the trunk of the car. She fought to regain her composure, telling herself she wasn't a little girl anymore, and took a measured step forward. The pigtailed girl hid her face in the president's pant leg.

"Mom? Dad?" Addie choked out.

But before she could say another word, her mother rushed at her, wrapping her in a tight embrace. "Addie. My baby. Oh my God." She buried her face in Addie's hair and breathed in deeply. "It's really you. You still smell the same. I can't believe it. I never thought I would—I would—" Her mother's quiet sobs sounded foreign to Addie, her voice like a stranger's. But she tucked Addie's hair behind her ears with those slender-fingered hands, that achingly familiar gesture—

It took Addie a moment to recognize the painful swell inside her chest that made tears sting her eyes. It swept over her like waves crashing over rocks, and she felt her whole body go limp as she rested her head on her mother's shoulder. *Relief.* A voice inside her that she thought had died long ago whispered: *It's finally over. You're safe.* Another set of arms wrapped tightly around them. The president's. He kissed the top of Addie's head. They stood there for several minutes, just clinging to each other and crying.

No. This was all wrong. She'd prepared for this. She needed to be in control. Yes, she should be crying... but not like this. She willed herself to stop as soon as possible. Real tears only got you hurt.

"Addie," the president said. Her name caught in his throat. He coughed and tried again. "I can't believe it. Sweetie, I've missed you every day...."

Addie looked up, disoriented. Somehow the memory of his voice didn't seem as muddled by the years. It was soft and gravelly, so different from the one he used for stump speeches and television ads—the only times she'd heard him speak in the past eight years. "I know," she said. "So have I. I can't—I don't even know what to say."

The president was very still, gazing at Addie like she might disappear again at any moment. "You're home," he said, brushing the tears off her cheek. "That's all that matters. All that matters is you're home now."

Addie felt her back stiffen. The past eight years mattered. They mattered a hell of a lot more than the first eight. And did they really think that Addie *wouldn't notice* that Elinor wasn't there? She tried to shake off her momentary weakness as her mother nodded and wiped her own face with the back of her hand.

"Addie, there's someone we'd like you to meet." Her mother waved to the pigtailed girl, who was now standing by herself on the opposite side of the vestibule. She watched them with big hazel eyes and an expressionless face.

"Mackenzie," Addie's mother said. "Come say hello to your sister, Addie."

Mackenzie walked over, staring at Addie the entire time.

Addie kneeled face-to-face with the little girl. She looked so much like Addie at that age, it was like a tiny stab in her heart. As though the *before* was standing right in front of her.

"Hi, Mackenzie," she said. "It's nice to meet you. I always wanted another sister."

Addie glanced over her shoulder at her mother. "Where's Ellie?"

There was silence for a moment, before the president said, "She's away. At boarding school."

Addie's jaw clenched. Only home for ten minutes, and already they were lying to her.

"She can't wait to see you, though," her mother said. "She'll be home as soon as we can get her here. It's just . . . complicated. . . ." Liz's eyes flicked to Mackenzie. The little girl was studying Addie intently.

"What are you doing here?" she said.

"What?" Addie blinked and stood up. Liz Webster scooped Mackenzie into her arms.

"Mackie, we talked about this," she said. "Addie lives here now. She's your sister." The little girl buried her face in her mother's neck.

"I'm sorry," Addie's mother said. "This has all been a lot for Mackenzie to take in. Why don't we go inside? Somewhere we can all get to know—" She cut her words short.

Addie looked quickly at her.

"I mean talk," her mother said. "Let's go somewhere more comfortable than the elevator vestibule."

Addie followed her family through a long narrow room furnished with a grand piano, leather chairs, and built-in bookshelves. It was hard not to be distracted—and somewhat intimidated—by the opulence of it all. The Versailles drapes. The fresh flowers in heavy brass vases. The crystal chandeliers. This wasn't just any house. It was the White House. And now it was Addie's house.

The family walked through a set of arched doorways into a smaller, more intimate room decorated with an antique sofa and matching armchairs. Addie hesitated, unsure what to do with herself, then sat in a chair. The president sat opposite her. Mackenzie curled up tight into her mother's side on the couch.

The next hour passed with more tears, hugs, and forced small talk.

Yes, it's beautiful here. I would love to help select some artwork. Of course I'd enjoy homemade macaroni and cheese for dinner; it's still my favorite.

But it was the spaces between the words that held the most. Addie could almost hear her family crying out with every pause and silence: *What happened to you? Are you okay? Are you still Addie?*

In a way, she wished they'd just go ahead and ask; stop being so polite. Say something real. But she was sure they'd been coached: Don't push. Let her come around when she's ready. Give her time and space.

But it wasn't making Addie calm. It was wearing her out.

"I'm kind of tired," Addie said. "Is there somewhere I could rest for a bit?"

"Oh my goodness, yes." Addie's mother stood. "Why don't I take you to your bedroom? Then after dinner we can give you the grand tour."

"That sounds perfect," Addie said.

The president also got to his feet. "I'm going to pop

downstairs and check in with Cheryl," he said. "I'll be back up to join you for dinner. Macaroni and cheese, right? No peas." He smiled and hugged Addie.

"Wait..." Addie said as she pulled away. "Cheryl? As in Fergusson?"

"That's right. You remember," President Webster said. "She'll be glad to hear that. I know she and Darrow can't wait to see you. When you're ready, of course." Addie's heart skipped a beat. *Darrow.* The last familiar face she'd seen, *before...*

Would he even know her now? Maybe he'd forgotten all about her, too. Just like the rest of them. Carried on. Found her replacement.

Addie's mom nodded at Mackenzie. "You want to come with me to show your sister her room?"

The little girl shook her head and the pigtails flopped from side to side. "I've got homework."

"They give homework in kindergarten?" Addie said.

"I'm not in kindergarten. I'm six. I'm in first grade," Mackenzie answered. "And yes, they do."

"Okay, come with me, Ad." Her mother took Addie by the hand. Addie held on limply, letting Liz lead her back through the central hall and another arched corridor like she was Mackenzie's age rather than a sixteen-year-old. They stopped at a set of double doors. Liz pushed them open. Addie had to catch her breath. She'd seen some lavish rooms in her travels, but nothing compared to this.

Straight ahead, a huge four-poster bed sat in the middle of the room, with thick red brocade curtains tied back at the sides with tasseled ropes. A Louis XVI dresser, two side tables, and a matching desk completed the set. Gilt-framed art was displayed

46

on the walls. A crystal chandelier hung from the center of the ceiling, surrounded by an intricate leaf medallion.

"What do you think?" her mom asked. She almost sounded nervous. "We didn't have much time to set things up before you got here, but—"

"It's beautiful," Addie said.

"I know it's sort of impersonal right now. But we'll make it yours, okay?"

"Sure," Addie said.

"Let me show you a few more things and then I'll let you get some rest." Her mom led her through the room to a large closet. "I had some clothes delivered for you. I'm sorry, I had no idea what you like. I hope they're okay."

Addie cringed inwardly as she looked over the rows of dresses, knit tops, and leggings. She hadn't worn anything like this in years. Well, not since she was eight.

"They're fine, Mom," Addie said. "Perfect."

Her mother sighed. "No, they're not, are they? I'm sorry. We'll go shopping later, okay? And if there's anything you need, just tell me. Anything at all."

Addie took a deep breath. "Mom? How much have they told you about what—what happened to me?"

Liz's breath hitched, but she quickly arranged her face in a neutral expression. "I know a few things, baby. But you don't have to tell me anything you don't want to."

Addie nodded quickly. "I've told the Secret Service anything I can think of that will help find . . . *them*. But there are other things that won't really make a difference. . . ." She trailed off.

Her mother just looked at her, an open expression that invited Addie to continue.

Addie swallowed. "The worst thing, besides missing you, was just, like, the isolation. I feel like I don't know anything about the world, anything that's happened since—" Her voice broke. "I feel so stupid. I don't *know* anything anymore."

"Oh, sweetie." Liz took her hand. "None of this is your fault. The last thing you should feel is stupid. Let me see what I can do about getting you a computer, to help you get caught up on everything you missed. How does that sound?"

"Okay," Addie said in a small voice. Triumph washed over her.

Her mother sat down on the bed and patted the space next to her. Addie lowered herself onto a cloud-soft mattress, carefully leaving a few inches of space between them. The bed was so high off the ground that only her tiptoes reached the floor. Addie stroked the silky duvet cover, avoiding her mother's gaze. She needed to be alone. She needed to think. After all this time, Addie didn't know what she had expected, but it wasn't ... this. The awkward attempts at kindness; the haunted look in her mother's eyes.

When Liz finally spoke, her voice sounded stronger than it had before. "Kiddo, I know all of this is overwhelming—I know, well, there's a lot of catching up to do, and there's a lot I don't know about you anymore. But ... I want you to know that I'm here, whenever you're ready. I've missed you so much, baby. You're home now, and I promise it will get easier."

"Thanks, Mom," Addie whispered. The traitorous feeling, the *wanting* to believe her, was back, but Addie pushed it away. Things didn't get better unless you made them better. Which was exactly what Addie was going to do. Still, she let her mother fold her in her arms until a small voice interrupted.

"What'll get easier?"

Mackenzie stood in the doorway, a small teddy bear clutched in her hands.

"Mackie," Addie's mother said. She walked over, wrapped her arms around the little girl's shoulders, and gave her a hug. The girl stayed stiff and held the bear out to Addie.

"I thought you might want this," she said, walking up to the bed.

Addie took the ragtag bear in both hands and ran her fingers over its matted fur and scruffy face. The felt nose was rubbed away from all the times Addie had slept with him under her pillow. Her hand began to tremble as she remembered those first two months alone in that dark, silent room . . . the nights she'd ached to hold Mr. Fluff.

"This is really sweet," Addie said. "Thanks for sharing your bear. What's his name?"

"He's not mine, he's yours," Mackenzie said.

"Don't you remember Mr. Fluff?" her mother said.

"Oh, right." Addie said. "Yeah, I remember him now. It's been a while. Mr. Fluff . . ."

"I call him Brown Bear," Mackenzie said.

"I guess Mr. Fluff is a pretty silly name, isn't it?" Addie said.

Mackenzie nodded. "He's really not very fluffy."

"No," Addie said with a sad smile. "But he used to be. A long time ago." She rubbed Mr. Fluff's head and held him out to her little sister. "Here. I think you should keep him. He's Brown Bear now."

Mackenzie just looked at her with those wide eyes. "No," she said. "I don't want him. He's yours."

With that, she turned and walked out the door and back down the hallway. Addie bit her lower lip, put the bear on her dresser, and sat on the edge of her bed. Suddenly, Mikey's face popped into her mind. He'd worn the same wide-eyed look when they'd first met, too. Addie's stomach knotted and she angled herself away from her mother's gaze. She couldn't think about him right now. The day had overwhelmed her enough already.

"Addie, let me explain. About your sister." Her mother sat back down next to Addie and took her hands. Addie couldn't help but notice they both had the same long, thin fingers, nails bitten to the quick. Just like how they both had long, black hair that fell in waves over their shoulders.

As far as Addie knew, that was pretty much where the similarities ended.

"It's not you, okay, Addie?" her mom said. "Mackenzie is just...how can I put this? She processes things differently than other people. She's like a walking computer. Emotions are tough for her. Does that make sense?"

"I guess so," Addie said.

"Give her time. She'll come around."

Addie nodded and Liz inspected her face.

"What is it?" Addie said.

"Elinor," Liz said. "I'm sorry we couldn't give you a straight answer earlier. I know you saw right through it. We just don't like to discuss it in front of Mackenzie."

"What's the matter with Elinor?" Addie said, surprised by her mother's sudden honesty. "Is she okay?"

Her mother took a deep breath. "Ellie, she's—well, she's

been through a lot in the past few years. I don't want to overwhelm you, but it's not fair to keep it from you either. Your sister has struggled with addiction." Liz sucked in a sharp breath. "And a month ago, she had a dangerous overdose."

Addie's heart clenched. Elinor. Her almost-twin and constant shadow, always hidden in plain sight behind the glare of Addie's spotlight. It could only have gotten worse when Addie performed the ultimate attention-grabbing feat: disappearing. Addie pictured Ellie's honey-brown hair and gray eyes and wondered what the years had done to her sensitive little sister.

"Overdosed on what?" Addie whispered.

"She got hurt running track last year," her mother said, her voice faint. "Her doctor warned us that the pills could be addictive, but we never thought—"

Liz ran her hands distractedly through her hair, then put her hand on Addie's leg. "She's going to be okay," her mother said. "She's in one of the best residential rehab programs in the country. And she's so happy that you're home. She can't wait to get back and see you."

Addie nodded. "I can't wait to see her, too."

The phone buzzed in her mother's pocket. Addie watched her mother's face twist to the side as she attempted to ignore it. The ringing finally stopped, but immediately started right back up again. Addie's mother checked the screen.

"I'm really sorry, Ad," her mother said. "We've had issues with the transition at Nova ever since I stepped down as CEO. . . ."

Addie cut her off. "It's okay. You can take it. I'm fine." Of course it was work. Even though becoming First Lady had meant Liz Webster could no longer run the day-to-day operations of the company she founded, Addie knew her mother better than to think she could just walk away. Addie felt an insane urge to laugh at the familiar feeling rising up in her, the resentment she'd felt as a child whenever her mom automatically shelved whatever the two of them were doing for her work. Almost everything had changed, but some things never would.

Addie's mom pressed the phone to her ear. "Liz here." She leaned over, quietly kissed the top of Addie's head, and mouthed, "I love you."

Then left.

Addie leaned back on the bed and closed her eyes. She was surprised at how tired she actually was. When she woke up, the room was quiet. She looked at the clock, and saw she'd been asleep for a half hour. There was nothing to do besides stare at the ceiling, so she decided to walk around the residence and check things out. She quietly padded down the halls, feeling oddly like an intruder, even though technically this was her home.

She wandered past a variety of rooms, poking her head inside several living rooms and sitting rooms, and rooms that seemed to have no purpose other than to just hold more stuff. The sheer opulence of it all was breathtaking and disgusting at the same time: antique furniture, crystal chandeliers, and priceless art everywhere she looked. Didn't they realize how quickly all of this could come crumbling down?

She passed the dining room and kitchen, where she could hear the staff cooking and preparing the table for dinner. She headed back through the common area, passing the elevator and what she recognized from pictures as the Lincoln

Bedroom—maybe the most famous room in the White House residence, thanks to the fact that it was practically a hotel room for top campaign donors.

At the end of the hall, Addie stopped short at the sound of her mother's voice coming from behind a partially closed door. From the one-sided conversation, Addie could tell she was still on the phone. She was about to walk away when she heard her name.

"I don't think Addie's ready," her mother said.

Ready for what? Addie pressed her back to the wall, moved closer, and listened.

"I don't know, Mark," her mom said. It was the president on the other end. "I don't think it's a great idea. She just got here. We need to give her time to adjust. We don't even know—"

Pause.

"Yes, I understand the public will want to see how she's doing." Pause. "I know Cheryl thinks . . ." Another long pause.

"Look, Mark," her mother said, voice rising. "I read the psychologist's report, too, and I'm concerned. Yes, I know her answers were perfect. *Too* perfect. The doctor said they have control questions to determine when someone's trying too hard. And it was inconclusive, but they thought maybe she was."

The blood rushed to Addie's face. She knew all those people questioning her had been trying to trick her into doing or saying something stupid. And obviously, she had.

"Why don't you just do the press conference alone?" her mother said. "The public will totally understand that Addie isn't up to having a bunch of cameras in her face. I mean, who would be? Not after what she's been through."

Pause.

"Jesus, Mark." Liz sucked in a breath. "They think an appearance will prompt chatter in the terrorist networks? Why not just call it what it is? You want to bait these shits with Addie, and I'm not going—"

Addie rapped on the door, pushing it open. Her mom jolted and spun around in her chair. She was sitting at a large desk covered with stacks of paper and a computer. A pile of envelopes toppled over and hit the floor. It always amazed Addie that her mom could look so disorganized, yet had founded one of the most profitable companies in the world.

"Oh my God, Addie," Liz Webster said. "How long have you been standing there?"

"A minute," Addie said. Her mother's face grew pale.

"So you heard . . . ?"

"Enough."

"Honey, let me call you back," her mom said into the mouthpiece.

"No, wait," Addie said. "Is that Dad?" Her mom nodded.

"Good. Tell him I want to do it," Addie said.

Her mom's eyebrows knit together. "Do what?"

"The press conference," Addie said. "That's what you're talking about, right? A press conference about me? Tell Dad I want to be there."

"But, Addie . . ."

"No," Addie said, standing up straight. "Put Dad on speaker. Please."

Her mother set the phone on the desk and pushed a button.

"Addie?" The president's voice crackled through the speaker.

"Hi, Dad," Addie said. "I just told Mom, I want to do the press conference."

The president was silent for a moment. "Addie, honey, are you sure about that? I don't want you to do anything you're not comfortable with."

Of course you don't, Addie thought. That's why you were just arguing that I should be paraded around in front of a bunch of nosy reporters. Once again, Addie was witness to the many faces of Mark Webster: slick politician, caring father, chameleon.

"I'm positive," Addie answered. "This is important to me. I want the world to see I'm okay. And if it helps find the people who took me, even better."

Liz flinched. But Addie swore she could actually hear the president smiling through the phone. His approval ratings were going to shoot through the roof. And if he had any hope of being reelected after the events of the last six months, he was going to need the boost.

"Well, only if you're sure," he said slowly. "Websters are tough, but you know I wouldn't mind if you sat this one out, right?"

Now it was Addie's turn to flinch. But only on the inside. Outside, she smiled. The perfect daughter. Before. After. And now.

"I know," she said. "But it's important. To me." She backed out of the room, waving to her mom. "I'll see you at dinner. Sorry for interrupting."

The first lady hesitated, casting a concerned look in Addie's direction, then resumed her conversation with the president, keeping the phone on speaker as she typed up notes on her laptop. Addie moved to the other side of the door and listened. Her mom started going over the menu for an upcoming state dinner until the president broke in.

"Hey hon," he said. "I'm sorry. I've got to run. Cheryl is here. She's been on the phone with Jenkins at the *Post* all morning. Someone came forward to claim responsibility for Saturday's attack."

"What, someone did?" Liz said. "Who?"

Addie froze, leaning forward to listen to the president's response, but Liz had turned off the speaker.

"Cerberus?" Liz said, her lowered voice incredulous. "The anonymous hacktivist group? Why on earth would they attack a Republican fund-raiser?"

Addie longed to hear what the president was saying in response. Her mother began speaking again.

"Yes, but watch what you say, Mark," she said. "A few nutcases may not be a threat to national security, but they can do a number on public opinion. Look what almost happened six months ago. . . ."

Disgust rose up in Addie's chest. With everything that had happened, they were only worried about the PR spin? Addie turned in frustration toward the hallway. A set of big hazel eyes stared at her from the door to the opposite room.

"Mackenzie," Addie said with a jolt. "I didn't see you there."

The little girl didn't blink. "You really shouldn't spy on people, you know," she said.

"What do you mean? I wasn't spying," Addie said.

"Yes you were. I saw you," Mackenzie said.

56

"And how would you know that? Were *you* spying?"

"No." Mackenzie pursed her small lips. "I was just going to the bathroom. You shouldn't spy. It's not nice and it will get you in trouble. Dad says so."

"Am I in trouble with you?" Addie asked her sister.

Mackenzie narrowed her eyes. "Not this time."

"Phew," Addie said, pretending to look relieved. Her sister didn't crack a smile.

As she watched Mackenzie's small form continue down the hallway, the words came back to Addie as clearly as if they'd been spoken yesterday, even though she'd only been a few years older than Mackenzie when she'd learned the truth.

What would people do without anyone looking over their shoulder? Can you imagine that world, little one?

Mackenzie might not like spies, but she had no idea just how much she needed them.

CHAPTER 10

A hush fell over the crowd of reporters assembled in the White House Rose Garden as Addie walked out of the Oval Office flanked by the president and first lady, holding her little sister's clammy hand. They walked along the colonnade between the white columns and down the steps, picture-perfect: Addie in a gray Tory Burch dress, Mackenzie in Burberry plaid with a matching headband, President Webster in his usual navy suit, and the First Lady in a pale yellow sheath dress by Janie Liu, the latest up-and-coming designer Liz had decided to make famous.

Addie, her mother, and her sister sat in a row of chairs facing the audience. President Webster took his position at the podium, drew in a heavy breath, and briefly closed his eyes. When he opened them, he smiled warmly.

"Thank you," he said. "Thank you for joining me here on what has proven to be the most monumental week of my life. The end of a long nightmare, the worst any parent can face."

Addie watched his face work through a range of emotions: sadness, joy, determination. If he hadn't become a politician, he would have been one hell of an actor. He certainly had the part of "president" down—the full head of hair flecked with just the right amount of distinguished gray, the charming smile, the ability to make people he'd just met feel like they were his oldest friend.

In fact, as Addie looked around at the reporters gathered in rows of folding chairs before her, at the crab apple trees in full bloom around the garden, the whole event struck Addie as little more than a Hollywood production. She touched the back of her own hair, which had been brushed smooth of its waves and tucked into a neat chignon by a White House stylist. Her face was caked with high-definition makeup designed to make her look like she was wearing almost none at all. A hint of cherry-blossom pink colored her lips and cheeks, and Addie was certain that the dove-gray dress that had appeared in her bedroom that morning was the result of multiple conversations behind closed doors. The tasteful neckline, cap sleeves, slenderizing little peplum, and knee-brushing hemline conveyed just the right balance of innocent yet grown-up, demure yet strong. Addie hated it.

But in a way, that made things easier. She was merely dressed up for a show, scripted into the scene by President Webster's staff. A supporting role in the grand drama that was Mark Webster's life.

All Addie had to do was play her part.

Just as the president played his.

At the podium he paused, letting the silence dramatically fill the air. "Eight years ago, our precious little girl was stolen from us. Yesterday, I was reunited with the strongest and bravest person I know." His voice broke, and Addie could almost see the reporters leaning forward, hanging on his words. "Our Addie is finally home."

Cameras flashed. A chorus of voices began calling out. "Mr. President, can you tell us . . . ?" "Mr. President, where has she been . . . ?" Another reporter broke in. "Mr. President, what is your response to the recent attack carried out by Cerberus, and their assertion that your administration's intelligence failures are to blame?"

President Webster held up his right hand. "Please," he said sternly. "Out of respect for my daughter and everything she's gone through, I ask that we keep this conference on-topic, and that you refrain from asking questions at this time. My press secretary will be available afterward to answer your inquiries."

The reporters quieted.

"Right now," President Webster continued, "I would like to focus on moving forward. And to say how deeply proud I am of my daughter. Not only for never giving up hope, but for growing into the courageous young woman you see here. Despite everything she's been through, it was her idea to be here today. In doing so, she is a reminder to us all of the resilience of the human spirit. She is a reminder to me of everything that is right in the world. Addie"—he turned to face her, hand on his chest, tears in his eyes—"your mother, sisters, and I are overjoyed that you are home. Words cannot express how much we love you and have missed you all these years. We never gave up hope. And we will not stop until the people responsible for taking you from us are apprehended and justice is served."

Addie's mother wiped her eyes with the back of her hands. Addie's own hands trembled. But she knew what she needed to do. It was time. The family was heading to the Clifton house tomorrow morning, just as she'd requested. Clutching her fingers together, she rose to her feet.

"I'd like to say something, if I could," she said in a quiet voice.

"Of course." The president looked slightly surprised. He quickly moved over, making room for Addie at the podium. He held his arm out to her. Addie stood at his side.

"Thank you, Dad," she said. "Mom. Mackenzie. My sister Elinor, who couldn't be here today. And thank you to everyone for keeping up the search. For never giving up on me. It's what kept me from falling apart during the last eight years. Knowing that somebody out there still cared." Her eyes welled with tears and she gripped the podium. President Webster put his hand on her shoulder.

"You don't have to continue," he whispered in her ear. She shook her head.

"I do," she said, taking a deep breath and speaking louder. "Because I also have this to say." She turned to the reporters, looking directly into the television camera set up between the chairs. "To my captors: You robbed me of my childhood. You robbed me of my innocence. But you can never rob me of my family. Of love. Of who I am. Your actions cannot define me. Only I can." Addie held her head high, thrust her chin forward, and smiled, a single tear rolling down her cheek. She lowered her right arm, pressing her hand against her waist, and quickly opened and closed her fingers. Twice.

A thousand camera flashes went off at once.

It would become the picture of the decade, gracing a thousand front pages and magazine covers, playing on television screens around the world. . . .

Including the screen she knew someone would be watching right now.

CHAPTER 11

He sat on the edge of her empty, unmade bed, switched off the television set, and just stared for a moment at the blank screen. It felt surreal to watch her up there, posing primly in a designer dress, hair perfectly combed, tears in her eyes. He didn't think he'd ever even seen her in a dress. And he hadn't seen her cry in years. The last time she had, it was on his behalf, not her own. But he saw the signal. She would be there. Two days from now. Six P.M., as planned.

Michael looked around the room. Her black T-shirts were strewn all over the floor. Jeans lay crumpled in the corner. Empty Red Bull cans littered her dresser. Even the power light on her computer still pulsed green.

It was like she was coming back.

But he knew better.

He got up and started scooping the clothes off the floor, folding them and putting them away. He couldn't help himself. He hated messiness. Disorder. Things not in their proper places. Not to mention he'd spent so much time cleaning up after her, it had become second nature.

He didn't want to miss her, but he did. As stubborn and opinionated as she could be, she was his best friend. His only friend, if he was being honest with himself. She was the one person on earth who had the guts to stand up for him. It almost made up for the fact that she was the favorite. The one who always got her way. When there were two bedrooms, she got the bigger one. When he'd been forced to endure school, she got to stay home with a tutor.

And when she ran away, he'd paid the price.

He rubbed his fingers over the thin raised scars that snaked across his lower back. Three lines. One for every time she had tried to run. He shuddered. In his mind, he could still hear the crack of the belt. The sound of her screaming *stop*.

Now seventeen, six feet four inches tall, he was too big to lash anymore. His once dirty-blond hair had turned a deep brown, his eyes a stormy blue. When he looked in the mirror, he no longer saw a scared little boy; he saw the heir apparent to an organization with the power to bring this country to its knees. Michael's fingers brushed lower to the tattoo. He couldn't see it, but he knew it was there, watching from its many beastly eyes.

Voices drifted in from the kitchen, where Father was meeting with one of his top lieutenants. The group's inner circle was small—only the vetted few who could be trusted face-to-face. But the ranks of foot soldiers were in the hundreds, scattered over the globe, united by their superior hacking skills and the knowledge that the security of the world relied on them. And now, Michael was their point man.

He stood and walked to her computer. With a jiggle of the mouse, the screen popped to life. He tapped his long fingers over the keyboard, posting an update to the others. Phase one of the plan had gone off without a hitch. Phases two and three were being coordinated. And by the time the final phase launched, the Webster administration wouldn't know what had hit it. Michael set up a new secure chat area in preparation. Ha. Not even difficult, either. For the first time in nearly a week, he smiled. Who said she was the best, anyway?

So what if he missed her. Maybe it was okay that she wasn't here. Maybe he was actually better off with her gone.

Finally, he would have his chance.

The chance to prove, once and for all, that *he* was the better one.

CHAPTER 12

Addie pulled a book from the shelf, sat in a chair, and tried to read. Her mom was opposite her on the sofa, computer in her lap. The president sat in another chair, glued to his smartphone, as he had been most of the weekend. And Mackenzie was sprawled on the floor clicking Legos into place, tongue poking from the side of her mouth in concentration.

The family was gathered in the study of their Clifton, Virginia, estate, taking a reprieve from the intense media glare back in D.C. Not that it made much difference. President Webster had been fielding phone calls from his advisors nonstop. Even though the administration had been riding high on a wave of positive public sentiment, thanks in large part to Addie, the attack on the Republican fund-raiser had cast a pall over her miraculous return. The president's opponents smelled blood in the water and they were circling, calling the administration's insistence that the attack was an isolated incident both foolish and naïve.

Addie shifted uncomfortably in her chair. Even though it had been her suggestion to spend the weekend at her childhood home, being here made Addie feel like Alice after she tumbled down the rabbit hole. The kitchen countertops seemed too short, the bookshelves too low; her bed was too small and narrow. Of course, Addie knew logically that it was only because she had grown. But somehow, it felt like everything else had shrunk instead, and if she blinked for too long the walls would close in on her. She needed a distraction.

Addie put down her book and nodded in her sister's direction.

"Whatcha making there, Mackenzie?" she said.

Mackenzie held up an airplane and flew it back and forth.

"Cool," Addie said.

On closer inspection, she could see it was *Air Force One*. The miniature Boeing 747 was an exact replica, right down to the American flag on the tail, the thick blue stripe on the side with UNITED STATES OF AMERICA emblazoned above, and the Presidential Seal. Well, it was an exact replica except for the left wing, which was still in a pile of gray blocks around Mackenzie's feet. She pulled open the plane's tiny door and pointed inside.

"See? This is where Daddy sits," she said. "He has an office in there. So does Mommy. And guess what?"

"What?" Addie said.

"They can even put fuel in the plane while it's flying, so Daddy doesn't have to stop!" Mackenzie said, eyes wide. "It could stay in the air forever if it had to."

"Seriously?" Addie said. "That's really awesome. I didn't know that."

"Anything you need to know about *Air Force One*, just ask Mackie. She's our resident expert," the president said. "Possibly knows more about it than my pilots."

Mackenzie smiled and nodded. It was one of the first smiles Addie had seen on her sister's face since she'd arrived home. It was like a little burst of sunshine. Addie couldn't help but smile back. She looked at the hundreds of tiny blocks that made up Mackenzie's toy. "I bet that took forever to build."

"Six hours and twenty-five minutes, actually," Mackenzie said. "So far."

"Hey," Addie said. "I've got an idea. Want to take a break for one of those minutes and play a game with me?"

"Okay." Mackenzie set her plane down on the floor. "But can we play for longer than one minute?" she asked.

Addie grinned. "Sure. But you'll probably beat me in less than a minute. My game skills are a little rusty."

"What does that mean?" Mackenzie said.

"Means I haven't played in a while," Addie said.

"Oh." Mackenzie stuck the Legos in the box and put it back in its place on the shelf. Her small hand ran across a row of board games. Monopoly. The Game of Life. Chutes and Ladders. She stopped at Connect Four. Addie's heart involuntarily skipped a beat.

"This is a good one," Mackenzie said, pulling the old box out.

"Yeah." Addie nodded, trying to swallow down the memory that was creeping up as a lump in her throat. "That used to be my favorite, too."

Addie and Mackenzie sat down in leather chairs opposite each other at a walnut poker table. Mackenzie sorted the checkers while Addie clicked the plastic grid into place. Not easy when her hands wouldn't stop shaking. What was wrong with her? She really needed to pull herself together. Addie glanced back toward her parents. Thankfully, they weren't watching. For once.

"What color do you want?" Mackenzie said.

"You choose," Addie answered.

Mackenzie shoved the red checkers across the table. "I'll be black," she said. "Black goes first."

"Right," Addie said. "Smoke before fire, isn't that what they say?"

Mackenzie scrunched her face. "That doesn't make sense," she said. "You can't have smoke without a fire."

"You're right. It doesn't make sense," Addie said.

"I like things to make sense," Mackenzie answered.

"Yeah, me too." Too bad they rarely did. Addie secured the latch on the bottom of the grid. "Your move."

Mackenzie dropped a black checker in the center. It clacked all the way down to the bottom row. Addie followed suit, dropping a red right next to it. Suddenly, her heart began to thump loudly in her ears. She shook her head. She had to get a grip. Mackenzie placed another checker, eyes squinting in concentration. They took turns and the grid filled.

But as each piece fell into place with a scrape and click, Addie's heartbeat grew even louder. She picked up another checker with a shaking hand and dropped it in, paying no attention to where it fell.

Clink, clack, went the checker.

Ba-boom, ba-boom, ba-boom, went her heart.

Addie put her hands over her ears. *Make. It. Stop.*

Mackenzie smirked, holding a black checker above the board. *Clink, clack...*

Click.

Mackenzie's checker fell into place. Four in a row.

"I win!" she said.

The pounding in Addie's ears got so loud she couldn't hear anything else. Her vision blurred, and all at once the only thing she could see in her mind's eye was the grid toppling, checkers flying through the air, a set of small feet pounding down the hallway.

And the hand.

The hand that had reached out of the darkness and clamped over her face, silencing her scream, making Addie's world go black.

Addie let out a gasp and stood, pushing her chair away from the table, not able to speak. Sweat beaded on her forehead, and her breaths came out short and stuttering.

"Hey," Mackenzie said. "Where are you going?"

Addie slowly backed up to the couch and sat opposite her mother, trying to keep from hyperventilating.

"Addie?" Her mother glanced up from the computer screen. "Are you okay?"

Addie was anything but okay. She nodded anyway.

Mackenzie scowled, her tiny face just a half-moon peeking from above the big card table. "Just 'cause you didn't win doesn't mean you can leave," she said. "You've got to help me clean up."

"In a minute," Addie said. She rubbed her eyes. She was still seeing spots. And the car trunk in which she'd woken up, covered by a heavy blanket. Her lungs squeezed tight like they were fists preparing to throw a punch.

"Mom," Mackenzie whined, "that's not fair. When you play a game, you're supposed to help clean up. Tell her to help clean up!"

Addie's mother and the president gave each other a look. *The* look. The one they'd been giving each other ever since Addie had come home. The one Addie hated. The one that said the words they didn't dare say out loud: that Addie was broken, lost. A shell of her former self. A victim. Forever ruined.

"Mackenzie," her mom said, putting her computer on the coffee table. "It's okay. I'll help you. Your sister just needs a minute."

"No," Addie said, wiping her forehead with the back of her hand and forcing a smile. She wasn't broken. She wasn't lost. She was stronger than all of them. She exhaled and willed herself to get up and sit back down at the card table with her little sister.

"I'm fine. Got a little dizzy when I stood up too fast. That's all," she said, scooping checkers haphazardly into the box. "Mac's right. I should help." But the pounding in her ears just wouldn't let up. Or the voice that came along with it.

Play fair, little one. . . .

She glanced at the clock and her heart stopped. It was five minutes past six. Where had the time gone? She was late. And she could not be late.

"Thanks for the game," Addie said quickly, her pulse racing. "I'm going to go rest for a little while before dinner, if that's okay."

"Of course, honey," her mother said. "Don't forget, Cheryl and Darrow are coming to join us. But if you're not up for guests, we can cancel."

"No, I can't wait to see them," Addie said. "Please don't cancel."

Addie slipped into the hall, managing only four steps before she broke into a sprint. The stairs were straight ahead. She took them two at a time and ran down the hall toward her bedroom. She paused, willing herself to breathe normally, chest rising and falling as she steadied herself. She strode across the room, past her old twin bed to the window on the other side, and climbed onto the seat below. She slid the glass up and a rush of cool air washed over her, sending goose bumps down her bare arms.

It was already dusk, and the trees in the distance were beginning to fade into the darkening sky. Addie was terrified— she was already five minutes late, and *he* despised tardiness. But she was even more terrified of what would happen if she didn't make it at all. Failure wasn't an option. And she had no one to blame but herself. With one last glance over her shoulder and another deep breath, she slipped out of the window to the branches of the old oak tree outside and shimmied down. When her bare feet hit the ground, she didn't look back. She just ran, fast and hard, as though her life depended on it. Because it did.

The house disappeared behind Addie as her feet pounded against the gravel road. She was only eight, but she was fast. And smart. So why had he left the boy to watch her? He was only nine himself. Shy and nervous. Addie's breath fogged in the cold air. There'd been no time to grab a jacket. She'd sent the boy into her room for a chocolate bar. He loved chocolate. But as soon as he'd gone in, she'd locked the door behind him and started running. It was dark outside. She could barely make out the road. Still, she ran, until the flash of headlights blinded her and she froze. Tires crunched against the gravel along the edge as the car rolled to a stop. Addie's knees shook and tears stung her eyes.

No no no no no—

The driver's side door swung open and she heard a low, familiar voice.

"Where do you think you're going, little one?"

And just like that, a pair of cold hands pulled her kicking and screaming back into the nightmare that her life had become.

CHAPTER 13

The wheels of Darrow's BMW Z4 hugged the curves of the road as he drove toward Clifton. He'd always had a love-hate relationship with this car. It was too showy in all the wrong ways: deep red, with rich leather seats, elongated hood, convertible top. A real *look-at-me* car if ever there was one, and Darrow wanted to be noticed for who he was, not what he drove. The engine might be a quiet purr, but the statement the car made was loud and clear: he was untouchable. And not a day passed that he wasn't reminded of it, of where he might be now if it weren't for his mother's money and power.

But right now, he was grateful for the roadster's tight turn radius. The shoulderless road leading to the Webster estate snaked through the tall trees like a discarded ribbon, barely wide enough for one car, let alone two. He eased around a hairpin turn, a little too fast. The tires squealed. His mother, who was tapping her smartphone in the passenger seat next to him, glanced up and gave Darrow a look.

His mother was the master of silent messages. She didn't

have to say anything to communicate that she knew exactly why he was speeding. And that he'd better slow down.

Darrow eased up on the gas pedal. He had waited a long time for this. So why couldn't he let himself feel excited? All he felt was a swirl of anxiety. As they approached the Webster estate, he could barely make out the roofline amid the tall trees that surrounded the house. He and Addie had spent countless days at this country home when Mark Webster had been the governor of Virginia. Darrow's thoughts flashed back to the forest—running through it with Addie, going down to the creek to collect frogs and tadpoles, playing hide-and-seek under the leafy trees, with Elinor a half step behind, if she managed to catch them at all before they ran off into the woods. But it felt unreal somehow. Like peering into a stranger's living room window from a passing car, a fleeting glimpse into a life that wasn't his own. Not anymore, at least.

His thoughts shifted to Addie, strong and defiant on the television screen days earlier. But even she didn't seem quite real up there either. Too stiff and scripted, not the Addie that Darrow remembered. More like an Addie puppet, invisible strings controlling her every move.

Darrow turned onto a gravel driveway and pulled to a stop in front of the Websters' gates. A Secret Service agent sat in a small booth to the left. He approached the driver's side of the car. Darrow lowered his window.

"Good evening, sir," the agent said.

"Good evening," Darrow answered. He held out two IDs. "Darrow and Cheryl Fergusson."

"Yes. Welcome, sir; ma'am," the agent answered. "The president and first family are expecting you. Please come in."

The agent returned to the booth, and the heavy wrought-iron gates swung open. Darrow drove through and eased into the long circular driveway, pulling up in front of the house. It was farmhouse style, yellow with white trim and a front porch dotted with Adirondack chairs. Where the White House was grand and intimidating, the Webster estate was grand but cozy: it was all window seats with paisley cushions, reading nooks, and fireplaces. There were plenty of places to play and hide. Darrow and Addie had spent countless hours curled up in corners of the house, reading their favorite books and playing make-believe.

Darrow stepped from the car and walked around to the passenger side to open the door for his mother. They climbed the front porch steps in silence, Darrow's heart rate accelerating. He was finally going to see Addie again. Before he could lift a hand to knock, the front door swung open.

"Darrow, Cheryl, come on in." It was President Webster, ushering them into the bright warmth of the foyer. He was out of his usual blue suit with its crisp white shirt and tie, instead dressed in country casual—a light sweater, jeans, and leather driving shoes.

Cheryl gave the president a hug and stepped inside the foyer. Darrow shook his hand and followed his mother inside, eyes casting around for a glimpse of Addie.

"She's still in her room," the president said. "Wanted a little quiet time before dinner."

"Yes," Cheryl said. "I'm sorry, we're a bit early. . . ."

"It's no problem," the president said. "Please, make yourselves at home in the living room. Liz and Mackenzie are in the kitchen putting the finishing touches on dessert. I'll get Addie. Actually..." He paused. "Why don't you get her, Darrow? She's really been looking forward to seeing you."

"She has?" Darrow's heart unexpectedly leapt into his throat. He swallowed hard.

"She has," President Webster said. "You remember where her room is, right? Top of the stairs, to the left at the end of the hall."

"I remember," Darrow said. "Are you sure it's okay?"

"I'm sure," the president said, giving him a gentle smile. "Go ahead. It'll give your mother and me a chance to discuss a few things before dinner."

Darrow nodded and headed up the hardwood stairs leading to the second floor. He could hear his mother and the president begin talking about the attack on the Republican fund-raiser. When he reached the top, he could see Addie's closed bedroom door at the very end. He took a tentative step. And then another. He could almost hear the echo of his and Addie's laughter in every creak of the hardwood floor.

You can't catch me, Dare! You'll never find me! Double-dog Dare you!

He stopped at the end and knocked gently on the door. "Addie?"

No answer.

He knocked a little louder.

"Ad, are you in there? It's me...." He cleared his throat. His voice had dropped an octave since the last time they'd talked.

She probably didn't even recognize it. "It's me, Darrow. Your dad asked me to get you."

Still no answer.

Darrow wondered if she was still sleeping. He hated to wake her up, but... oh, the hell with it. Darrow grabbed the doorknob, not aware his palms were sweating until they slipped on the metal. All at once he was nine years old again, pushing open the hatch to an empty tree house. He wiped his hand on his pants, pinched his eyes shut and open, then turned the handle and opened the door.

Addie's room was on the other side, just as he remembered it from all those years ago, like a shrine to young Addie—the yellow eyelet duvet, the boy band poster above her desk, the old computer and stacks of books on the nightstand. Everything was exactly the same, right down to the hopscotch rug in the center. Except for one very important thing:

Addie wasn't there.

CHAPTER 14

Darrow stood there for a beat, trying to process the sight of the empty room, an all-too-familiar fear washing over him. It couldn't be happening. Not again.

A flutter in front of the window seat caught his eye. It was the yellow curtain, blowing in the breeze. The window behind it was open, cool air rushing inside. Just outside, the branches of the old oak tree that he and Addie had snuck down to play in the woods reached toward him like a hand full of twisted fingers.

Darrow ran to the window and looked down, and his heart leapt back into his throat; a fresh set of footprints was pressed into the muddy earth two stories below, moving away from the house. Without hesitating, he squeezed through the window onto the nearest tree branch.

Darrow moved lower, the next branch sagging beneath his weight. He wobbled, hit with the realization that the last time he'd attempted this, he'd only weighed seventy pounds. He grabbed another branch for support and shimmied down to the ground, landing with a thud.

Straight ahead, the lawn sloped away from the house and

into the dense forest. Darrow squinted into the darkness, picked up the trail of footprints that led across the damp grass, and took off running. But at the edge of the tree line, the trail came to an abrupt stop in the blanket of pine needles that covered the ground. The woods loomed dark and foreboding ahead of him.

Darrow paused, trying to silence his breathing, and listened. Something rustled in the leaves up ahead. A chill crept up Darrow's spine as he realized, if someone had gotten to Addie again, he might not be out here alone. He pulled his keychain from his pocket and curled his fist around his silver house key, ready to stab someone in the eye with it if need be.

"Addie?" Darrow said into the darkness.

There was another rustle. Darrow began blindly running in the direction of the sound, nearly tripping as his feet caught on the gnarled roots. It had been years since he'd run through this forest and it was unfamiliar to him now, overgrown and changed. A bird squawked overhead and swooped through the trees, startling him.

Darrow heard something that sounded like a voice, muted but close, followed by rapid footsteps. He trained his eyes toward the sound.

"Addie!" Darrow shouted. There was a shriek in response. Darrow was unsure if the noise was Addie, or if it was just another bird and his mind was playing tricks on him. He thought he heard something coming up behind him, crunching the dead leaves and twigs, but when he looked back, no one was there. He ran faster, deeper into the woods, branches pinging against his arms. The light from the house was far away now, and Darrow could barely make out where he was going.

Suddenly, his foot caught on something and he pitched forward. The keys flew from his grip, and his bare hands scraped across the dry ground as he tried to catch himself.

"Ow," he muttered as he sat up, grabbing his keys and looking back at the thing he'd just tripped over. He blinked and tried to make sense of what he was seeing in front of him. It wasn't a stump. Or a rock.

It was a girl, crouched in a ball, hands clutched over her head. She was barefoot, wearing just a pair of jeans and a thin black T-shirt. Her dark hair hung in a curtain around her face.

"Addie?" he said.

The girl whimpered.

"Addie?" Darrow moved closer and reached out a hand, touching the girl's back. She jolted, head tilting sideways. The green eyes he'd waited so long to see were wide with fear.

"Addie, it's okay. I'm sorry," he said. "I didn't mean to scare you. It's me—Darrow. Darrow Fergusson. Your old friend, remember?"

"Darrow?" she said in a low whisper.

"Yes. It's me. Darrow."

She looked around the dim forest, dazed. "Darrow? What are you doing here?" she said.

"Looking for you," Darrow said. Something crunched in the leaves nearby. Darrow's back stiffened. Instinctively, he moved closer to Addie. "What are you hiding from?" he whispered. "Is someone else out here?"

"No. No, just me," Addie said. Another shuffle of leaves and twigs.

Darrow, still rattled, got up and held out a hand, helping

Addie to her feet. As she stood, her warm breath grazed Darrow's cheek and his heart strained against his rib cage. It took everything in his willpower not to scoop her up and clutch her to his chest, just to make sure she wasn't a figment of his imagination.

"Are you okay?" he said, the words immediately sounding stupid in his own ears. Of course she wasn't okay. He had just found her barefoot, crouched and hiding in the middle of the woods.

"Yeah, I'm okay," Addie said with a shaky half-smile.

"What are you doing out here?"

"I don't know exactly." Addie shook her head and looked away. "I was playing with Mac. Then I went to my room to take a nap. I must have had a bad dream. I woke up all confused and was about to head downstairs when I heard unfamiliar voices in the foyer. . . ." Her voice trailed off. "It must have been you. But I guess I got spooked. Last thing I remember, I ran out here and hid. I just kind of tuned everything out after that. I'm sorry. I didn't mean to freak you out." She wrapped her arms around herself and shivered.

"You've got nothing to be sorry about," Darrow said. "I'm just so glad you're here, that you're . . ." He couldn't finish. "I really . . ."

"I know, Dare. I really missed you, too."

Addie's eyes met his, and this time Darrow did reach out and hug her, folding her narrow frame into his arms. She felt so warm, so alive—so real—that Darrow was afraid to let go. Like she might just disappear if he did.

Shouts echoed from the house.

"Addie! Darrow! Where are you? It's time for dinner."

Darrow released her from his grasp. "We'd better get back inside."

"Right," Addie said. She lifted her head, rubbing her eyes as though she'd just been awakened from a dream, and walked with Darrow across the lawn. But as they approached the front porch, she stopped suddenly and grabbed his arm.

"Wait," she said.

"What is it?"

"My parents," Addie said. "Your mother. You can't tell them."

"Tell them what?" Darrow asked, confused.

Addie motioned over her shoulder. "That you found me out here . . . like that."

"What are you talking about?"

She shook her head. "You don't know how it is. They're terrified of me. They act like I'm made of glass. If they knew I ran off like that and hid, it would just get worse. I've put them through enough."

"But you didn't put them through anything," Darrow said. "The people who took you did." He felt a rage swelling up in his chest, the same rage he'd spent so much time trying to shove back down, to channel into something useful—the lacrosse field, homework. Anything that wouldn't land him in trouble. Anything that wouldn't leave him feeling helpless like he had the day she disappeared, like he did right now, wishing he could punch a hole in something.

"It doesn't matter," Addie said. "Please. *Please* don't give them one more thing to worry about. I just can't handle it."

Darrow hesitated. Addie kept her determined gaze fixed

directly on him, and for a brief moment, he saw the old Addie. He knew that look. It was the same one that sent him three branches too high up the tallest tree, or three feet too far into the deep end of the pool.

Double-dog Dare you....

"Well, what am I supposed to tell them we've been doing out here instead?" Darrow said.

"I don't know," Addie said. "Just say we were so excited to see each other, we climbed down the tree and ran into the woods. Like when we were kids."

"Addie..." Darrow began. "But you're not even wearing shoes. They're never going to believe that."

"Sure they will. People believe what they want to believe." Back in the darkness of the forest, something rustled. Another bird? Or was it something else?

"Please," Addie said. "I'm begging you. Please, Dare. Do this for me."

The front door swung open, and the president was standing on the other side. "Oh, there you two are," he said. "We've been looking all over for you. Dinner is ready." The president forced a smile, an attempt to hide his obvious concern that Addie hadn't come when he'd called.

And there Darrow went, blindly up to the top of the tree, the hard ground too far away. No one to catch his fall. Just like when he was eight.

"I'm sorry, sir," he said. "It's my fault. We just got so excited to see each other again, we ran down to the creek. Like the old days."

The president's shoulders relaxed. "Sounds like fun. Now come on inside. It's a little chilly to be out here barefoot."

Darrow and Addie walked through the front door. As they did, Addie leaned over and whispered in Darrow's ear.

"Thank you," she said. "I knew you'd understand."

Darrow nodded. But he didn't understand. Burned in his mind was the other look Addie had given him—the terrified one when he'd tapped her on the back just moments earlier. As though he'd caught her doing something. As though for a minute she'd thought he was the bad guy.

CHAPTER 15

"*In this house we have rules, little one,*" *he said.* "*I know you're not used to hearing the word 'no,' but I can't protect you if you don't follow the rules. Understand?*"

Addie nodded. Her shirt was torn where he had grabbed her and pulled her into the car, then up the front steps and into the kitchen. Now she sat on a wooden chair, legs too short to reach the ground, feet swinging back and forth. Remnants of fiery tears still burned the corners of her eyes. Her mouth was dry from screaming. Mikey sat opposite her, head down, a smudge of chocolate on one cheek, the red imprint of a hand outlined on the other.

The man rounded the kitchen table and kneeled in front of Addie. He grabbed her swinging legs.

"*Stop fidgeting and listen to me,*" *he said.*

"*Yes, sir,*" *she said, willing herself to hold perfectly still.*

"*Yes what?*" *he said.*

"*Yes…*" *Addie glanced briefly away, confused. She could see Mikey out of the corner of her eye, mouthing something. She pushed her eyebrows together. He mouthed the word again. Addie looked back at the man.*

"Yes, Father," she said, swallowing the bile rising up in her throat.

"That's better," he said with a smile. "Now, what was I saying?"

Addie stayed silent, afraid to open her mouth.

"Yes," he said. "Rules, little one. In this house we have rules. Do you remember the first and most important rule?"

Addie nodded.

"Let me hear you say it," he said.

Addie ran her dry tongue across the roof of her mouth. It felt like sandpaper. "Always listen to Father," she said.

"That's right," he said. "And did you listen to your father today?"

"No," she said.

He tilted his head to the side, eyebrow arched.

"No, Father," she quickly corrected herself.

"Good," he said. "Now listen, little one. The rules are not meant to make you suffer. We have rules because they provide order. You are still learning and don't know any better. But you will come to understand. Now go to your room and think about what I've told you. Think about the consequences of your actions."

"Yes, Father," Addie said.

She slipped from the chair and stood on wobbling legs. As she walked down the hall toward her dark room and went inside, she could still feel where his hands had gripped her calves. She shut the door. Moments later, she heard the lock latch from the outside. She began to shake, not knowing how long he would leave her in there. Locked up. Alone. Sometimes when he was displeased, he left her for days.

She lay on the bed, shivering, until another sound made her jolt upright.

"No, Father! Please!" Mikey pleaded.

There was a scuffle and something banged into the door. Addie began shaking harder.

"*Michael, we talked about this,*" *an eerily calm voice said.* "*You, unlike her, should know better. You were given a simple task, and you failed. You understand that now you must be punished.*"

"*But it wasn't my fault,*" *the boy whimpered.* "*She tricked me. I did what you asked.*"

"*Never,*" *he said coolly,* "*never blame others for your own failures.*"

"*But...*"

"*Accept your punishment now, Michael,*" *he said.* "*Unless you wish for it to be worse.*"

"*Yes, Father,*" *Mikey said shakily.*

"*Raise your shirt.*"

Addie heard muffled sobs, another shuffling noise, followed by the crack of the belt against Mikey's bare skin. Her entire body quaked with fear. She pressed her hands tight over her ears, rocking back and forth, as he cried out in pain.

CHAPTER 16

Darrow jogged down the front steps of his brick row house, taking a right on P Street and a left on 35th. He sucked in the fresh spring air, feet slapping against the slate sidewalks. The morning sun filtered through the rows of trees above his head; daffodils sprouted in the flower beds; fresh-faced tourists wandered the historic Georgetown streets, snapping photos and pointing out landmarks.

But Darrow didn't notice any of it.

All he saw was Addie, crouched in the woods, hands over her head. Sure, she'd seemed perfectly fine when they'd gone inside moments later. Maybe too fine. As though nothing had ever happened.

But it *had* happened.

Darrow knew that better than anyone. He'd lived with the guilt of Addie's disappearance for so long—nearly half his life—that it had become like a second shadow. Even when he willed himself not to think about her anymore, the shadow lingered, casting darkness over everything he did.

Darrow jogged to the intersection of M Street and turned

left toward Pennsylvania Avenue. He would follow the road all the way to the White House, then loop back home, where he'd shower and change for school. Usually a morning jog helped clear Darrow's head, get him ready for another day at Cabot. Not today. His thoughts were more scrambled than ever.

To Darrow's right, the Potomac River flickered in and out of view. Boats glided along the water and bicyclists zipped down the path alongside. But Darrow was oblivious to it all. His head was so full of Addie he didn't even notice the group of middle school girls on a field trip giggling and waving when he ran past.

He definitely didn't notice the government-issued blue sedan with tinted windows, rolling along slowly on the street beside him. The man sitting in the driver's seat with dark sunglasses, watching. Or the small camera he held up discreetly, a series of clicks documenting Darrow's every move.

CHAPTER 17

The Foggy Bottom Metro station was clogged with people. Typical Monday morning rush hour. The young woman in medical scrubs, fresh off the night shift at GWU, stood shoulder to shoulder with dozens of other commuters. Her feet were sore and she was anxious to get on board and sit down. Eight months pregnant and big as a house, she didn't know how many more twelve-hour shifts of changing bedpans and attaching IV lines she could take. Finally the warning lights flashed and the Blue Line train pulled into the station, wheels screeching on the metal tracks as it came to a stop.

"Doors opening," an automated voice announced.

The double doors in front of her parted with a whoosh. A few passengers filtered out as the mass of humanity on the platform pushed its way in. The woman looked around the train car. Every seat was taken, and no one ever bothered to get up for a pregnant lady anymore, so she found an empty inch of silver pole to hang on to with one hand. She put the other on her lower back for support as more people pushed into the empty spaces around her.

"Excuse me—ma'am?" a voice said.

She turned toward the sound to see a young guy, probably a college kid, in a GWU sweatshirt with a blue-and-yellow backpack at his feet. He nodded toward her and stood.

"Here. Have my seat, please," he said.

She smiled as the boy stepped aside. "Thanks. You have no idea how much that means to me." She lowered herself into the seat, happy to take the weight off her aching legs, and closed her eyes. The automated voice came over the loudspeaker.

"Doors closing. Please stand clear of the doors."

Trying to get comfortable, the woman shifted her body, tucking her feet beneath the seat. They bumped into something. A blue-and-yellow backpack. She quickly grabbed it and stood up, looking for the guy.

"Hey!" she said, scanning the crowded subway car for his GWU sweatshirt, unable to find his face among the commuters. She turned toward the window, just in time to see the boy running across the platform and up the escalators, probably late for class.

"Hey!" she yelled again, even though she knew he couldn't possibly hear what she was saying. "You forgot your backpack!"

She sat back down. Poor kid. Did something nice, and now he was probably missing his homework. She placed the backpack on her lap and flipped it around, hoping there was some sort of identification in it so she could return his stuff. Maybe give him a gift card to Starbucks, too. Thank him for being nice.

She yanked the zipper and her heart leapt into her throat. She stared at the open bag in her hands with disbelief.

No books.

No papers.

Just...

The train lurched forward and the backpack tipped upside down. A single silver canister rolled out, biohazard symbol clearly imprinted on the side. The woman placed her hands protectively over her belly, body shaking, and screamed. As her fellow passengers turned in her direction, trying to figure out why the pregnant lady was yelling frantically—was she in labor?—the train's loudspeaker crackled back to life.

But the familiar female voice had been replaced by an eerily robotic male one.

"Now departing Foggy Bottom," it said as the train hurtled into the dark tunnel ahead. *"There will be no next stop."*

CHAPTER 18

"How are you doing this morning, Addie?"

Dr. Gregory Richards, behavioral psychologist, stroked his bearded chin and peered thoughtfully from behind his wire-rimmed glasses. A small tape recorder sat on the table next to his chair. Addie sat opposite him on the sofa. The First Family had returned to D.C. from Clifton first thing this morning. Addie had hoped she would just get to go home with them. Instead she'd been driven here, to Dr. Richards's Georgetown University office, a small bookshelf-lined space cluttered with dusty journals and old books.

Behind the frosted glass of the closed door, Addie heard students chatting and laughing in the hallway, occasionally gliding past like dark shadows. Ghosts of a future Addie knew she would never have.

Addie shrugged. She still hadn't figured out how much she could trust Dr. Richards. The last shrink type they'd sent to see her at the safe house was the one who'd given her that stupid test—and immediately reported the results right back to her mother and the president.

But Richards seemed different. Sure, he wore the clichéd tweed jacket and khaki pants of a rumpled professor. But the getup seemed perfectly natural on him: the frayed lapels, the slightly disheveled hair. Like he rolled straight out of bed every morning looking like Indiana Jones. Probably born with a pipe in his mouth and eyebrow arched, asking the delivery room staff how they were feeling.

"Okay," Dr. Richards said. "Don't really want to talk?"

Addie's eyes flitted to the tape recorder. Dr. Richards followed her gaze.

"I see," he said. "Does that thing make you nervous?"

Addie shrugged again. Dr. Richards picked up the recorder.

"Eh," he said, "I don't like it either. Can't stand hearing the sound of my own voice." He scratched the fuzz on his chin and rolled his eyes. "Actually, if you ask my daughter, she'd say there's nothing I love more than the sound of my own voice. But that's a different story."

Addie knew she was supposed to laugh. She didn't. Unfazed, Dr. Richards clicked off the recorder and stuffed it in a drawer.

"Better?" he said.

Addie nodded.

"Listen, Addie," Dr. Richards said. "I want you to know this is a safe place, okay? I'm not here to investigate. I'm not here to judge. I don't work for the FBI or the Secret Service. Or even your parents. I work for you. You can talk or not talk, okay?"

Addie nodded again.

"Just know that whatever you say in here stays between you and me . . ." Dr. Richards pointed to a shelf above his head, at a weird-looking striped stuffed animal with a zipper for a mouth. "...and of course, Sorgenfresser over there."

"Sorgen-what?" Addie said, surprised by the sound of her own voice. "What's that thing?"

"Sorgenfresser," Dr. Richards said, pulling the bear down, "is a worry eater." He unzipped the mouth. "See, you write down your worries and drop them in there, then Sorgenfresser eats them for you. My little clients love him. Well, come to think of it, lots of my grown-up ones do, too. He's kind of cool, huh?"

"Maybe you should give him to my parents," she muttered.

"Oh yeah? Do they worry a lot?"

"Yes."

"About what?" Dr. Richards said. "I mean, I get your father has plenty to worry about as leader of the free world, what with the attack at the Reagan Center last week. But what is it that *you* think your parents need Sorgenfresser for?"

Addie went back to shrugging.

"You think they worry about you, is that it?" Dr. Richards said.

Addie nodded.

"Does that make you uncomfortable?" he asked.

Addie nodded again.

"I wonder why?"

"Because..." Addie's back stiffened. "I can take care of myself."

"I see," Dr. Richards said. "You've had to take care of yourself a lot these last eight years, haven't you?"

Addie looked away.

"It makes perfect sense that it's difficult to have other people concerned about you now," Dr. Richards said. "But it's okay, you know, to let other people care for you. You aren't alone."

Addie began to pick at the sofa cushions, chewing her bottom lip.

She was alone, trapped in this bedroom for more days than she could count since her escape attempt. But her pillowcase was no longer damp with tears. She'd stopped crying for Mommy and Daddy in her sleep. It was clear they weren't coming. They didn't care. Nobody did. They'd never find her, anyway. She wasn't even sure where she was. Somewhere far away, where the only sounds she'd heard had been her own sobs. Until she couldn't cry anymore. But now the silence was worse, like a fist clenched around her chest, squeezing her tightly until even the will to scream was gone.

The door to her room opened, and he walked in holding a tray. He came three times a day bearing simple meals. Oatmeal in the morning; bread with some meat and cheese and a piece of fruit in the afternoon; a bowl of soup at night. She sat up. Even though she hated his dull food and still feared his presence, she'd grown to anticipate his visits. At least for a few minutes, she wasn't alone.

"I have something special for you today, little one," he said.

"Yes?"

He pointed at a large candy bar on the wooden tray, propped next to the steaming soup bowl. "Marabou dark chocolate," he said. "My favorite as a child. I hope you enjoy it." He smiled and set the tray on the small desk across from her bed.

"Thank you," she said.

"You're welcome." He held out something else. A thick book, pages

*dog-eared at the edges, cover faded with time. "You enjoy reading?"
he said.*

*She nodded and accepted the book eagerly. Trapped with her own
thoughts for so long, it would be a welcome distraction to experience
someone else's.*

*"Yes, I also loved to read as a child," he said. "We are so much
alike, you and I." He gently stroked her hair. And for the first time since
she'd arrived, she didn't recoil. It had been so long since anyone had
touched or held her in a normal way, like a parent or babysitter would.
"This book was my favorite," he said. "I hope you enjoy it."*

*She looked up at him and met his cool blue eyes, this time without
fear. "Thanks, Father," she whispered. He nodded, and patted her head
one more time before leaving. She felt a rush of disappointment as the
door closed behind him. Then she remembered the hardbound volume
in her hands—*The Count of Monte Cristo. *Ignoring her soup, she
went straight for the chocolate bar, slipping smooth, rich squares into
her mouth as she immersed herself in a tale of revenge.*

Dr. Richards leaned forward, extending Sorgenfresser in his
hand. "So how about it?" he said. "Want to give it a try?"

Addie jumped. "I'm sorry. Give what a try?"

"Sorgenfresser," he said, handing Addie the bear and a
piece of paper. "Let him have one of your worries."

Addie tried not to roll her eyes. "I'm not eight years old
anymore," she said, wondering how much longer this session
was going to last.

"No, you're not," Dr. Richards answered. "But you were,
once."

Addie sighed. "Okay. Fine." She took the ridiculous bear,

paper, and pencil, and looked around the room, thinking. Addie worried about plenty. Mikey. Her sisters. Innocent people that needed to be protected from evil. But she couldn't stuff that into Sorgenfresser's zippered mouth. For starters, it would never help. Also, she was sure Dr. Richards would read it as soon as she left.

She tried to think of something to write, but her mind wandered to Darrow and stuck there a moment, like it had been doing ever since she'd seen him the previous night. Over the years, she'd occasionally allowed herself to imagine what he had become, what it would be like if she saw him again. Somehow her idea of Darrow had never changed much in these fantasies. He was just an older version of the lanky, nerdy little boy who had been her partner in crime for so long, the one person in the world she knew she could always count on. So the tall, deep-voiced guy she'd encountered last night had come as a pretty big shock. She couldn't believe he'd found her like that. Of all the people . . . still, once she'd gotten herself together, Addie couldn't help but notice the way his shirt stretched across his broad chest, the ripples of muscles beneath the fabric. He'd grown out his thick black hair so it fell to the nape of his neck in soft curls. The baby fat had disappeared from his face, and his cheekbones and strong jawline were more pronounced.

His eyes hadn't changed, though—still deep brown flecked with gold, like they contained tiny shards of sunlight. Still thoughtful and kind. And he hadn't looked at her the way everyone else had. That look of pity, concern, fear. Darrow simply looked at her like he wanted to understand.

But how could he, living here in his little bubble? It was impossible. He'd never know what it meant to be afraid. Like last night, when Addie realized the full implications of her failure; she had arrived in the woods too late for the handoff. Fear had taken over—she had been terrified that *he* was somehow going to come for her, punish her then and there. No one had come, but she knew that didn't mean her mistake would be forgotten. Addie shifted uncomfortably. She cupped her hand around the paper on her lap and wrote, the sharp point of the pencil digging into her thigh.

As Dr. Richards watched with a smile, Addie folded the note and fed it to the bear. She handed it back to the psychologist, but he shook his head.

"Keep him, Addie," Dr. Richards said. "Use him when you need to. And when you're ready to talk, we'll talk. I'm here to help you."

"Okay," Addie said.

But talking didn't solve anything. Addie knew that now. Only action did.

And it was up to Addie to act.

She inhaled deeply and glanced out the window at the manicured campus that stretched between the brick buildings. Students crisscrossed along the paths, holding coffees and books. They stopped and chatted, perfectly content, their futures laid out before them like shiny prizes at a carnival. Addie hated them, in a way. For being what she could have been, if *he* had just left her alone. But she knew that wasn't possible. And maybe she didn't even care. Sometimes it was better to know the truth. Justice wasn't blind. It was only achieved with eyes wide open.

Dr. Richards was gazing benignly at Addie, waiting for her to speak.

She let out a slow breath. "I want to be normal," she finally said. "Like them," she added, pointing out the window. "I don't want to be 'Addie Webster, kidnapping victim.' I want to be a regular teenager. But I just don't see how it's possible, you know?"

"Anything is possible," Dr. Richards said. "As long as you're willing to put in the effort. Are you?"

Before Addie could answer, there was a knock on Dr. Richards's door. The handle twisted and Addie drew back reflexively, curling into herself as the door flew open. Agent Alvarez stood on the other side, face serious.

"I'm sorry to interrupt," she said. "But I need to take Miss Webster back to the White House."

Addie glanced back and forth between Alvarez and Dr. Richards. "Don't we still have a few minutes left?" she said, even though she'd been anxious to leave since the moment she'd arrived. She didn't like the way Agent Alvarez was keeping her hand close to the weapon Addie knew was tucked into her waistband. She didn't like that fierce look in the agent's eyes.

Alvarez shook her head. "We have a situation," she said. "And it's critical we get you to a secure location. Now."

"Okay." Addie stood, trying to steady her shaking knees as she walked to the door.

"Thank you, sir." Alvarez nodded at Dr. Richards. "I advise you to remain in your office."

Alvarez left the bewildered psychologist behind and led Addie quickly down the hallway, one hand on her elbow, eyes darting from student to student as if any one of them might have explosives hidden in their backpacks. When they reached the motorcade, Alvarez practically shoved Addie into the backseat, then sat down next to her and slammed the door.

Addie swallowed hard. "What's going on? What sort of situation?" she said, voice hitching. "Am I in danger?"

Alvarez took her eyes off the scene outside and trained them on Addie.

"Hijacking on the Blue Line," she said, and went back to watching random people milling about on the nearby walkway. "We don't know what's going on yet, but we don't take chances in situations like these." She tapped the seat in front of her and motioned to the driver. "Let's roll." The limo lurched forward, sirens blaring.

The train barreled around a corner and screeched to a stop, sending the passengers in all six cars lurching forward. Some cried; some screamed in terror; others just sat, gripping their seats, immobilized by shock.

Several jumped to their feet, trying to pry open the locked doors, but the emergency exits had been disabled. People continued to punch hopelessly at their cell phones, but the signal had been jammed as soon as they'd departed Foggy Bottom. In desperation, a woman gave the train's emergency call box another try, only to be greeted by dead silence on the other end.

The train's loudspeaker crackled back to life and the passengers went silent, listening.

"We are Cerberus," the robotic man's voice said. *"We have control of this train. Do not try to escape; do not attempt to move. Do as we say and you will not be harmed."* The speaker sputtered off and back on again. *"Disobey and we will kill you."*

There was another moment of silent disbelief, punctuated by muted sobs and whimpering. Then a man in a gray business suit jumped to his feet, yelling, "No way! No way am I going to die on a damn train!" He took out a heavy black laptop from his bag and bashed it against the nearest window. More passengers began to scream and cry. Another man attempted to restrain him.

"We've got to stay calm!" he screeched.

"To hell with that!" the man answered. He shoved the other man away. "I'm getting out of here." He pounded at the window again. Several other passengers got to their feet and began to help, smashing at the windows with anything they could find.

Suddenly the train lurched forward, slowly and deliberately. The man with the laptop fell sideways as the lights flickered off. The voice came over the loudspeaker, uttering just four words before cutting out again:

"You have been warned."

The canister at the pregnant woman's feet popped and hissed. She curled into herself, sobbing. So this was it. This was how she was going to die—at the hands of terrorists. All her life, twenty-six years, she'd lived in this city, and she'd never been afraid like she was right now. She rubbed her belly.

"I love you, baby," she choked out as a sickly sweet gas filled the train's compartment.

CHAPTER 19

The motorcade raced through the streets of D.C. Outside, Addie could hear sirens wailing. The limousine's tires screeched as they took a hard turn onto Pennsylvania Avenue. Addie desperately wanted to ask Alvarez for more details, but the agent was busy watching every passing motorist, every pedestrian that crossed their paths.

The White House loomed ahead. The gates swung open, swallowing Addie's motorcade and slamming shut again. Addie's limo pulled to a stop in the secure parking garage. She was quickly hustled from the car and led into the elevator, up to the residence. As the door opened into the vestibule, Alvarez spoke into her mouthpiece.

"Songbird is back in the nest," she said.

Addie's mother stood on the other side.

"Honey." She rushed forward and folded Addie into an awkward embrace. Addie went limp. She wasn't used to being hugged; not like this. Liz pulled away. The elevator door closed behind them, but instead of heading back downstairs like usual, the Secret Service followed Addie into the residence, spreading out and listening to instructions coming from their earpieces.

"What's going on?" Addie said. "Agent Alvarez said a Metro train was hijacked?"

Her mother nodded. "Six-car train departing Foggy Bottom," she said. "That's all I know."

Addie's eyelids began to flutter. "Are we in danger? Why was I rushed back here?"

Liz rubbed Addie's shoulder reassuringly. "The campus wasn't secure. We're in lockdown mode here. But we're free to move around the residence," she said, a little too earnestly. "You're safe."

More lies. She'd never be safe. Anywhere.

"Where's Dad?"

"Situation Room with his advisors," her mother said. She took Addie's hand. "Why don't you come with me? Mac and I are watching a movie in the playroom."

Addie let her hand slip out of her mother's grip. "No. Thanks," she said. "I'd rather go to my room, if that's okay. I have a headache."

The corners of Liz's mouth turned down. "Okay. If that's what you'd like. Can I get you an Advil or anything?"

Addie shook her head and walked away, picking up the pace as she went. She had to find out what was going on.

She nodded curtly to the agent posted outside her room, pulled the door shut, and sat at the Louis XVI desk. A shiny silver laptop was waiting for her, the gift her mother had promised when they'd returned from Clifton. Addie opened it and tapped the trackpad. The screen glowed a welcoming blue. Her fingers flew over the keyboard. A line of code, another click, and she sailed right past the firewall her mother had set up to limit Addie's Web browsing to certain sites.

Addie headed straight to the news. A live report was streaming in from the Arlington Cemetery Metro stop. Of course he'd picked the cemetery. Addie's throat tightened. At least it wouldn't be these people's final resting place. Not this time. Onscreen, several yards from the station, dozens of people were running toward the emergency vehicles parked nearby, hands clutched over their mouths, coughing and gagging.

The reporter spoke into her microphone, shouting over the chaos. "We're here live at the Arlington Cemetery Metro, where just minutes ago a hijacked Blue Line train pulled into the station."

She paused and gestured behind her.

"This is what we've learned," she said. "The train's operating system was hacked after departing Foggy Bottom a half hour ago, leaving the conductor with no control. The hijackers were apparently able to remotely operate the train. They stopped it in a tunnel between Foggy Bottom and this station, at which point they detonated several canisters of what is now believed to be harmless gas." She held her hand to her ear, squinting. "And I've just received word that Cerberus is again claiming responsibility, and has provided the media with copies of e-mails and texts allegedly detailing how they planned this attack, right under the noses of the very people tasked with protecting this country. We'll have more as the situation develops."

Addie clicked over to YouTube. Already, dozens of people had posted shaky cell phone videos of the attack—passengers huddled together in fear as the canisters exploded on the train, terrified people running from the Arlington Cemetery station, children crying. Addie had to close the window. It was too much. In her mind's eye, she couldn't shake another all-too-familiar series of images: terrified faces covered in blood, mangled remains of small children. She heard the screams, the wails of the sirens. The stretchers carrying lifeless bodies. The smoke twisting from the underground wreckage, reaching out like ghostly fingers clawing at the daylight. *He* had made her watch it on video—so many times, the scene had been seared into her memory. Sometimes she even dreamed it was her face covered in blood, her screams piercing the morning calm.

Addie rubbed her temples, pushing the thoughts from her mind, and opened a new window. She typed her own name into the search engine. A string of news articles came back. She clicked the top link. A pretty generic news story about her return, along with the expected questions about where she'd been, who had taken her. She clicked more, making sure to leave no trace of her activity in the browser's history. She was good at covering her tracks. The only person she couldn't fool was *him*. He always knew when she had searched for something forbidden.

She scanned reports about the ongoing investigation. According to "inside sources," the FBI was actively questioning members of an unnamed domestic terror group. So far, the leads had turned up nothing.

Addie clicked on the comment section, raising an eyebrow as she read:

She's an imposter. Just look at her! Looks nothing like the real Addie.
Reply

Obviously the White House is hiding something. How does a kid disappear without a trace for eight years and then show up out of nowhere?
Reply

The real Adele Webster died eight years ago. The one you see in the White House today is an expensive clone, created in a secret lab in the Mojave Desert. Don't be fooled! #conspiracytheory
Reply

You mean to tell me one day "Elinor" ships off to boarding school and right after that "Addie" turns up, just in time to get the president's approval ratings out of the toilet? Right. Keep drinking the Kool-Aid, sheeple.
Reply

Elinor. Addie tried to imagine what her sister must be like now. Even though she'd seen photographs around the house of a smiling teenager with blunt-cut, highlighted brown hair, the only image Addie could conjure up of Ellie was the little girl with serious gray eyes who had watched quietly from the corner while Addie and Darrow played. Addie ached to know her sister was okay. But her mother had been clear—even she and the president weren't supposed to contact Elinor until she came home.

Addie exhaled, reminding herself that she had work to do. She launched another site, an obscure cooking blog that never saw any traffic, save for the random bored housewife that stumbled upon it by accident in search of a new meatloaf recipe.

Addie scanned the page for the symbol. She found it hidden in two zeros in the bottom right corner, and clicked. The screen went black, except for a single blinking cursor. Addie's heart rate accelerated, beating in time with the flashing rectangle. She quickly typed in a string of letters, followed by an encryption key.

A new screen popped up, blue with another blinking cursor. Addie entered her code name and waited. Within moments, a line of text appeared.

You missed your rendezvous. What happened?

Addie wiped her palms on her jeans and answered.

Couldn't break away in time. Sorry.

That is unfortunate. We will have to make an alternate plan. What is the progress with Shi?

Assessing situation. Gaining trust. Will take time to locate.

Her heart pounded. There was a pause. The cursor blinked ominously. Finally, another line of text appeared.

Can we still meet our target date?

Addie sucked in a breath. Just weeks away. She was surrounded by people watching her every move. But Addie was smarter than them.

She had to be.

Yes. April 15. On target.

Very good. April 15. Never forget....

Never forget.

How could she?

Addie had learned her lesson. She knew better—probably better than anyone—the consequences of guarding your front gate while leaving your back door unlocked.

CHAPTER 20

"You gonna finish those?" Harper Cutting tucked her blue-tipped blond hair behind her ear and gave Darrow a friendly poke when he didn't reply. "Everything okay, D?" she asked, helping herself to the thick-cut fries Darrow piled onto his plate every day at lunch. Of course, the Cabot cafeteria offered a wide selection of healthy choices, but Darrow and Harper were both fried-food devotees and usually made a beeline for the grill.

They were sharing a small table in the corner underneath the wide arched window. Despite the Cabot Friends School's reputation as educator of D.C.'s elite, the cafeteria was modest and austere, much more in keeping with the school's Quaker roots. Round wooden tables adorned the high-ceilinged room, the students clustered around them laughing and chatting. The last things Darrow felt like doing.

"I'm ... not sure, to be honest," he said.

Harper dipped a fry in ketchup and popped it into her mouth, chewing thoughtfully before responding. "I know the feeling," she said. "Want to talk about it?"

Darrow rubbed the back of his neck. He and Harper had

been best friends since sixth grade. And even though Darrow had a lot of friends, Harper was the only one he could really talk to. About anything. She was the only one he could trust with the truth about who he was and the things he'd done. Harper understood. She had her own secrets.

"I saw Addie last night," he said.

Harper glanced up sharply. "And?"

"And," he said, "it was just . . . screwed up. We went to their Virginia place. Addie, she's . . . kind of quiet and everything. But if you didn't know what had happened to her, you'd think nothing had happened to her."

"That's probably just her way of coping," Harper said gently. "I'm sure she just wants to feel like a normal person."

"Yeah, that's the thing," Darrow said. "It's like she wants everyone to think she's got it together. But right before dinner I found her hiding in the woods outside the house. All freaked-out, saying she'd heard voices downstairs and she got scared and ran. She begged me not to tell her parents."

"Jesus," Harper said. "Did you?"

"No. I couldn't."

"Good. I mean, unless you think she's, like, a danger to herself, I would leave it. God knows I wouldn't want my parents hearing about everything I did. They'd probably pull me out and send me to a real Christian school. None of this Quaker 'friends' bullshit."

Darrow snorted. Harper's father, who'd made a fortune running a telecom start-up, had then turned around and used his billions to secure the junior Senate seat from South Carolina six years ago. Once there, he'd quickly become the unofficial spokesperson for the far right. Blonde, beautiful, and doe-eyed, Harper was every inch the perfect Southern belle, and her sweet smile was stamped all over her father's campaign materials. If the senator ever found out his daughter had a secret belly button ring, a tattoo on her lower back, and a girlfriend, his head would probably explode. Darrow was the only person Harper was out to, and he'd guard that secret with his life.

Two more guys and a girl pushed their trays onto the table and sat down with Darrow and Harper. The rest of their usual crew: Connor, Luke, and Keagan. Like pretty much everyone else here, they were the children of Someone Important: Connor, the son of two high-powered lobbyists; Luke, whose mother was the South African ambassador to the U.S.; and Keagan, offspring of the head of the World Bank. It sometimes gave Darrow a headache, being surrounded by so much importance. Even though he was technically the kid of someone important, too, he didn't really see himself that way. His mother had come from nothing, his father from even less.

"I hate you both," Connor said with a dazzling grin. "Coach has me off anything that's even come close to a deep fryer." He was tall and sandy-haired, and had a long, angular face with oversized features that would have looked misplaced on anyone else. But Connor's confidence radiated from him like the sun, and nothing about him seemed awkward or unintentional. Darrow had never seen Connor in anything but seasonally appropriate sports gear—fall meant Redskins, winter the Caps, and spring the Nats. Today he wore a CABOT TRACK AND FIELD sweatshirt in anticipation of the meet that afternoon.

"Fine line between hate and love," Harper said, picking

up another fry. She leaned in to waft it in Connor's face before seductively popping it into her own mouth. Harper and Connor flirted so shamelessly that people often assumed they were together—a rumor Harper did nothing to dispel.

Keagan shot a quick glance at Darrow as Luke reached into his bag, pulled out an AP Chemistry textbook, and began scribbling furiously in a notebook.

"So," Keagan began, anxiously twisting a lock of bright red hair around her finger. Darrow knew what was coming. Keagan was one of the nicest people he knew, but she had a wicked addiction to gossip of every kind. She was an avid follower of the "Addie Webster mystery," as tabloids and gossip Web sites liked to call it. And though she usually had enough sense not to bring it up around Darrow, he knew she wouldn't be able to help herself today. "Have you seen Addie yet?" she asked in one breathless gush.

"Yeah, last night," Darrow said, mouth pressed in a line.

"Okay," Keagan said. "Okay, good. So it's really her. Is she, um, doing all right? Is it true what they're saying online about—"

"You know as much as I do," Darrow cut in, his voice sharper than he meant it to be.

"Keagan," Luke said, barely looking up from his chemistry. "Let up. Pretty bloody obvious Darrow doesn't want to talk about it."

"Don't put words in his mouth," Keagan snapped back. "Darrow, you don't have to tell me anything, I just thought you might want to, because—well, you were the last person to see her before she was taken and that can't have been easy, so I just wanted to say I'm here for you. If you want to talk."

112

Darrow shot Harper a pleading look. She nodded slightly, grabbed her tray, and stood.

"Sorry to break up the lovefest, but I've got to go set up for this afternoon's podcast," she said. "Darrow, can you come with? I need someone to help with the sound check."

Darrow stood and joined her, saying good-bye to the rest of the table before dropping their trays on a conveyer belt on their way out.

"Thanks," Darrow said.

"No worries," Harper said. "I've got your back."

They walked through the hallway toward Harper's "recording studio," i.e. a retrofitted janitor's closet, at the end. Despite its humble origins, Harper's two-year-old podcast had gained a following far beyond the walls of Cabot. With her unique access to the capital's leaders and a finger on the pulse of current issues, Harper's show covered everything from happenings at Cabot to the latest political storm brewing on Capitol Hill. Her loyal followers included even the most influential political bloggers, who occasionally scooped CNN based on something they learned from Harper's show. Her dream was to become a Pulitzer prize–winning investigative reporter, and she'd already been accepted into Northwestern's undergrad journalism program.

As Darrow and Harper made their way toward the senior hallway, a security guard in a dark blue uniform turned the corner, nodding at them as they passed. Thanks to the recent attacks, there were guards on every floor of Cabot now. Darrow knew it was an extra precaution to ensure that the children of the city's Important People were kept safe. But between the lockdown here and at the White House, Darrow wasn't sure whether he felt secure, or like a prisoner.

"So, have you heard anything from Elinor?" Harper asked. "How's she taking Addie's return?"

"Hard to say. She barely talks to me anymore. But she texted last night," Darrow said. "Wanted to know if I'd seen Addie."

"What did you tell her?"

"That I had," he answered.

"That's all?"

"What else was I going to say?" Darrow said defensively.

Harper raised an eyebrow. "So are you going to tell Addie about you and her sister?"

Darrow shrugged, uncomfortably aware of Harper's pointed expression. He could still picture the cold, hard look Elinor had given him when he'd confronted her about the pills and threatened to tell her parents if she didn't stop. The way she'd just narrowed her gray eyes at him and walked away. The last thing he'd expected was for her to turn around and down a handful of pills later that night, landing herself in the hospital with a tube down her throat. Darrow vacillated between feeling guilty and thankful that at least now Ellie was getting help.

Harper stopped at her locker. "Let me grab my stuff," she said, turning and reaching for the handle. Then her hand suddenly dropped and she pulled something from her pocket. She stood there a moment, back to Darrow, shoulders hunched and head tilted down.

"Harper?" he said. "Is something wrong?"

Her back straightened and she faced him, bottom lip quivering. She closed her eyes and held out her phone; there was a text message from a blocked number.

"Not again," Darrow said.

Harper just nodded. Darrow took the phone and read:

You don't see me, but I see you
And all the secret things you do
Mind your step and watch your back
You never know when I'll attack

CHAPTER 21

General James McQueen sat at his desk in the Eisenhower Executive Office Building, a view of the West Wing visible through the window behind him. He stared at his computer, the outline of his strong cheekbones, square jaw, and eight-dollar buzz cut reflected in the screen. Jiggling the mouse, he toggled between the half-dozen windows open in front of him, each displaying evidence Cerberus had sent to media outlets around the world—text messages, e-mails, discussion board postings—detailing how they'd overtly planned and carried out the attacks on the Republican fund-raiser and the Metro train. Everything had been laid out plain as day, time-stamped and dated in the weeks leading up to the assaults. It was a regular shitstorm.

Of course, the press was eating it right up. Fingers were pointing in every direction; the right was claiming the administration was weak on security, while the administration was quick to blame the intelligence community. But McQueen knew better. The NSA, CIA, DIA could only do so much. Their hands had been tied the day President Webster took office and made good on his campaign promise to severely curtail the nation's electronic surveillance policies. You couldn't catch what you didn't monitor: a fact that Cerberus was gleefully pointing out to anyone who would listen.

An alarm on McQueen's phone sounded: 8 A.M. McQueen paused what he was doing and pulled a bottle from his desk, dumping two pills out and tossing them into the back of his throat. He took a swig of water, swallowed hard, and shook his head. Damn arrhythmia. After tours in hostile zones all over the world, a piece of grenade lodged in his thigh, and two knees with zero cartilage left, the last thing McQueen ever figured would end his military career was the flu. But it had. Five years earlier, a freak bout of myocarditis after contracting the H1N1 virus had weakened his heart, forcing him to retire just before he pinned on his third star, and leaving him to pop pills twice a day for the rest of his life.

But maybe it was for the best. Out in the civilian world, the former Special Forces intelligence officer had quickly established himself as an international expert on cybercrime. It wasn't just that McQueen had a knack for coding and all things technical. He also possessed an uncanny ability to read other people, to ferret out their hidden motivations. In the early days of his military career, McQueen had personally recruited several key assets, knowing exactly when to use charm, when to rely on coercion. Now the battlefield had changed, with modern wars waged anonymously via keyboard strokes and drone strikes.

But McQueen understood something most of his younger colleagues didn't. The key to winning the battle wasn't just to out-code, outwit, or terrorize your opponent—it was to get inside the head of the other guy. Figure out what made him act. And stop him before he did.

McQueen turned his attention back to his computer and clicked open a timeline. Cerberus had been on his radar for about six years: a loosely structured organization that had grown to approximately two hundred anonymous members worldwide. Members didn't appear to know each other in real life, and communicated only with code names, using a series of ever-changing secure message boards. While McQueen had never been able to identify any of the members, he knew the code name of the group's leader—a man or woman going by the name of Dantes.

Until recently, the group had been largely known for disrupting terrorist-run Web sites using repeated denial-of-service attacks, as well as alerting authorities to potential plots. While McQueen didn't entirely approve of their methods, he couldn't deny that these so-called ethical "white hat" activists got the job done. For most of the group's existence, McQueen had been satisfied to keep a watchful eye on them, making sure they didn't venture into criminal territory.

Then, six months ago, something had changed. A group of jihadists had pulled off a late-night hack into the nation's power grid, gaining control of dozens of nuclear power plants. The entire country had been on the brink of multiple catastrophic meltdowns. The potential death toll had been staggering—millions would have died immediately, and even more faced long, agonizing deaths from radiation poisoning. But while the government had been scrambling to respond, someone else had hacked into the grid and shut the operation down. That someone was Cerberus.

Shortly after, Cerberus had sent several news outlets screenshots of the chat room where the jihadists had planned the attack, showing that critical pieces of intelligence had been missed in the days leading up to the near-catastrophe. The political fallout could have been huge. But thanks to a tip from a reporter at the *Washington Post*, the Webster administration had been able to put its own spin on the story before it went far and wide, claiming its people had been well aware of the plot, and the public had never been in any danger. McQueen had been quickly hired as special advisor to the president on cybersecurity to quell any lingering fears. And the public, who had no clue how bad things had almost been, went back to living their daily lives.

From what McQueen could tell, that's when Cerberus had gotten pissed off, suddenly going dark—until last week, when they'd attacked the fund-raiser.

And then Addie Webster had reappeared.

Coincidence? Maybe. But McQueen had spent enough time in the field to be suspicious of anything that didn't quite add up. And something wasn't adding up. Not that he could say anything to President Webster or his cronies yet. Not without concrete evidence. It hadn't taken long to figure that out. Just yesterday, when McQueen had tried to subtly raise his concerns at the morning briefing, he had been slapped back down so fast—by the press secretary, of all people—it had made McQueen's head spin.

Well, if that was how they wanted to play it, fine. McQueen

was going to do his job, with the administration's permission or not. They could worry about their opinion polls. McQueen would worry about what was really going on.

He had just begun another attempt to decode the origin of one of Cerberus's e-mails when the phone on his desk rang. He picked it up and cradled it between his shoulder and ear.

"Davis," he said. "Talk to me."

The voice of NSA Director Chuck Davis came over the line. The retired Colonel Davis and McQueen had leapt from airplanes together back in their younger days.

He listened intently to his buddy and nodded.

"Interesting," he said. "Can you send it my way?"

"You got it," said the voice on the other end of the line.

McQueen hung up. A few moments later, an e-mail alert popped up on his computer. He clicked it open, heading straight for the attachment. A black-and-white security video filled his screen, the tall trees of the Websters' Virginia estate coming into focus. McQueen watched, the creases between his eyebrows deepening as a slight figure came into view.

As he watched it move along the perimeter, apparently searching the darkness, one thing became increasingly clear to McQueen. Addie Webster was playing at something.

What, he wasn't sure.

But it definitely wasn't a game of hide-and-seek.

CHAPTER 22

Addie fidgeted in the back of the limo as her motorcade turned off Wisconsin to 37th toward the side entrance of Cabot Friends. The morning sun filtered through the tinted windows, warming Addie's cheeks. Even so, a chill worked its way down her spine as the Town Car pulled through the tall gates. The fifteen-acre campus loomed straight ahead, not nearly as grand as Addie had pictured—simple brick buildings, surrounded by neatly trimmed trees and green fields—but it still scared Addie in a way she hadn't expected. The glossy-brochure normalcy of it all. The idea that, somehow, she had to fit in. She felt like an alien that had crash-landed on another planet.

Addie sat up straight, reminding herself how hard she had worked to get here. It had taken a careful performance to make Dr. Richards suggest that school would help integrate Addie back into regular life, and the Cerberus attacks had nearly derailed those plans. But Addie had pleaded with her parents— after all those years locked up, how could they turn around and lock her up again? And so, after the Secret Service had guaranteed that the quiet Quaker school would be locked down as tightly as the White House itself, they'd agreed to let her go. The motorcade pulled up directly in front of the school. Even though they'd arrived a half hour early, students were already starting to mill about outside. Addie's car honked at a group of kids blocking its path. One by one her classmates turned, elbowing each other and pointing. Addie's shoulders tensed. Way to make a subtle entrance. At least her parents hadn't come. They'd wanted to, but Addie had begged them to stay home, knowing it was an even bigger production whenever the first lady or president showed up anywhere.

Agent Alvarez, on the other hand, was in her usual seat right next to Addie, watching the scene outside. Addie couldn't help but wonder if she'd be parked next to her in homeroom, too.

"So, here's the drill," Alvarez said, as though reading Addie's mind. "I'll escort you inside and ensure you get to your classes, then I will make myself invisible. We'll have two agents out here in a vehicle guarding this entrance. Another will be situated out front, and two more on the adjacent streets. And we'll be coordinating continually with Cabot security."

Addie nodded. "So you don't have to come to class with me?"

"Nah," Alvarez said. "I've been to high school already. Once was enough. Trust me."

A small laugh escaped from Addie's lips.

"The whole idea is to keep you protected and let you experience school like every other student," Alvarez said. "I'll be nearby keeping an eye on you at all times, but I won't be right in your face. If I'm doing my job, you won't even know I'm there."

Alvarez pulled a shiny gold smartphone out of her bag and handed it to Addie.

"Cool," Addie said, turning the phone over in her hands. "I've never seen one like this before." She began to swipe her finger across the touch screen to unlock it, then quickly caught herself. "Well, I guess I really haven't had a cell phone since the kind you flipped open to use."

Alvarez smiled. "This phone is one of a kind," Alvarez said. "Designed just for the Secret Service. You can thank Nova for that."

Addie ran her fingers over the ubiquitous star logo of her mother's company on the back. Goose bumps popped up on Addie's arms. She flipped the phone back over. Alvarez swiped her finger across the screen.

"Pretty easy," she said. "You activate it like this. Phone, text, camera—all that is right here. And check this out—the phone's been retrofitted with a special button." She pointed to the side, just below the toggle switch. "Any danger, just push it for one second and it will sound a silent alarm. We'll be with you instantly. Hold it for five seconds and it will produce a siren loud enough to raise the dead. My direct cell number is also plugged in there if you need anything non-emergency-related. Like maybe my opinion on which ballet flats match your leggings."

Addie looked at Alvarez's feet, clad in a pair of rugged combat boots. She laughed. "Will do." Addie dropped the phone in her pocket, smiling to herself as she felt the cool metal against her palm. She didn't care about ballet flats any more than Alvarez did. But she could definitely do a lot more than buzz the Secret Service with this thing. She couldn't wait to jailbreak it later and load it with some real apps, not Notepad or whatever lame stuff was on it already.

The limo rolled to a stop. As Addie and Alvarez stepped from the back, the chattering students congregating outside fell silent. Addie immediately wanted to hop back in the car and race back to the White House. But she couldn't. She had to prove she was okay. She kept her back straight. Her head high. She had to keep marching forward, even if she was on her own personal parade into hell.

Addie climbed the steps to the main administrative building. It was solid brick, like the rest of the buildings on campus, with CABOT FRIENDS written in simple block letters above the double oak doors. Addie kept her gaze focused straight ahead as she and Alvarez walked down the hallway to the office, still feeling the burn of eyes watching her. Nobody actually said anything right to her face. But they didn't have to. Addie could still hear them. What they whispered to each other when they thought she was out of earshot.

Did you see her?

That's Adele Webster.

What do you think happened to her?

She looks normal enough.

Really? You call that normal? Is she in mourning for her lost childhood?

Addie's face burned. Her fitted black T-shirt and dark coated skinny jeans had seemed like the safest bet this morning, but now she realized they were all wrong. Cabot might not have a uniform, but there was certainly an unofficial one, and Addie was pretty sure she was in violation. The dress here was simple and unassuming, but in a preppy sort of way: button-downs tucked into skirts for the girls, and chinos and polo shirts for the boys. Addie tried to shake it off. It really didn't matter what she wore. She was going to stand out. She just had to learn to deal. Fit in. At least for another week or two. Until this whole thing was over.

When they reached the office, a frizzy-haired receptionist handed her a printout of her schedule. She scanned her classes and the attached map. This place was a lot bigger than it looked from the outside. The paper shook between her fingers. This was ridiculous. With everything she'd been through, *high school* was throwing her for a loop? She took a deep steadying breath and looked up, then jumped.

Darrow was standing right in front of her. How the hell did he keep sneaking up on her like that?

"Sorry, didn't mean to scare you." He was wearing a crisp white shirt and a cautious smile. A backpack was slung casually over one shoulder.

"Hey," she said. "No worries."

He looked at her carefully, and Addie felt her breath catch in her throat. Those golden-brown eyes never seemed to miss anything.

"First days suck," he said bluntly.

"Yeah, they do," she said, letting out a pent-up breath with a laugh. It was nice to be around someone who didn't sugarcoat anything.

"What do you have first period?" Darrow asked.

"British Literature," Addie read.

"Cool," Darrow said. "Me too. I'll walk you there." His eyes flicked to Christina. "If that's okay with your friend, of course."

Alvarez nodded. "She's all yours, Fergusson. Just don't lose her between here and the playground at recess."

"Recess," Darrow said with a snort. "Funny. Who says Secret Service agents are a bunch of stiffs?"

"I don't know," Alvarez said, standing up straight and tapping her concealed firearm. "Who does?"

Darrow's eyebrows shot up. "Uh . . ." he stammered.

Alvarez laughed.

"Go on, get out of here," she said. "I don't need my charge getting a detention on her first day. I've got things to do after school. Need to get home in time for the Ellen show, you know."

Darrow and Addie grinned, then headed back into the hall. Alvarez followed ten steps behind.

"I like her," Darrow said.

"Alvarez?" Addie said. "Yeah, she's pretty cool. Not bad if you're going to have someone trailing your every move."

Addie cast a glance over her shoulder. Yep. Alvarez was there, combat boots clomping down the wood floors, causing the other students to stop and stare. Not exactly invisible, that was for sure. Addie shoved her schedule and map into her pocket and followed Darrow into another part of the building.

First bell was now just a few minutes away, and the hallway was growing more congested. Addie could still see Alvarez keeping pace, but she was surrounded by dozens of students. They held cell phones in front of their noses, bumped into each other, dug books and papers from their backpacks, laughed and high-fived. A few spotted Addie and pointed in her direction.

Fine. Addie straightened and brushed her long hair out of her face. As she met each of their gazes, they quickly turned away.

Darrow's hand touched her arm. "Almost there."

They rounded a corner and stopped at a classroom. "This one."

Addie felt more eyes digging into her as they walked inside. There were a few hushed comments. Sideways glances. A group of girls in front turned and stared, elbowing each other, but Darrow shot them a look. All but one, a pretty blonde wearing a blue sweater and red lipstick, turned away. The girl shot a narrow-eyed look right back at Darrow.

"What's up with her?" Addie whispered. "Your girlfriend or something?"

Darrow hesitated, not looking directly at Addie.

"No," he said and dumped his backpack on a table. The tables were arranged in a big U, conference-style, with about twenty chairs around them. The girl kept staring.

"Huh," Addie said.

"Well, we hung out a little last year. Nothing serious." Darrow pulled out a chair, still not meeting Addie's gaze. "Here. You can sit next to me."

Addie slipped into the seat and pulled her chair forward. The blonde girl sat on the opposite side, still watching. Addie wasn't sure what it was, or had been, but it sure didn't look like "nothing serious." Addie knew it shouldn't bother her if Darrow had had a girlfriend—of course he'd had one after all this time, probably *more* than one. But it still hurt Addie's heart a little, this latest realization that time hadn't stood still while she was gone.

The bell rang. A teacher wearing a loose floral dress, her gray hair arranged in a messy bun, glided through the door.

"Good morning." The teacher's eyes flicked around the room. Addie cringed, wondering if the woman was going to make her stand up and introduce herself.

Hello, my name is Adele Webster! I don't have anything for show-and-tell. Except this phone. Watch—I can push this button here, and every one of you can experience the exhilarating feeling of a Secret Service agent's P229 pistol in your face. Cool, right? Other than that, I'm just your average junior.

"For those of you who don't know me, I'm Miss Hastings," the teacher said, giving Addie a small nod and smile. "Now, as for the rest of you, please pass your essays to the front."

Addie watched as the students around her pulled papers from their backpacks and passed them forward. Miss Hastings collected them and placed them on her desk, then sat on the edge facing the class. She pulled out a book.

"Last night's reading," she said, holding up a copy of *Hamlet*. "Anyone care to take a stab at the major themes of the play?"

"To be or not to be!" one student called out.

"Yes," Miss Hastings said. "That *is* the question." The class laughed. "Who else wants to share their profound insights? What do you think *Hamlet* is about?"

"Revenge," a student said.

"Mortality," said another.

"Madness," said a third.

"Very good," the teacher said. "Anyone else?" Her eyes scanned the room again, pausing for a moment on Addie. Addie's throat tightened. She shrugged like she had no clue, even though she'd read *Hamlet* four years ago. Twice. The teacher skipped past her.

They were missing one.

Deception.

CHAPTER 23

Officer Reynolds waited just past the Braddock Road entrance of the I-495 HOV express lanes in an unmarked Dodge Charger, sipping his coffee. Two EZ Pass readers were positioned in his back window, and a computer was mounted on his front dash. Reynolds kept one eye on the computer, the other on the morning rush-hour traffic driving past.

The screen in front of him displayed an alert: oncoming motorist in the HOV lane, which meant at least three riders needed to be present in the vehicle. Reynolds glanced at the passing car. Sure enough, just one guy. That hadn't taken long. Didn't even get to finish his coffee. Reynolds hit his siren.

Hope saving that four bucks was worth it, buddy, Reynolds thought as he pulled out after him.

The officer eased the Charger behind the car, a white BMW X3 with Virginia tags, and sounded his siren. He watched the driver's eyes flick toward him in the rearview mirror, as if to say, *Who, me?*

Yep, that's right. Pull it over. Reynolds motioned for the driver to move to the side.

The guy looked at the officer for one more beat, then turned his focus back to the road. He hit his right turn signal. But instead of pulling over and slowing down, he got in the breakdown lane and sped up.

"Oh, come on," Reynolds groaned.

He blared his siren again and took off after the HOV violator. Reynolds's day had already started off badly. Chief had put him on nights for the next two weeks, which meant Reynolds would miss Mason play in the NCAA Sweet Sixteen. He definitely wasn't in the mood to deal with some entitled jerk who was too important to be late to his morning meeting. The only consolation was the look Reynolds envisioned on the guy's face when he gave him not one, but two—make that three—tickets; might as well throw in some "reckless endangerment" in addition to "evading arrest," along with a summons to appear in court.

The BMW weaved back into traffic and Reynolds followed. He couldn't imagine how this guy thought he could get away. To the right, the highway's main lanes were bumper-to-bumper traffic, cars moving at a slow crawl as they approached the intersection with I-66. No escape in that direction. Reynolds radioed ahead so another officer would be ready and waiting at the end of the HOV lane. And if the guy tried to get off the highway altogether, Reynolds would be on him like a fly on shit.

The BMW dodged around a few more cars, then without warning cut across an access path into the main lanes of I-495, where it promptly got stuck in rush-hour traffic. Reynolds snorted, easing the Charger onto 495, and pulled behind the BMW. He switched on his microphone.

"Virginia State Police," he said. "Please pull over and remain in your vehicle."

A set of eyes looked back at Reynolds in the rearview mirror again, and the BMW shifted lanes into the center.

What the hell was wrong with this guy?

Well, if that was how he wanted to play it, Reynolds would just tail him all the way to work and introduce himself to the guy's boss. Reynolds changed lanes, leaned back in his seat, and followed the BMW at the whopping speed of five miles per hour. The guy up ahead took one more look in his mirror and... smiled?

Just then, the Charger jolted. Reynolds sat up straight, gripping the steering wheel. Had he just been rear-ended? He checked his mirror. The guy behind him was a car's-length distance away. His car jolted again, and the computer on his dash flashed. A message popped up.

Let's just see how fast this baby can go, shall we?

The officer's eyes went wide as the car suddenly lurched forward, nearly slamming into the back of the BMW. Reynolds's chest was flung against his seat belt. His coffee flew out of the cupholder, splashing hot liquid all over his pants. Reynolds cursed and lifted his foot off the gas pedal. He hit the brakes, but the car didn't slow down.

"What the hell?" he yelled as he pointlessly pumped the brake pedal up and down. The car slowed down briefly, long enough for another message to flash across the screen.

Just don't hit anything... unless you want to go BOOM!

A picture of an explosive device, duct-taped to the bottom of the Charger, appeared below the message. The car sped up

131

again. Reynolds looked frantically for somewhere to go. Siren blaring, he jerked the car to the right, forcing a slow-moving Jeep to swerve out of his path. Reynolds could hear the distinct sound of metal crunching behind him, but he couldn't stop. He kept going until he made it to the right breakdown lane, where his car accelerated even faster—twenty, thirty, forty...up to fifty, sixty, seventy miles an hour now. The left tires of the Charger thumped wildly over the warning strip, the picture of the explosives still on his screen.

Reynolds tapped the radio to call the emergency dispatcher. "Officer in distress," he yelled. "Vehicle out of control!"

He jerked the car to the right again, avoiding a piece of blown-out tire in his path and narrowly missing the guardrail.

Dispatch answered. *"Sending assistance. Please remain in your location."*

"Can't remain in location! And send the bomb squad!" Reynolds hollered as the car barreled forward onto an overpass. He could barely hold the vibrating steering wheel with his sweaty hands. A large orange sign came into view:

WORK ZONE AHEAD. RIGHT SHOULDER CLOSED.

"No!" he yelled, pounding the brakes to no avail. He narrowly missed the sign, only to see rows of orange cones and a flashing barricade coming up fast. Behind the barricade, dozens of construction workers were raking fresh concrete. Reynolds's heart pounded. He had no choice. There was nowhere to go. It was either mow down a bunch of guys, crash into the guardrail, and cause an explosion, or head back into traffic.

He was nearly on top of the construction site now, the flashing lights of the barricade spotting his vision, orange cones ricocheting off his front hood. He could have sworn he could see the whites of the construction workers' eyes, wide with fear as they dove to the side. With a quick prayer, Reynolds hit the brakes again and jerked the car to the left. He heard the crunch of metal as his car shoved another out of its path. His front end clipped a second vehicle as he pushed across all four lanes, where mercifully, the Charger came to a sudden stop in the left breakdown lane.

Entire body shaking, Reynolds jumped out of the vehicle and looked underneath. The bomb was there, still taped in place. Breathing heavily, Reynolds stood and turned around, surveying the terrifying scene behind him: a tangle of smashed cars, fenders dented, smoke curling from the hoods. The chain reaction had caused a pileup as far as Reynolds could see. The officer's only hope was that the slow-moving traffic had kept anyone from being seriously injured. He shuddered at the thought of having harmed anyone. At least the bomb hadn't detonated.

Reynolds could hear the wail of fire trucks, police cars, and ambulances approaching. But he didn't wait. He made his way through the wreckage, looking for anyone who needed help.

Above his head, the digital traffic sign went black. The 3 MILES/15 MINUTES TO I-66 message disappeared. A new one flashed yellow in its place.

YOU HAVE BEEN WARNED.

CHAPTER 24

President Webster sat in a plush leather chair at the head of the twelve-person conference table in the Situation Room, rubbing his temples. Cheryl Fergusson sat to his left. General McQueen, NSA Director Davis, and the directors of the CIA, FBI, Secret Service, and the Department of Homeland Security rounded out the group. They silently watched the news footage of the trooper's wreck on 495 play out on the television screens surrounding the room.

The president broke the silence. "Okay people, give me the latest."

FBI Director Justin Lassiter responded first. "Our team on the ground has verified the 'bomb' strapped beneath the car was harmless," he said. "We're analyzing security footage from the precinct to see if the vehicle was tampered with there, but we suspect whoever did this accessed the car while it was parked overnight at the trooper's residence."

President Webster nodded. "Keep me posted on any developments." He glanced at DHS Director Rebecca Ashland. "And what about Homeland Security?"

"Mr. President, sir," she said. "As you know, we've upped the threat level both in the city and nationwide. We've increased security at all train stations, Metro stations, and airports."

"And Cabot?" the president interjected.

"Locked down as tight as the White House," said Robert Wilson, director of the Secret Service. "We've got additional patrols stationed around the campus, and Agent Alvarez will not let your daughter out of her sight. Of course, this is in addition to Cabot's own security, which as you know is extensive. If we have any reason to be concerned, we will pull Addie out of there immediately."

"Good," President Webster said. "Sorry—please continue, Rebecca."

Director Ashland began speaking again. "As you already know, we've also advised major malls and public venues to up their security. And we've stepped up our 'If You See Something, Say Something' campaign. However, the problem is . . ." She paused and shifted in her seat.

"Yes?" the president said.

"The problem, sir," Ashland said, "is that we can increase security in all the obvious places, but it's nearly impossible to prevent Cerberus—or anyone else, for that matter—from attacking places we can't completely secure. Just like we saw this morning."

The room fell silent again. McQueen cleared his throat.

"Excuse me, Mr. President," he said. All eyes turned toward the retired general. "I disagree. It *is* possible to predict and prevent these attacks." He thumbed through the updated daily intelligence briefing on the table in front of him. "In fact, we have pages of evidence right here, detailing exactly what was going to happen before it ever did," he said. "Text messages, e-mails between Cerberus members..."

The president held up a hand, quickly shutting McQueen down. "I think I've already made my position on this matter clear. Our current level of electronic surveillance is sufficient. Anything more far-reaching would be unconstitutional."

"Sir, with all due respect, this is pretty clear evidence that the current levels are *not* sufficient," McQueen said. "These e-mails and messages are proof that—"

"—they are trying to manipulate us into doing just what you're proposing," the president cut in. "We're not going to give them what they want. I refuse to play into their hands and spy on citizens. What I expect is for you to do your job and shut these people down."

"Yes, sir," McQueen said, clenching his jaw.

"Cheryl," the president said. "How is this playing out in public opinion?"

"Our poll numbers are still down," Cheryl answered. "I suspect they will drop further after this morning's attack. The public doesn't want to hear theories right now. They want an arrest. Something that shows we're taking action."

FBI Director Lassiter cut in. "Sir, as you know, we have a lead on the Republican fund-raiser attack," he said. "It may go nowhere, but we've finished interviewing everyone who worked the party that night—except one. A busboy. We missed him on the first go-round because he apparently clocked in using someone else's time card. But his description fits the one Burke gave us of the kid he witnessed running out, and his coworkers say he hasn't returned since that night. We're putting all of our resources into locating him."

"Good," the president said. "I want to be made aware the minute you have him in custody."

"Mr. President," Cheryl said, "I also think it would be a good idea to get out in front of today's attack with a press conference as soon as possible. We need to show the public we won't be bullied by terrorists. They need reassurance from you."

The president leaned forward on his elbows. "Set one up for this afternoon. And please stick around so we can go over talking points." He nodded toward his advisors. "Let's reconvene here this evening to assess the situation again. Thank you."

As the president began going over notes with the chief of staff, the rest of the group gathered their papers and filed out the door. NSA Director Davis caught up with McQueen in the hallway. The pair of former intel officers exchanged a dark look before heading through the lobby, not speaking, and out the door into the parking lot. There was a chill in the air and the sky was gray, a light mist falling. McQueen popped a black umbrella open and held it over his and Davis's heads. They stopped at a dark blue government-issued sedan, and Davis cast a glance around. McQueen lowered his umbrella, obscuring their faces, as Davis pulled a file folder from his briefcase.

"About our conversation the other day . . ." he said, handing the folder to McQueen. "You might find this helpful." McQueen glanced inside before discreetly slipping it into his overcoat.

He smiled at his old friend. "Good to see you haven't lost your touch."

CHAPTER 25

After British Literature, Addie broke away from Darrow for French. Ninety more minutes of class and lunch was next. Addie followed the map to the cafeteria, an airy room filled with wooden tables and surrounded by tall windows. Addie wasn't very hungry, but she slipped into the line of students anyway, grabbed a tray, and stacked a chicken salad and iced tea on top. As she moved along the line toward the register, someone tapped her shoulder. Addie turned to see the blonde girl from British Literature smiling at her.

"Hey," the girl said. "Sorry to bother you. I just wanted to apologize for staring at you in class."

"Oh. It's okay," Addie said, cheeks turning pink. She could already feel every eye in the place on her. One more set hardly made a difference. "You're not the only one."

"No," the girl said as they slid their trays forward. "It's just ... I was just surprised. I was expecting you to look more like her, you know."

"Excuse me?"

"Elinor," the girl said. "I thought you'd look more like

your sister. Sorry." She held out a hand. "Anyway, I'm Olivia Gardner. Elinor and I are friends."

"Oh," Addie said, shaking her hand. "Nice to meet you." The stabbing in Addie's heart started back up again. She had forgotten that Elinor had been a student here—before she was shipped off to rehab. Addie tried to picture her sister roaming these halls, filling a tray with food, hanging out with friends . . . but she came up blank. The fact was, Addie didn't know Elinor anymore.

Addie slid her tray to the register and paid. Olivia did the same, and tilted her head toward a table of girls across the room.

"You can sit with us if you want," she said.

"Thanks," Addie said. "But I'm supposed to meet someone here."

"Let me guess," Olivia said, eyes narrowing. *"Darrow."*

"Um, yeah," Addie said. As if on cue, she caught sight of him waving from a table by the window.

"No worries, some other time," Olivia said with a fake smile. Then she leaned in and added in a loud whisper, "But if you want my advice? Watch your back. Darrow has a habit of sticking his nose in places it doesn't belong."

Before Addie could respond, Olivia flicked her hair and walked away. Addie headed in the other direction, trying to steady the tray that had begun to wobble in her hands. The other students turned and stared, then quickly looked away as Addie passed. She felt like a walking freak show.

When Addie got to the table, Darrow slid his chair over, making room for her. She exhaled and sat down.

"You okay?" Darrow asked quietly, casting a glance in Olivia's direction.

"I'm fine," Addie said with a small smile, aware that the rest of the people at Darrow's table had stopped talking and were now staring at her.

"Hey, you going to introduce us, D?" said a sandy-haired guy in a Caps jersey.

"Sorry, guys," Darrow said. "This is Addie."

The girl next to her, a blonde with blue-tipped hair, held out a hand. "Harper," she said. Addie shook it as Darrow introduced everyone else: Connor, the guy in the Caps jersey; Luke, a kid with dreadlocks and a calculus book open on the table in front of him; and Keagan, a petite girl with long red hair and blue eyes.

"Nice to meet you all," Addie said.

"You too," Harper said, looking right at her. "We've heard a lot about you." Addie appreciated how direct this girl was.

"Yeah, I bet," Addie replied. "I'm everywhere these days. Can't even avoid myself."

Harper grinned. "You probably want to sometimes, huh?"

Addie rewarded Harper with a real smile, the first she'd worn all day. "You have no idea."

A group of girls sat at the next table. Connor glanced up from his lunch, clearly checking out one in particular, a pretty sophomore named Ruchi that Addie recognized from Biology class. He watched the girl, ignoring everybody else, as she poured dressing onto her salad. Luke glanced at Keagan, held a finger to his lips as he unscrewed the top of the saltshaker, and then dumped it into Connor's Coke.

Connor made eye contact with Ruchi and smiled. As she slowly grinned back, Connor picked up his Coke and took a huge sip, promptly spewing soda everywhere. The girl cringed and quickly looked away.

"What the *hell*!" Connor sputtered, wiping his mouth.

"Just doing you a favor, mate," Luke said with an impish smile. "She's already said yes to Sam Bergmann, and this way you're spared a public rejection."

Everyone at the table cracked up—except Addie, who wasn't in on the joke.

"Prom," Darrow explained. "Connor's been plotting to ask Ruchi for weeks now."

"Guess you're stuck with us," Keagan said.

"Wait, you want to go with me, Red?" Connor said with a smirk.

"Dream on," Keagan said.

The group laughed again. Harper nodded at Addie. "You should come with us," she said. "To prom. We all go together."

"Yeah?" Addie said. "That sounds cool. When is it?"

"April fifteenth," Harper said.

"April fifteenth. Count me in," Addie said, a small smile creeping across her cheeks.

Luke's phone buzzed. "Hey," he said, tapping the screen. "You guys see this? News alert. Some cop went insane near 66 on the Beltway. Barreled through a bunch of backed-up traffic. Caused a pileup a half-mile long."

"What?" Connor said, color draining from his face. "My parents drive 495 to work every day." He took out his own phone and began typing. "I've gotta make sure they're okay...."

"According to this, there were no serious injuries," Luke said. "Just major traffic delays. It's only getting cleared up now."

"Thank God," Keagan said.

"But get this," Luke said, still reading. "Cerberus is taking credit. They say they operated the car remotely. And there's more coming if people don't listen to them. . . ."

Harper shuddered. "More attacks?"

"Guess it's a good thing our new friend here comes with a security detail. . . ." Connor nodded toward Agent Alvarez, who was standing by the wall, watching with arms folded across her chest.

Nobody laughed. An uncomfortable hush fell over the table.

"Not funny, dude," Harper said.

"Sorry, I didn't mean anything by it." Connor pushed up his jersey sleeves, cheeks burning red.

"It's okay," Addie said softly. She looked down at her hands, suddenly realizing she had ripped the napkin in her lap to shreds. She crumpled it into a ball and tossed it on her tray, wondering why Christina hadn't yanked her out of here yet, like she had that day at Dr. Richards's office. Must be security was better here than over on Georgetown's open campus.

The bell rang, and the students emptied their trays and streamed into the hallway. Darrow stayed close to Addie, as though trying to protect her from some unseen enemy. When they reached her next class, he stopped outside the door, touching her elbow. An unexpected tingle went up her arm.

"I hope that wasn't too weird for you," Darrow said. "They take a little getting used to, but I promise, they're cool."

"It's okay, Dare," Addie said. "I'm sure I take a little getting used to, as well."

Darrow shook his head and gazed down at her, his eyes

warm but somehow sad. "Not for me," he said. "I'm not sure I ever got used to *not* having you around."

Addie's heart gave a lurch. She had expected Darrow to tiptoe around the past like everyone else, but his openness was catching her off guard. After all these years, she had figured on Darrow having mostly forgotten her, a shadow of his past, but it seemed like the opposite was true.

She couldn't stop herself from wondering—if losing her once had affected him this much...what would it be like for him to lose her twice?

CHAPTER 26

Darrow raced to the White House intern office that afternoon. He was ten minutes late, but only because it had taken an extra twenty minutes to get through all the added layers of security. He couldn't park his car until it had been thoroughly checked by explosive-sniffing dogs *and* Secret Service. At the employee entrance, in addition to running all of his personal items through the X-ray machine and walking through a metal detector, his bag had been manually searched and security had patted him down three times.

Even though Darrow knew he presented no threat at all, the whole experience made him twitchy, as though no one could be trusted. Every time he turned around, someone was speculating about the Cerberus attacks—on the news, in the hallways at school, in the packed corridors of the White House. His mother was as stressed as he'd ever seen her, barely getting home before ten o'clock every night, and leaving each morning at the crack of dawn.

Darrow checked in with the intern advisor and was immediately shuffled out of the West Wing to the Eisenhower

Executive Office Building next door, where he spent the next hour stuffing envelopes for some gala that the vice president was hosting next month. Darrow's fingers were dry from rubbing against card stock, his back stiff from sitting hunched over a box. Not to mention he'd developed a strange crick in his neck that he couldn't pop no matter which way he twisted his head.

Whoever thought being a White House intern was all glamour and parties clearly had never spent a day in Darrow's shoes. At least he only had one more box to stuff; then he was out of there.

Darrow stood, cracked his back, and stretched. The rest of the VP's staff was in a meeting somewhere else, so it was just Darrow in the high-ceilinged conference room, alone at the massive table that sat atop a heavy Persian rug. Alone, that is, until a hulking outline filled the doorway.

"Mr. Fergusson?" a voice said.

"Yes?" Darrow answered.

A large man stepped into the room. Darrow immediately recognized him by the off-the-rack blue blazer that strained to cover his broad shoulders. In a building full of tailored Armani suits and manicured nails, the guy stood out like a pit bull in a litter of kittens. General James McQueen. Special advisor to the president on cybersecurity.

"May I have a moment of your time?" General McQueen said.

"Sure, sir," Darrow answered. He groaned inwardly, wondering what sort of pet project was about to be thrown his way. Whenever these guys spotted an intern roaming the halls, they moved in like lions on an injured gazelle. Nothing like getting your work done for free.

General McQueen pulled the door shut behind him. It creaked ominously.

"Have a seat," he said.

"Yes sir." Darrow sat back down at the conference table. The general pulled up an armchair on the other side and set a manila folder on the tabletop. Great. Just when he thought he was getting out of here.

"There's something I'd like to discuss with you," General McQueen said.

Darrow wondered what it would be. Filing? Licking stamps? Sorting notes from a congressional hearing? Running to Starbucks for a triple mocha extra-foam latte? Nah, McQueen looked more the type to just slug back a packet of instant coffee and wash it down with whiskey.

"Or rather, someone," McQueen continued.

Darrow wrinkled his nose. Someone?

"Adele Webster," McQueen said.

"What about Addie?" Darrow said in a rush. He had spent so many years trying to avoid thinking about her that even now, hearing her name out of the blue made him freeze up. It was almost like he had to remind himself that he was *allowed* to think about her, now that she wasn't dead, that she was wonderfully, incredibly alive, and probably somewhere in the White House at this very moment.

McQueen leaned across the table, gray eyes squinting. "Pretty interesting, her miraculous return. Don't you think?"

"What do you mean, *interesting*? I think it's awesome," Darrow said.

"You don't find it a little odd?"

Darrow's back stiffened. He cast a glance at the closed door and back at the pockmarked face of the general in front of him. This whole thing was beginning to make Darrow extremely uncomfortable. "No," he said. "What I think is odd is that you're in here asking me questions about the commander in chief's daughter. Do you want something?"

"Yes," McQueen said. "I want to know what she's up to."

A slice of anger cut through Darrow's confusion. *"Up to?* What would *you* be 'up to' after crazies held you captive for eight years?" After all she'd been through, what right did this guy have to ask *anything* about her, besides how she was doing?

"I'm not sure," McQueen said. "But nothing about your friend's story explains some of her recent actions."

"What are you talking about, 'recent actions'?"

"I'm not at liberty to say, kid."

Darrow crossed his arms over his chest. He was getting tired of this conversation. This McQueen dude may have been an ex-general tough-guy type, but Darrow was young and strong and could have him in a headlock in no time flat. So what if maybe he wouldn't do it. He still didn't like being pandered to. "That seems pretty convenient."

"Okay," McQueen said, obviously changing tack. "So what are your impressions, then? You've spent some time with Addie, right?"

"Yeah, some," Darrow said. "I see her at school."

"Mmm." McQueen nodded. "And you guys hung out at the Virginia estate the other night. Playing hide-and-seek out in the woods, or something?" He let out a friendly chuckle. "Sounds fun."

"What?" Darrow said, not liking where this was heading.

"Oh, sorry," McQueen said with a wave of his hand. "I just

saw the security video from the estate that night. The president said Addie was outside goofing off with you. Which I admit is a little odd, because the video appears to be time-stamped two minutes after your arrival. But hey, sometimes I guess these things can be off, right?" His gray eyes bored into Darrow's. All the color drained from Darrow's cheeks, and he struggled to pull himself together as he pictured Addie crouched in the woods, hands over her head.

"Well, I still don't see what any of this has to do with me," he said with his best poker face.

"No?" General McQueen leaned back and smirked. "Like I said, I want to know what she's up to."

"So why don't you ask her father? Your boss. The president."

"You and I both know I can't do that," McQueen said. "Come on, you're a smart kid. Figure it out. I want you to do a little digging for me. Find out what she's doing in her free time. Other than hanging out with you in the woods."

"What?" Darrow got to his feet. "You're asking me to *spy* on—"

"Calm down," McQueen barked. "Do you really buy this story of hers? A couple of wackos kept Addie Webster for eight years for no apparent reason? No ransom. Didn't kill her. Just kept her locked up for the hell of it, until one day she gets lucky and runs away. That's it? Give me a break. I've been around the block a few more times than you, kid. And let me tell you, nobody makes a move in this world without an endgame."

A wave of horror and disgust washed over Darrow. The idea of Addie locked up anywhere, that strangers could have done anything to her, made him crazy. Whoever those sickos were, he hoped they got what was coming to them. That was the only endgame Darrow cared about. Still, he couldn't help but wonder...what *had* Addie been doing the night Darrow found her hiding?

"Seems like maybe I've struck a chord with you, kid." General McQueen's gruff voice broke into Darrow's thoughts.

Darrow met McQueen's eyes. "Not at all," he said in a cold, even voice. Maybe there was something up with Addie. Maybe there wasn't. But there was no way Darrow was selling her out to this jerk. She was still his friend, and Darrow stood by his friends. Well, most of the time. His stomach churned. He wouldn't make the same mistake twice—sell someone out to save his own ass.

"I don't know what your endgame is," Darrow said. "But I want no part in it. And you are going to regret this conversation when I tell—"

"You're not going to tell anyone," McQueen said.

"Really."

"This isn't a request."

Darrow was having trouble controlling his breathing. He forced his voice back to calmness. "What is that supposed to mean?"

"Oh, you know," McQueen said. "Had an interesting little chat with one of my buddies at the NSA recently. Seems you're not exactly the golden boy everyone thinks you are."

"Excuse me?" Darrow's skin crawled and his cheeks burned.

"I know—crazy, right?" McQueen said. "Who would ever guess that the son of the chief of staff for the president of the United States has a juvenile record that was conveniently buried?"

"It wasn't buried," Darrow said, blood pressure rising. "It was expunged. I wasn't guilty of anything."

"Typical 'he said, she said' kind of thing, I guess. I'm sure the rest of those guys who were hauled off to juvie weren't guilty of anything, either," McQueen said with an exaggerated shrug. "Doesn't really matter. You should know by now that nothing in this day and age ever really goes away. All you have to know is how to look in the right place. Actually, I'm not sure Georgetown would have to look that hard at all—not if I just sent it to them."

"You can't do that," Darrow said. "I could sue you in federal court. The president—"

McQueen put up his hand. "Save it for debate club, kid," he said. "Let me make this simple for you. If you want that little run-in with the law you had in Southeast when you were fourteen to stay buried, you'd better keep your mouth shut. And you'd better find out what the hell Adele Webster is playing at."

Darrow gripped the edge of the table, hands shaking.

"It's not a difficult decision, really," McQueen said. "You help me, and I'll make sure you keep that early-admission slot to Georgetown that you've got all lined up. You may think they'll be sympathetic, but you can't bank on it. And word is, you're on the fast track to get into politics yourself someday. Stuff like this comes out, you won't get elected to the student council, let alone the Senate. I'd hate to see a bright future like yours go down the toilet. All for some idiot move you made because you fell in with the wrong crowd."

Darrow lowered himself into his chair, angry and terrified. His entire life played out in his mind—all he wanted was to do something good in the world. Stand up for the little guy. Maybe be president himself someday.

But there was a time he *hadn't* wanted that, when he'd

wanted nothing to do with this world where everything was handed to him on a silver platter, everything except the one thing in the world he actually wanted: relief from the suffocating guilt that had haunted him since he was nine years old. When he'd turned fourteen, he'd started lying about where he went after school. He'd made new friends. But none of it had made him feel better about Addie. It had all just led up to that night when everything unraveled. And now Addie was back, somehow managing to be the best thing that ever happened to him, somehow managing to still screw up his life.

Darrow rubbed his temples.

"I don't know how you expect me to do that," he said. "The White House is keeping her pretty secluded."

General McQueen grabbed his folder and stood. "You're a smart kid," he said. "Youngest White House intern ever, right? Top of your class at Cabot. Captain of the crew team."

Darrow said nothing, lips pursed with anger.

"I'm sure you'll find a way," McQueen said. "Oh, and if you're still considering running to Mommy or the president with any of this, think again." McQueen pulled something from his file and dropped it on the table.

Darrow looked down. An eight-by-eleven photo of him on his daily jog teetered atop the stack of half-stuffed envelopes. Darrow gasped and opened his mouth to speak.

"Spare me another lecture, kid," McQueen said as he headed to the door, a threatening smile on his face. "Just remember: We have eyes. Everywhere. This isn't some sort of game I'm playing here. Get close to Addie. And be in my office by five P.M. on Monday with something I can use."

CHAPTER 27

Addie sat at her computer, the glow of the screen reflecting off her pale cheeks. She was supposedly doing homework before dinner. Instead, Addie was scanning the White House network, looking for the one computer she wanted. Finally, it popped up in her menu: LCWebster.

Select.

Her desktop changed. A picture of Liz, President Webster, Elinor, and Mackenzie on the South Lawn popped up. A lump formed in Addie's throat. All this time gone, and she wasn't even a background photo anymore.

"See, little one?" he'd said the last time he discovered her searching for her mother's name. *"She's back at work. She's moved on. They have a new baby. It's time you accepted that* this *is your family."* He'd leaned over her shoulder and Addie could see his pale face reflected next to hers on the computer screen, matching dimples in both their cheeks, matching slopes to their narrow noses. *"We are much more alike than we are different,"* he'd said. *"I have so much to teach you. . . ."*

Addie pushed down the memories and started typing.

Her mother had set up an extra layer of security on her

personal computer, but Addie didn't have trouble bypassing it. Why would she? Addie had learned from the best. She'd even taught him a thing or two. With a few keystrokes, she was breezing through Liz Webster's master directory. She paused and glanced around the room nervously, then shook her head. Stupid. Who did she think was watching in here, anyway? The ghost of Calvin Coolidge?

Addie licked her dry lips and read the program names in alphabetical order.

SafeguardPro

Seeker

SPQ

Addie rubbed her temples.

It wasn't there.

She searched another directory. And another; zip. Her next search came up empty. It made no sense. He'd told her she would find it on her mother's personal computer. So where was it? Maybe she had named it something else?

Addie read through every program in the directory, clicking on several. But none were right. She flicked the screen. What if it didn't even exist? What if she was going through all this for nothing? She tried a few more directories to no avail.

A knock on Addie's door interrupted her typing. She logged out and closed the browser just as her mother's head poked in.

"Hey," Liz said.

"Hey, Mom," Addie answered.

"Mind if I come in?"

"Sure." Addie closed her laptop and tried to smile casually. Her hands were still damp with sweat. She folded them in her lap. "What's up?"

"You've got a visitor," her mother said. "Finished up work early, and wants to know if you'd like to hit Shake Shack with his friends."

"Darrow?" Addie said.

Her mother nodded. "What do you think? Want to go?"

Addie was about to say no, that she should do her homework. She was nervous. She was running out of time, and there was no sign anywhere of Shi. Her mother placed a hand on her shoulder, misreading her anxiety.

"We'll double down on the security detail," Liz said, clearly trying to push back her own worries. "You'll be perfectly safe."

"I'm sorry, what?" Addie said.

"I've already talked to the Secret Service," Liz said. "They'll send an advance team to ensure the restaurant is secure, and you will have a full detail in sight at all times. So what do you think? Do you want to go?"

Addie wanted to stay exactly where she was and keep looking for Shi. But she could see from the expression on her mother's face that, despite her fears, she desperately wanted—maybe even needed—Addie to go. It was exactly the sort of thing normal teenagers did.

"Sure, sounds great," she said, giving her mother a small smile.

"Good," Liz said. "I'll call down. The driver and Christina and the rest of the detail will be ready to bring you in thirty minutes."

Forty-five minutes later, Addie, Darrow, Luke, Keagan, and Harper sat crammed together on two long benches at a scuffed wooden table in the corner of Shake Shack. The popular Dupont

Circle burger joint was packed with an eclectic mix of Hill staffers, families with little kids, and teenagers.

She hadn't been in a place like this since she was a little kid herself—warm, buzzing with people, smelling like grease and French fries. *He* didn't approve of pedestrian fare. A handspun black-and-white milkshake sat in front of Addie, and she hadn't been able to focus on much else since it had arrived. She gripped the sweaty paper cup in both hands and slurped through the straw.

"This shake is the best thing that's ever happened to me," she said, setting it back down.

Connor grinned. "No, it's not. But it's about to be." He glanced over his shoulder at Agent Alvarez, who was sitting unobtrusively a few tables away with two other members of the detail, eating a cheeseburger and pile of crinkle-cut fries. Three more agents were posted outside, keeping an eye on the perimeter. Addie suddenly felt bad for them. The smell of fast food wafting out there had to be torture. Connor turned around and pulled something shiny and silver from his front pocket.

"What's that?" Addie said.

"Shhh," Connor answered, holding a finger to his lips.

"Seriously?" Keagan said, giving Connor a disapproving look that didn't hide her amusement. "With the First Kid here? I am *so* tempted to make a scene right now, see what Coach thinks of that," she said.

"Don't hate," Connor said, unscrewing the cap, and Addie suddenly felt like an idiot. It was a flask. "Ladies first." He poured a splash of something that smelled rich and nutty into Keagan's shake.

Darrow glanced at Addie and raised an eyebrow. "Only if you want to," he said.

Addie shrugged as Connor discreetly spiked the others' shakes. This was probably the most normal night she would ever have in her life; she might as well enjoy it.

"That's my girl," Connor said when she held out her cup, and he poured twice as much into Addie's shake as he had into the others'. She decided to take it as a compliment. He poured a generous splash of golden liquid into his own milk shake, then topped off everyone else's. He raised his cup.

"To the weekend!"

"It's only Thursday," Harper said.

"Then all the more reason."

They raised their cups. Addie sipped, the cool milk shake now burning slightly as it slid down the back of her throat. She coughed a little. Discussion turned to the latest Cabot gossip, from who had hooked up over spring break, to a plagiarizing scandal at the school newspaper. It was all so incredibly normal, and that somehow made it fascinating. She watched how Darrow and his friends interacted. They were so comfortable with each other; they'd clearly been close for years. She wondered what it would be like to have friends like that, to have so many inside jokes and stories that you could practically speak to each other in shorthand. For a few minutes, she pretended that she really was one of them; that these were her jokes, too. After a while, Darrow leaned in and whispered in Addie's ear.

"I hope you're not getting bored," he said. "I know you don't have a clue who half these people are."

Addie shook her head, which was already feeling light from the little extra something in her milk shake. Nearly an hour had passed, and she had barely noticed. "No," she said, slurping up the last of her shake. "In fact, this is the best time I've had in ... well, a long time."

Darrow grinned at her. He looked so happy that, in that moment, she wanted more than anything to make him believe she was the girl he thought she was—that things might really go back to normal and they could pick up where they'd left off, continue the story of what might have been.

"Thanks for inviting me," Addie said, and a sweet, floaty feeling of serenity drifted over her. Her head was suddenly resting on Darrow's shoulder, and just then she couldn't think of a single thing that would convince her to move it.

Darrow swallowed, then raised his hand and gently stroked her hair.

"I missed you, Ad," he said, his voice low and soft.

Addie felt a deep ache in the pit of her stomach and a tingle that spread to the tips of her fingers. A loud voice brought her back to reality.

"Don't laugh about it," Harper said, her alto voice an octave higher than usual. "They're dangerous. No one knows what they really want."

The attacks. The conversation was bound to come around to them at some point. What was Addie thinking? Did she really believe she could just slip into a new life because she felt like it? This was all pretend. She was just a player on a stage. And there were more important things at stake, people she couldn't let down.

Harper opened her mouth to continue, but something beeped in her pocket. She pulled out her phone and tapped the screen. All the color drained from her face.

"I've got to go." She grabbed her jacket and stood.

"Wait, what?" Darrow said. "Why?"

Harper shoved her phone into her pocket. Her bottom lip trembled and Addie could see she was fighting back tears. "It's nothing," she said. "I've just got to get home."

"It doesn't look like nothing," Darrow said, following Harper to the door. Addie watched them as they talked, Harper shaking her head, Darrow seeming to plead with her to do something. Finally, Harper pulled out her phone and showed it to Darrow. His face screwed up tightly with anger. Harper attempted to leave again, but Darrow caught her by the arm, saying something with more force now.

Curiosity getting the better of her, Addie slipped her own phone out of her pocket and tucked it beneath the table. She tapped the screen, keeping one eye on Harper and Darrow, and one on the phone. She scanned the Bluetooth devices nearby. C'mon . . . there it was. She typed in a series of commands. She just needed a few more seconds . . .

Across the room, Harper shook herself free of Darrow's grasp and hurried out the door. Darrow stormed back to the table, cheeks red and eyes burning. Addie tapped her phone. Got it.

"What's up?" Luke asked. Darrow's jaw was clenched, his hands balled into fists.

"I can't say, but I've kind of lost my appetite. Let's roll," Darrow said.

As the limo rounded the corner onto Pennsylvania Avenue, Addie turned her back on Darrow and Christina, who were sitting opposite her. Darrow was still too angry to talk, and Christina was busy watching the road outside.

Addie tapped the screen on her phone. Just before Harper left the restaurant, Addie had found a back door into her e-mail. And now she knew what had Harper and Darrow so upset. A single, grainy video of Harper. Kissing a girl at some music festival on the Mall. With an attached message: *"just wait till daddy finds out."*

Addie's gut burned. And this time, it wasn't the whiskey. She liked Harper. From the moment she'd met her, the girl had made Addie feel welcome. Harper didn't sneak looks at Addie and then cast her eyes away whenever she looked back, like pretty much everyone else at school. Addie stared intently at her phone. The e-mail had come from a generic address, but Addie didn't have any trouble tracing it to an Instagram account. With a name. A name that made her want to throw up all over the limo's leather seats.

Elinor Webster.

CHAPTER 28

Darrow sat in the limo, silently fuming. What the hell was Elinor thinking? He knew she hated Harper, blamed his friend for "turning him against her," but he couldn't wrap his mind around this. Had Ellie always been this cruel?

The car slowed and approached the White House gates. In the darkness, the glow of Addie's phone reflected on the tinted window next to her and Darrow's mouth dropped.

He could have sworn the video Harper had shown him was on Addie's screen.

He tried to look again, but Addie had the phone in her lap now, angled away from him. She was typing, eyes intent on the screen. Darrow shook his head. She must have been looking at something else. There was no way.

The car pulled through the back gate and took a sharp turn into the White House garage. The phone in Darrow's pocket buzzed. He pulled it out. A text from Harper.

Call me. ASAP.

Darrow barely said good-bye when the limo pulled into the

parking space and rolled to a stop, instead hurrying to his own car, where he called Harper. She answered on the first ring.

"Harper," he said the second she said hello. "I am so sorry. I had no idea she would pull something like this. I'm going to—"

"Whoa," Harper said. "Slow down. That's why I texted. Elinor already called me."

"What?"

"Yeah, she was pissed. Accused me of hacking into her computer and deleting the video," Harper said.

"Did you?" Darrow said, impressed.

"Um, no," Harper said. "I don't know how to do that."

Darrow paused, thinking. "Weird. Think she deleted it herself by accident?"

"Nope," Harper said. "Because get this. She also accused me of replacing the file with some cat video." Harper giggled. "So it was no accident."

Every hair on the back of Darrow's neck stood on end. It was definitely no accident. The whole thing made him uneasy, reminded him of something. And then it hit him: Parker Carrington getting a face full of chocolate milk in the third grade when he'd spread a lie about Darrow.

Revenge exacted by the same person who had just been huddled over her phone in the limo next to him.

But how the hell did Addie Webster have the tech savvy to do that, after spending the last eight years locked in a room, virtually alone on some compound, entirely off the grid? It just wasn't possible.

Unless General McQueen was right.

And Addie was lying.

CHAPTER 29

It had been a long week. Darrow spread a stack of papers out on the table in his mother's White House office, knowing he should be happy it was finally Friday. But all he felt was dread. On Monday he had to report back to McQueen. And right now, Darrow had no idea what he was going to tell the man. He couldn't shake the image of the video he'd seen reflected in the limousine's window last night—just minutes before *someone* deleted it off of Elinor's computer. Darrow rubbed the back of his neck. He needed more time. Time to think. And he needed answers.

He pulled the phone from his pocket and typed.

We need to talk, E. That was low even for you.

He stared at the phone, waiting. She didn't respond right away. A knot formed in Darrow's gut. Elinor's silence, as he now knew, could be far more deadly than her bluntness. Ellie was never truly quiet, only quietly planning. The phone buzzed.

Thought you'd like it. Guess I have friends now who HELP ME instead of selling me out.

Darrow's jaw clenched.

So you used your friends to spy on Harper? To get back at me? How big of you.

Don't flatter yourself, Elinor replied. *Gotta find some way to pass the time here ;)*

Darrow stared at the message, anger rising, and considered writing back. Then he thought better of it. No point engaging in a word war with Elinor. He had bigger things to worry about. He shoved the phone back in his pocket. It buzzed almost immediately.

He blew out a sigh as he pulled the phone back out and checked the screen. But this time, the message was from Addie. The blood rushed to his cheeks.

Hey. No clue how to find the volume of a cube. Feel so stupid.

You're not stupid, Darrow quickly typed back.

Still need help . . . Please?!? In Dad's study.

Sure. Be right there.

Darrow stacked his papers, tucked them into his backpack, and headed down the hallway toward the Oval Office. It was six thirty and relatively quiet in the West Wing. Just the usual overachievers milling about, young staffer types with no families at home for them to worry about feeding or tucking into bed at night. They'd keep going until they moved over to Union Pub, where they'd toss back twelve-dollar pitchers of beer, stagger home to sleep, and get back up the next morning to do it all over again.

Darrow found Addie sitting on a sofa in President Webster's private study on the other side of the Oval Office. She had a computer open in front of her on the coffee table and a stack of papers next to it.

"Hey," she said, quickly slapping the computer shut.

"Thanks for coming." She moved over and made room for him next to her.

Darrow sat down and their shoulders bumped, sending a little tingle down his spine. He moved slightly away. But not too far. He dropped his backpack on the floor. "Let's see what you've got."

Addie pulled out a geometry worksheet and slid it in front of Darrow. He read the problem, then picked up a pencil and began to write out the answer, explaining each step, while Addie watched and nodded.

"Does that make sense?" he said when he reached the end.

"I mean, yes. But you make it look so easy," Addie said. "I'm too stupid to—"

"You are not stupid," Darrow said. "You're just..."

"Just what?" Addie said.

"Just going to need a little time to catch up." He handed the paper back to Addie, fingers brushing against hers. That little tingle he'd felt earlier ran up his arm. "Don't beat yourself up, okay?"

"Okay," Addie said softly. "Thanks."

"Sure." He leaned back, face flushed. Addie relaxed into the sofa next to him. They both stared straight ahead. The outline of Agent Alvarez's right arm was visible just outside the door. She lifted it, and Darrow could hear the agent mutter something into the mouthpiece on her wrist.

"Not quite the same as the tree house here, is it?" Addie said.

"At least it's more secure," Darrow said. Addie faced him, color draining from her cheeks. Darrow immediately regretted his words. "I meant with everything going on with the attacks. That's all."

"Right," Addie said and leaned forward onto her elbows, back trembling slightly.

"Are you okay?" Darrow said. He held out his hand and quickly pulled it back, wanting to touch her but losing his nerve.

"I'm fine," she said. "Just a little cold."

Darrow peeled his sweatshirt off, static crackling his hair and making it stick up. He smoothed it down and handed it to Addie. "Here. Have this."

Addie took the maroon Cabot sweatshirt and slipped it over her head. "Thanks," she said, pulling the long sleeves over her hands.

An awkward silence hung in the air. Addie leaned back next to Darrow again and he grew increasingly aware of her breath, the heat of her body so near his. He also became increasingly aware of the time. And the meeting with McQueen, getting closer by the minute. He had no idea what he was going to say. And the more time he spent here with Addie sitting shoulder to shoulder, the more conflicted he grew.

"So, have you heard anything from Elinor?" he asked cautiously.

"Ellie?" Addie said. "No. I have no idea how to get in touch with her."

"Nothing? No e-mail or anything?" Darrow said, eyes flicking toward Addie's closed computer.

Addie raised an eyebrow. "I don't have an address for her. Why, do you?"

"No," Darrow said, almost a little too quickly. "I mean, I

have her Cabot e-mail, but not her personal one . . ." His voice trailed off. Addie regarded him for another moment as his eyes wandered briefly to her laptop and then back to her. She stood, stretching her arms above her head. Darrow began to stand, too.

"Don't get up," Addie said. "Just need to run to the bathroom. I'll be right back, 'kay? Then maybe you could help me with a couple more problems?"

"Yeah, sure," Darrow said. He watched her walk away. Once she was gone, he looked back at her laptop, the green power light on the front blinking like a beacon. She'd slapped it shut so quickly when he came in . . . Was she hiding something?

He rubbed his palms on his jeans and peered into the hallway once more. He couldn't shake the feeling that Addie was lying through her teeth about Elinor. Well, there was one way to find out. He flipped the computer open and was greeted by a login screen.

With trembling fingers, he typed in the password Addie had used when they were little kids: *mrfluff.*

The screen immediately froze. Something flashed.

Invalid password.

Dammit. Darrow's heart pounded wildly as Addie's footsteps tapped down the hall, getting closer. He slammed the computer shut and pushed it away just as she entered the room, trying not to jump.

"Hey," she said, looking at the table. "What are you doing?"

"Nothing," he said. "Just waiting for you."

"All right." She raised an eyebrow, still staring at her computer, then walked around the coffee table and sat down next to him. "You ready to get back to work?"

"Of course," Darrow said, trying to slow his pounding heart.

After they wrapped up the last question, Addie stayed behind. She waited until Darrow's footsteps faded away, then flipped open her computer. Her lips tightened.

She knew it. He had been trying to log in while she was in the bathroom. The proof was right in front of her. She logged in, clicked the security program she'd installed, and read the report.

Unauthorized login attempt: "mrfluff", 6:47 P.M.

A picture of Darrow's guilty face appeared below, captured by the computer's camera as he'd tried to shut it down.

Addie closed the program. Darrow was suspicious of her for some reason. She ran her hand across the smooth silver finish of her laptop, thinking. What had he been looking for in here? The obvious answer: something to do with Elinor. Addie remembered Darrow peeking over her shoulder in the limo last night, and his questions today about whether Addie had been in touch with her sister. But why not come right out and ask Addie if she knew about the video?

The not-so-obvious answer: he suspected her of something else. Something more. Addie chided herself. She'd been so careful around everyone . . . except him. It was beginning to look like she'd underestimated her old friend.

That was a mistake she wouldn't make again.

CHAPTER 30

On Monday, Addie had the distinct feeling that Darrow was avoiding her. At lunch, instead of joining everyone at their usual table, he disappeared into the library to study, barely saying hello. He simply waved when they passed in the hallways. And he busied himself with his phone as soon as he sat down next to her in English. A guilty conscience for trying to get on her computer? Maybe, but Addie needed to be sure.

When the last bell rang she headed straight for the senior hallway, searching for Darrow's familiar dark curls among the crowd. She finally spotted him cramming books into his locker. As he turned to head for the door, she ran and caught him by the arm.

"Hey," she said. "There you are. I've barely seen you all day."

"Yeah, it's been busy," he said, keeping his eyes straight ahead.

"No kidding," Addie said. "Headed to the White House now?"

"Yep," he said. "Same place I always go after school. I'm like part of the furniture there."

Addie laughed. "Cool. I was hoping maybe we could work together again. You really helped a lot Friday. Think you could come to my dad's study?"

Darrow slowed. Students streamed past, bumping into them. "I'm sorry," he said. "I can't today."

"Why not?" she said. "Too much work? I have connections, you know. I can call off the dogs and get you a break."

"No," Darrow said. He came to a complete stop and turned toward Addie, looking intently at her face. She blinked, feeling the color rising in her cheeks.

"What is it?" Addie said.

"I've just got some stuff I need to take care of," Darrow answered. "I'll catch you later, all right?" He quickly turned and hurried toward the exit, backpack bouncing on his right arm.

"All right," Addie said to his retreating back. "Catch you later."

Alvarez caught up with Addie and tapped her shoulder. "Ready to go, girl?"

Addie nodded, still watching Darrow as he disappeared out the door. Alvarez followed her gaze.

"Something up with your buddy?" she said.

"Yeah, you could say that," Addie answered quietly. "Let's get out of here."

Darrow left the White House press office—he'd stuffed enough envelopes for the day—and made his way across the street to the Eisenhower Executive Office Building. Built from granite and slate, the elaborate structure had been heralded as both the best example of Second Empire French architecture in the country, and the ugliest building in America. But right now, as far as Darrow was concerned, it was a tower of doom. He stopped and hesitated at the bottom steps. He had no idea yet what he was going to say to McQueen. All he could picture was Addie's face when she'd looked at him in the hallway today, cheeks pink, asking for help with her homework. The way she'd rested her head on his shoulder at Shake Shack.

But then he saw that other Addie: the one crouched in the woods, the one on her phone in the limo, the one who was hiding *something*. . . .

Darrow pursed his lips and wrapped his fingers around the phone in his pocket. He wasn't sure what he was going to say, but he was sure of one thing: he wasn't going to let McQueen call the shots anymore.

Darrow jogged up the granite steps and went inside. He cleared security and headed toward McQueen's office, shoes squeaking down the black-and-white marble floors. When he arrived, he lingered just outside the door for a moment. He could hear the man's assistant on the phone scheduling an appointment. Darrow waited until she stopped talking and walked inside.

"Can I help you?" she said. She was a pretty, dark-haired woman in a Navy officer's uniform. Darrow hadn't seen her before, but then the staff around here was constantly changing; officers rotated in and out, particularly in the spring.

"Yes, ma'am," Darrow said. "I'm here to see General McQueen."

"And your name?" she asked.

"Darrow Fergusson."

"One moment, please." She picked up her phone and spoke into it, then put the receiver in the cradle. "You may go in," she said.

Darrow walked past the assistant's desk and down the hallway, to the general's office. He rapped lightly on the door.

"Come in," a gruff voice answered.

Darrow pushed the door open and walked inside. The general's office sat in a corner of the building, looking out over the West Wing of the White House. The bookshelves were lined with military memorabilia: helmets, mortar shells, challenge coins. A framed flag of the United States, folded into a triangle, hung on the wall. McQueen himself sat behind a large wooden desk, a computer and a stack of papers in front of him.

"So? What do you have for me, kid?" McQueen said.

Man, this guy didn't beat around the bush. Darrow considered what he'd seen over the course of the last several days. Some strange things, but . . .

"Nothing, sir," he said.

"Nothing," McQueen repeated flatly, unimpressed. "Were we not in the same room when I told you this girl could be compromising national security? You have two options here, kid. Be the hero who exposes a liability. Or lose everything you've worked your ass off to get."

Darrow shrugged, heart beating wildly in his chest.

"I guess Georgetown isn't as important to you as I thought," McQueen said, shaking his head. "This is why your generation is going to destroy this country. Damn trophies just for participating. You have no idea how to play to win."

Darrow fumed inside. So McQueen wanted a fight? Well,

Darrow would be happy to give him one. Time for Plan B. He fumbled his fingers on the phone in his pocket and tapped the button he'd gotten ready on his way in: *record*.

Addie sat alone in her room, laptop balanced on her knees. Darrow had always been a terrible liar. What was he really doing today? She tapped her keyboard to wake up her computer, logged into the White House intern office's schedule, and read until she found Darrow's name:

D. Fergusson: Press Office, monthly newsletter mailing

He wouldn't have blown her off for that. Addie clicked through a couple more screens until she reached his personal account. It didn't take long to find his calendar. There was only one thing on it: a meeting with General James McQueen at the EEOB. Addie looked at the time.

It was happening now.

She drummed her fingers on her computer. Okay, so maybe Darrow was doing a project for the guy. But if that was the case, why be so dodgy about it? And it wasn't on the official schedule, either. Addie drummed her fingers harder. This McQueen guy's name sounded awfully familiar.

Suddenly it hit her. He'd been brought in here six months ago, in response to . . .

Addie's fingers stopped moving. The blood drained from her face. She had to know what Darrow and McQueen were meeting about. *Now.*

It took her a minute to find the general's computer on the network, and another five to hack in. He was good—he'd added his own extra layer of security, just like her mother. But Addie was better. She sailed past it, wiped her forehead, and checked the time. 5:06. If McQueen was as prompt as Darrow, the meeting was already under way. She had to hurry.

Addie tapped a few more keys and activated the camera on McQueen's computer. An image of his pockmarked face filled Addie's screen.

"—jerking me around, kid," he was saying. "I know you have something on her. Or you wouldn't have come here today."

Addie's skin prickled. She listened intently.

"You know why I came." It was Darrow's voice, coming from somewhere else in the room. "The question is whether you're really going to follow through on your absurd threat."

"Oh, I see," McQueen said. "You're calling my bluff. Fine. Let me just show you the file I've prepared to send to Georgetown's office of admissions if you don't play ball."

Addie's chest tightened. She hadn't expected this. McQueen was blackmailing Darrow? He had no right. And McQueen was the last person she wanted on her trail. At least he hadn't gone to the president yet. . . .

McQueen clicked his mouse. Addie clicked hers. She opened another window, accessing McQueen's main file directory as quickly as she could type. She barely breathed, heart pounding, as she executed a search using Darrow's name.

C'mon. C'mon.

She could see McQueen in the corner of her screen, typing furiously.

A file popped up on Addie's monitor with Darrow's name on top. It was some sort of police report. Without even reading it, she hit *delete*, then leaned back and exhaled loudly. She performed a quick search on McQueen's computer for any other files that contained her friend's name. Nothing. It was clean. But she knew that didn't mean it was the end of things.

Darrow watched as McQueen pounded on his keyboard, face reddening. Whatever he was looking for, it was obvious he couldn't find it.

"What's the matter?" Darrow asked.

McQueen looked up, lip curled into a snarl. "Nothing's the matter, kid."

"Really?" Darrow raised an eyebrow, feeling his confidence grow. "It looks like you might have lost something."

McQueen stopped typing and folded his arms across his chest. "I haven't lost anything," he said calmly. "Like I told you before, nothing is ever truly gone. You just have to know where to look. So if you're thinking of backing out of our agreement, I'd suggest you think again."

"Our agreement?" Darrow said.

McQueen let out a frustrated breath. "Yes, our agreement. Did you bump your head at rowing practice today or something? You find out what's going on with Addie Webster and I'll make sure Georgetown never finds out about your juvenile indiscretions. Got it?"

Darrow slipped his hand into his pocket and palmed the phone. He stopped the recording and smiled.

"Got it."

CHAPTER 31

Addie couldn't sleep. Whatever McQueen had on Darrow, it was enough to make her friend consider spying on her. She had to make sure there were no traces of that police report. Anywhere. As the D.C. Metro Police's Web page lit up her screen, Addie created a backdoor into their servers, and after a half hour of searching she found Darrow's sealed file.

With a twinge of guilt, she opened the record. Maybe it wasn't any of her business what Darrow had done. He obviously didn't want anyone to know. Addie shoved those feelings aside. Sure it was. Darrow had made it her business the day he'd tried to log on to her computer.

She squinted and read the police jargon:

At 01:27 hours, Officers Blake and Parker responded to an alarm at JFK Junior-Senior High School, 2208 2nd Street SE. Officers located group of four males on the bleachers of the football field consuming alcoholic beverages. Officers approached, at which point suspects attempted to flee, striking Officer Blake in the head with a beer bottle, causing the officer concussion and severe bleeding. Darrow Fergusson, 14; Lance

Martin, 15; Daniel Lee, 14; Nick Anderson, 16, subsequently appre-hended by street patrol at 01:35 hours and charged with trespassing, consumption of alcohol by a minor, resisting arrest, and assault of an officer.

A lump formed in Addie's throat, picturing this other Darrow: the young teenager, stuck in a no-man's-land between the confident senior she knew today and the sweet boy she'd been friends with as a child. Addie couldn't help but feel respon-sible somehow, like her disappearance had knocked the uni-verse off its axis. First Elinor's addiction; now this. Addie had suffered, but they had suffered, too. Enough was enough.

One keystroke and Darrow's file was permanently deleted from the system.

Once she was done, she considered making contact. Maybe she should let them know she might have been compromised. But she quickly changed her mind. It was too risky. *He* didn't tolerate mistakes. Addie would handle Darrow and McQueen herself.

She logged in to the White House network and did one more fruitless search for Shi, then closed the computer and pushed it aside. But she still couldn't sleep. She threw off her covers and got out of bed, remembering the chocolate cake she'd skipped for dessert tonight. Maybe it was still in the refrigera-tor. Addie slipped down the hallway, tiptoeing for reasons she couldn't explain.

This is my house, she thought. *I don't have to sneak around.*

When she rounded the corner to the kitchen, she was sur-prised to discover the light on and her mother sitting at the table. Liz Webster turned around, mouth in the shape of an O.

"Hi, honey," she said, flushing. "Looks like you caught me."

"Caught you?" Addie said.

Her mother slid a plate out in front of her. "I might just be eating that piece of chocolate cake you didn't want tonight. Hope that's not what you're here for."

"No," Addie said, her mouth watering at the rich smell of chocolate. "I just couldn't sleep."

"Yeah, me neither," her mom said. "Here, sit down." She pushed out the chair next to her. "It's good cake. Grab a fork and join me. I can't eat this whole piece myself. Well, I shouldn't. It'll be just like the old days. Remember when we used to share cupcakes? I ate the bottom and you had the top?"

"Yeah, I remember," Addie said with a sad smile.

"Here." Her mom spun the plate around. "The frosting side is all yours."

Addie didn't really have the heart to tell her mom that she preferred cake to frosting now. Instead, she grabbed a fork and sat down, taking small bites. Her mother took a forkful, then set it down, silently watching Addie.

"What's the matter, Mom?" Addie said. "Do you want some of the frosting? I'm not five years old anymore. I can share."

"I know you're not five years old anymore. I mean, look at you. You're so grown-up. So beautiful." Liz Webster's voice caught in her throat.

"Mom?"

"I'm sorry," her mother said. "It just breaks my heart every time I look at you. All those years I missed and can never get back."

Addie didn't know what to say. "I'm sorry," she finally squeaked out.

"You have nothing to be sorry for," Liz said. "Nothing at all."

Addie's heart lurched around in her chest. It felt so good having a mother again. But it felt so wrong, too. Where had Liz been when Addie needed her? After Addie was stolen away from everything she knew and loved? When she'd cried in the middle of the night in a cold, dark room . . . alone.

Even when Addie had been little, before she'd been taken, her mother had been like a shadow in her life. The nanny had been the one to read Addie bedtime stories and hug her when she fell off her bike and skinned her knees; Addie's room and heart were left empty when Liz was flying cross-country on her many business meetings. She had barely known her mother then. She hardly knew her now.

Yet here they were, matching hands and forks reaching for bites of chocolate cake. Addie could feel the wall between them slowly crumbling. She didn't know whether to kick it the rest of the way down or hurry to build it back up.

The chocolate frosting was suddenly sticking to the roof of her mouth. She got up to pour herself a glass of milk, then realized she had no idea where the glasses were kept.

"Top corner cabinet by the sink," her mother said.

"Thanks." Addie filled her cup and sat back down.

"So . . ." Liz said with a hesitant smile. "It's nice to see you and Darrow hanging out again."

"Yeah," Addie said noncommittally, seeing the wheels spinning behind her mother's eyes. Everyone knew the whole Webster meet-cute story, and Liz was probably hoping for a repeat performance from her daughter. Her parents paraded it out for every election. Mark Webster and Elizabeth Chan, college sweethearts who fell in love when Mark accidentally broke Liz's brand-new glasses at the homecoming dance while trying to impress her with his not-so-graceful break-dancing moves.

Applause every time. Especially when Mark attempted to do the "robot" as demonstration.

"Hey," Liz said. "I want to show you something."

"All right," Addie said, wondering where this was headed.

Liz took her hand like they were a couple of best girlfriends and led her into the First Lady's Suite to the dressing room. Liz released Addie's hand and pointed at a brocade couch opposite the fireplace.

"Have a seat," she said with a grin. "I'll be right back."

Addie lowered herself onto the soft cushions and watched her mother disappear into the closet. She returned a few minutes later with a dress draped over her arm. She held it up by the quilted hanger.

"Well, what do you think?" she asked, twirling it around.

Addie actually gasped. The dress was an iridescent shade of seafoam green, subtly reflecting the light from the chandelier above her mother's head. It almost looked as though it was made of water. But it wasn't gaudy at all. Long and simple, with a sweetheart neckline, a plunging but tasteful back, and a subtle flare at the bottom.

"It's beautiful," Addie said. "You are going to look incredible in it."

Her mother laughed, almost sounding giddy. "No, silly," she said. "It's not for me. It's for you."

"For me?" Addie said.

"Yeah, I was going to save it as a surprise, but I just couldn't wait. You really like it?"

"Are you kidding?" Addie said. "I love it. But... what's it for?"

"Your welcome-home reception. I wanted you to have something to wear that made you feel special. It's by my favorite designer, Janie Liu. She has great taste, just like you."

Addie's cheeks flushed.

"I've been working with her on it," her mother continued. "Trying to design something that would really suit you. We had to do some guesswork on the sizing, but it can still be tweaked. Do you want to try it on?"

It was well past midnight, but Addie was wide-awake.

"Yeah, okay," she said.

"Good," her mother said. "You go ahead and change. I'm not done with the surprises yet. Be right back...."

Liz disappeared again. Addie slipped out of her pajamas and pulled the dress over her head. It even felt like wearing water, smooth and liquid. And it fit perfectly.

Addie was running her hands over the silky fabric when Liz returned. She stopped dead in the entryway.

"What?" Addie said. "Does it look awful?"

"Oh no, Addie," her mother said. "Not at all. You're breathtaking. Just look at yourself." Addie's mother pointed at a full-length mirror across the room. Addie stood in front of it, inspecting the dress. Her mother came up behind her and gently placed a hand on Addie's shoulder.

She was right. The seafoam color brought out the green in Addie's eyes and played up the contrast between her dark hair and fair, lightly freckled skin. "I've never seen anything more perfect," her mother said. "And the dress isn't bad either."

Addie snorted. "Mom. Lame." But she couldn't help looking again. She barely recognized the reflection staring back at her. The dress *was* perfect. And it was exactly what Addie herself would have chosen.

"I have something else for you," her mother said.

She held out her hand. Two jade chandelier earrings sat on her palm.

"These were Grandma Chan's," she said. "Actually, they belonged to Grandma Chan's great-great-grandma. They're very old, and they've been in our family a long, long time. I think they'd look perfect with this dress. I want you to have them."

Addie gazed at the earrings, suddenly unable to speak. They didn't belong to her. She shouldn't want them. And yet, she ached to put on the delicate green chandeliers and see how they looked.

"Here. Try them on." Before she could protest, her mother slid the earrings into Addie's ears.

Addie stared at her reflection. She looked like a stranger. A girl who had never been stuffed in a trunk, had never learned what happened when the horrors of the world were unleashed on innocents. What if she just kept on being that girl? What would happen?

"Yep," Liz said with a smirk. "Darrow isn't going to know what hit him. . . ."

"Mom!"

"I'm just saying," her mother said. "You never know . . . maybe he's the one."

"I'm not sure there's such a thing as 'the one,' " Addie said.

"Of course there is," Liz said. "Look at me and your dad. Twenty-five years and still going strong."

Addie's heart stuttered. "And all that time, you never doubted it?" she asked, trying to keep the edge out of her voice.

"Of course not," Liz said. "I've never doubted my love for your father."

"So there's never been anyone else?" Addie blurted out. "Ever?"

"That's an odd question," Liz said. "Why do you ask?"

"Just curious, I guess," Addie said. "Seems like lots of people I meet, their parents aren't together anymore. Like Darrow's. Just trying to understand. I'm sorry."

"Don't be sorry," Liz said. "I hope you'll always feel comfortable asking me anything that's on your mind. And I'll answer you as best I can. Deal?"

"Deal," Addie said.

"So, to answer your question . . ." Liz said.

Addie held her breath.

"Of course I dated before I married your father. But after— no, there's never been anyone else." Liz diverted her eyes from Addie for a moment before smiling. "It's always been Mark."

"Of course," Addie said. She faked a yawn. She'd heard enough. "I'm getting tired. I think I'd like to get changed and head back to bed. Thanks for everything, Mom."

"Oh, Addie." Liz hugged her daughter. "I was hoping we could play dress-up and gossip all night. But I understand. I'm getting tired, too."

"Okay. Thanks again, Mom."

"No, thank you, honey," Liz said. "It's been so good.

Talking to you like this. We should make this a regular date. This was just what I needed."

"Yeah," Addie said. "Me too."

It was exactly what Addie needed.

A reminder that her mother was nothing but a liar.

CHAPTER 32

The next day after school, Addie sat in the president's study. Her laptop was open on the coffee table, but she was staring past it at the television on the wall, where live news coverage of a White House press conference was under way. President Webster stood at the podium, flanked by American flags, the White House emblem displayed on the blue wall behind his head.

He addressed the room full of reporters, but looked straight at the camera.

"Thank you for being here today," he said. "As you know, we have been pursuing leads in the recent attacks on our nation's capital, carried out by a group calling themselves Cerberus. The perpetrators of these attacks believed they could use fear tactics to chip away at our core values. But they will never win. Today, I'm pleased to announce we've made a significant breakthrough in our investigation, with the arrest of an individual linked to the cowardly attack at the Reagan International Trade Center."

Addie sat up straight. An *arrest*? A murmur worked its way

through the crowd of reporters. Questions began to erupt from the front row.

Mr. President, how were you able to identify the suspect? Mr. President, can you give us a name? What is the alleged attacker's background?

"Jonathan will get to your questions in a moment," the president said, nodding toward his press secretary. "But first, I'd like to introduce FBI Director Justin Lassiter, who with the help of local law enforcement apprehended the suspect this morning, as he attempted to board a plane to Mexico at Reagan National."

Addie took several deep breaths through her nose as President Webster moved to the side and Lassiter took the podium. He placed a sheet of paper on top.

"Thank you, Mr. President, sir," he said and began reading from his notes. "At ten twenty-six this morning, we apprehended Tyler Randall, nineteen years old and of no fixed address, in connection with the attack on the Republican fund-raiser at the Reagan International Trade Center. Mr. Randall has been positively identified as the employee who was seen fleeing the room just moments before the artificial bomb detonated. Mr. Randall is now in custody and is being questioned. His laptop has been sent to the FBI forensics unit to extract any data that can lead us to other members of the Cerberus organization." He stopped reading and cleared his throat. "We believe today's arrest marks a significant turning point for the investigation into these attacks, and expect more developments to be forthcoming. Thank you, Mr. President, for the opportunity to speak, and to the members of the press for being here today."

The director folded up his paper, stuck it in his suit pocket, and stepped away from the podium with a nod. Press Secretary Jonathan Waite moved behind it.

"Thank you, Director Lassiter," Waite said, and turned to address the reporters. "I am happy to answer any questions you may have at this time."

A reporter with long black hair in the front row raised her hand.

"Yes, Anne," Waite said.

"Thank you," she answered. "Do you believe that the suspect in custody, Mr. Randall, is tied to all three attacks? And if not, do you believe he can lead you to the people who are responsible?"

Waite nodded. "Yes, we have good reason to believe Mr. Randall played a key role in the Cerberus organization, and based on what we've learned from him so far, we expect more arrests will be forthcoming."

More murmurs and hands being raised. Waite gestured at another reporter. Addie squinted at the television in disbelief.

The man stood. "So, does the administration believe that the threat has passed?"

"I believe we have Cerberus on the run," Waite responded. "And it's just a matter of time before we dismantle the entire organization."

Addie couldn't take any more. She flicked off the television. There was only one person who held all the power, and he would never let himself be known to someone like Randall.

She sucked in a breath and considered making contact. But suddenly it felt too risky. So she walked into the hall, where Christina was perched like a sentry. Addie didn't think she'd ever get used to dragging a Secret Service agent with her every-where she went. At least it wasn't forever.

"Hey, Christina," she said.

"How's it going?" Alvarez answered.

"Good," Addie said. "How long till I'm expected upstairs?"

"You've got about an hour," Alvarez said.

"Enough time for a run?" Addie asked.

"Yeah, sure," Alvarez said. "We can hit the track."

"Oh," Addie said. "I was sort of hoping we could go some-where more interesting instead. Like the Tidal Basin or the Mall. I'm starting to feel a little cooped up here."

"Sorry, Ad," Alvarez said. "Takes a little more planning to do an off-premises run. We can't just have you out there in the open without proper protection in place."

"Of course." Addie could only imagine. The Secret Service would probably have to shut down all of D.C. just so she could take a jog. "The track it is," she said. "Beats the treadmill."

Addie changed, and she and Alvarez exited through the glass doors of the Oval Office onto the South Lawn. A quarter-mile track circled the grounds, weaving its way between the gardens and trees, passing the tennis courts and swimming pool. Addie extended each leg one at a time and stretched her hamstrings. She sucked in a breath of spring air and raised her arms over her head, leaning from side to side. Okay, so maybe it wasn't a running path along a river through the woods, or a sandy beach, but it would do.

"See ya," Addie said with a little salute to Alvarez.

Alvarez nodded. "Enjoy your run."

Addie took off, feet flying and arms pumping. She had never been good at starting slow. Within minutes, her heart was pounding and sweat was beading on her neck. But she didn't let up. Soon, the endorphin rush would kick in. Her ragged breathing would yield to a runner's high.

And Addie would feel truly alive.

As she rounded her first lap, it occurred to Addie that her running skills might look a little too good for someone who'd been locked up for eight years. So she slowed her pace and let her mind go blank. Third, fourth, fifth lap. Addie listened to the birds chirping. The White House became a colorless blur that melted into the blue sky. Just another cloud, drifting along the horizon.

As Addie circled the track an eighth and final time, she paused by the east exit, inspecting the tall wrought-iron gate that kept the world out. Or did it lock her in? She wasn't sure anymore. For a split second, she wondered how high she'd need to jump in order to clear it. One good running start, and she would fly right over.

The muscles in her calves twitched as she remembered the last fence she'd jumped. Security had been terrible at that airport. The place was utter chaos. A jumble of people and luggage all clogged around customs, carts banging into each other, babies screaming. Addie had sailed through the lobby and right out the front doors before anyone had realized she was gone. But there had been nowhere to go. The ocean on all sides. Endless sky above.

She had stopped, surrounded by infinite blue. She was twelve. Alone. As she stared out at the ocean, she'd wondered if freedom smelled like the sea, all salt and fish and sun. If waves could cradle you in their arms and sweep you away somewhere safe. But just then a seagull had screeched overhead, startling her, and in its plaintive wail she'd heard the sound of Mikey's screams as the belt hit his skin. That was the moment she knew she couldn't do it.

There was no escape.

There never would be.

The waves would only crush her, until her lungs were filled with water and she could no longer breathe.

So she had turned around and run straight back, to the man she called Father. No, she didn't just *call* him Father. In that moment, she knew it was useless to try to deny it anymore. He *was* her father. And nothing would change that fact, no matter how far she might go.

Addie was jolted from her thoughts by the sound of someone yelling her name.

"Addie! Addie! Get down!"

Addie turned to see Alvarez running straight toward her, gun drawn, arms and legs pumping double time. Addie froze.

"I said, get down!" Alvarez yelled again. What? Did Alvarez think she was trying to escape? Was she getting ready to *shoot* her? But before Addie could even process what was happening, the Secret Service agent was on Addie's back, knocking her flat to the ground. Something whooshed overhead. Addie looked up in time to see what looked like a child's toy airplane fly directly over them and skid to a stop in the grass beyond the track. Alvarez shouted into her mouthpiece.

"We've got a breach," she said. "Drone on the South Lawn. Unknown whether device is armed."

Alvarez grabbed Addie's arm and pulled her to her feet.

"Let's go!" she said, not even giving Addie time to wipe away the gravel lodged in her palms. They sprinted across the lawn as Secret Service agents rushed out of the White House in the direction of the drone.

Just then the device exploded, sending a twist of bloodred smoke into the sky above it. Addie screamed. The Secret Service agents stopped in their tracks. Their earpieces buzzed. But instead of a message from the central office, a different voice broke into the communicators.

"You have been warned."

CHAPTER 33

McQueen sat at his desk. It was after midnight, but the retired general wasn't going anywhere—not until he'd figured out what these assholes were playing at. Today, they'd flown an unmanned drone over the White House fence and onto the South Lawn. McQueen figured the jerkoffs would be dancing in the streets after pulling off that stunt, especially since the drone had crash-landed right next to the president's daughter. But instead of sending out the usual after-the-fact missives to the press, Cerberus had suddenly gone dead silent. It didn't make sense.

Of course, President Webster and his close advisors were already declaring victory amongst themselves, convinced they had the hacktivists on the run. The boy in custody was giving up names fast and furious. FBI agents were already getting warrants for more arrests. And the forensics lab was dismantling the kid's computer, extracting all the data from the hard drive.

But the whole thing made McQueen suspicious. It was too neat, wrapped up like a Christmas present with a pretty red bow on top. There was no way that the kid the FBI had downtown was Dantes, nor was he likely to know his identity. And nothing McQueen had ever observed about Cerberus or its elusive leader had indicated that the next move would be to just...*go away.*

McQueen went back to his files, once again opening the e-mails and texts Cerberus had sent to the media after the fundraiser, Metro, and Beltway attacks. He lined them all up side by side and began the long process of tracing their original IP addresses. Again. Just like before, they pinged all over the globe, leading McQueen nowhere.

Except, hold on... he squinted at the screen and rubbed his eyes. A pattern was emerging. Breathless, he traced another e-mail. Bingo. McQueen smiled to himself.

Maybe they weren't so careful after all. Maybe they'd gotten a little too cocky—and had finally left a trail that would lead McQueen right to their front door.

CHAPTER 34

Michael had to grab the laptop to keep it from sliding off the table as the Gulfstream G650 banked left, beginning its final descent. Outside his window, the stone and marble monuments of the most powerful city in the world grew closer. The plane turned, running parallel with the Potomac River below. The cabin smelled like coffee, and Michael felt someone's hot breath on his neck.

"Any updates?" his father asked, leaning over Michael's shoulder.

"No," Michael said.

"Are you certain?"

"Yes, Father," Michael said, bristling at the words. He was tired of always being second-guessed. Of course he was certain. He wasn't stupid. But it had been three days since her last communication. Michael was getting nervous. If something had happened, if something had gone wrong, she wasn't here, but he was . . . Michael carefully weighed his next words.

"Do you think she's been compromised?" he said. "Could that guy actually have told them something useful?"

The pilot's voice crackled over the intercom. *"Please take your seats, fasten your seat belts, and prepare for landing."*

Michael's father stood up straight and walked to the leather seat opposite his son. He sat, pushing his glasses up the bridge of his nose, and leaned back, thinking. Michael and his father were the only two passengers on this private jet, which had spent the night hurtling across the Atlantic. Their breakfast dishes, half-eaten croissants, and empty coffee cups were still scattered across the table. No one would come by to clean them up until after they had landed and deplaned. Michael's father didn't like to travel with more than the bare minimum for a crew, which generally meant just a pilot, co-pilot, and flight attendant if necessary. The more outsiders you let into your circle, the harder they were to control. Michael's father was very careful about who he gave access to, within the top levels of Cerberus. It was important not to place trust in the wrong people, especially now.

Michael was used to it, though. The paranoia. The precautions. The world was a dangerous place. And this plane was their second home. Maybe their first, really. His father had associates all over the globe—most of whom, like Michael's dad, preferred to keep their meetings private.

"No," his father finally said. "The busboy doesn't know anything. I'm certain of that. And forensics won't find anything on his computer, either. I made sure. Hopefully your sister is just being careful. We're reaching the final stages and we have a lot at stake here. I don't think I need to remind you of that." The tattoo on Michael's back throbbed like a phantom limb. Three heads growling at him at once, mouths open, fangs bared.

"No, you don't." Michael began to type. The screen in

front of him changed, a string of messages from their members. Father had always handled communication with the rest of the organization, but he'd turned more of it over to Michael in the last few weeks, especially as their attacks on D.C. had escalated. Michael read, the color draining from his face.

"We have a problem," he said, shakily spinning the computer around. His father's expression hardened.

"She should have told us," he said flatly.

"So what do we do?" Michael asked.

The plane hit the runway with a jolt and slowed to a stop. Outside the window, Michael could see the Washington Monument and Jefferson Memorial silhouetted against the pale blue early morning sky. His father turned and watched the scene outside for a moment, too. When he shifted his gaze back to Michael, his face was cold.

"We fix it," his father said.

CHAPTER 35

Darrow was stuffing books into his backpack, getting ready for another day at school, when his phone buzzed. He glanced down. An e-mail alert from his White House account. He tapped the screen and cringed. McQueen.

Situation has changed. Meet me in my office. 8:15 A.M. Urgent.

Darrow's eyebrows bunched together. Damn right the situation had changed. Darrow had his recording, and he didn't have to take being blackmailed. Juvenile record or no juvenile record.

Darrow checked the time. It was seven. School started at eight, but the first period today was "morning meeting," the traditional Quaker meditation, and he didn't really need to be there for class until nine thirty. He grabbed his things and went downstairs for breakfast. His mother was in the kitchen eating a bowl of quinoa and reading the *Washington Post*. She folded the paper and set it on the table.

"Morning, hon," she said. "Join me?"

"Sure," he said. He grabbed a bagel, cream cheese, and a gallon of orange juice and sat down. He poured himself a glass of juice, drank it all in one long gulp, and poured himself another. Cheryl watched him, eyebrow arched.

"I was wondering where the last gallon went," she said. Darrow smirked as he filled a third glass. He spread some cream cheese on his bagel and took a bite, staring absentmindedly out the window. A bird fluttered from branch to branch on the big tree in their backyard, landing briefly on one, only to move to the next. There was something . . . off about McQueen's e-mail. If he just wanted to prove he hadn't lost Darrow's file, why make such a big production out of it? Why tell him the situation *had changed*?

"Hey," Darrow's mother interrupted his thoughts. "What's got you all distracted this morning?"

"Huh? What?" Darrow said. He shook off the question. "Nothing."

"Nothing. Of course," Cheryl said, glancing at the newspaper. The front-page headline was about the arrest of a man implicated in the Cerberus attacks, and hinted more arrests would soon be made. Darrow saw no mention of the fact that an unmanned drone had breached the White House perimeter. He wasn't surprised, though. His mother had told him they'd managed to downplay the story. For some reason, Cerberus hadn't come forward to take credit this time, and the administration was just playing it off as an accident. No one beyond a small circle of White House insiders even knew the drone had detonated. Or the fact that Addie had been just feet away when it did. Darrow shuddered. Had that drone been armed, she might be dead.

"She's okay, hon," Cheryl said, reading his mind. "Addie. I know you're worried about her, but she's fine. All right?"

"Sure," he said. Cheryl got up and rinsed her bowl in the sink, then slipped on her suit jacket and headed to the door. "I've got to run, but I'll see you tonight." She blew him a kiss.

"Have a nice day, Mom," Darrow said.

He sat there a little while longer before leaving. When he reached the EEOB, it was five minutes past eight. He didn't know what McQueen wanted now, but he was certain it wasn't to meet for coffee and doughnuts. At least this time, Darrow thought as he tapped the phone in his pocket, he'd be ready.

When Darrow entered McQueen's office, his assistant waved him through. "Go on in. He's expecting you," she said. "Been working here most of the night."

Darrow walked around her desk and down the hallway to the door of McQueen's office. It was partially closed. He could smell coffee brewing on the other side. Darrow rapped on the door with his knuckles and waited for the gruff response. It didn't come.

Darrow knocked again, and the impact pushed the door open slightly. McQueen's chair was turned away, but Darrow could see the outline of the general's broad shoulders. He walked inside.

"General, sir?" Darrow said. "It's Darrow Fergusson. You wanted to see me."

The man in the chair didn't answer. With growing trepidation, Darrow took measured steps toward McQueen's high-backed leather chair. Maybe he'd fallen asleep? His assistant had just said he'd been working late. But something about the angle of McQueen's head didn't look right. Darrow's heart pounded.

Darrow rounded the desk. An empty bottle of medication

sat on top, cap next to it. Darrow called out McQueen's name again and touched the chair. It spun toward him. The general wasn't wearing his usual suit, but a gray Army T-shirt and athletic pants. His head lolled unnaturally to the left. Darrow gasped. Frantic, he put two fingers on McQueen's neck. There was a pulse, but it was faint.

"Help!" Darrow yelled. "Somebody! Help!"

As Darrow moved the general to the floor, McQueen's assistant rushed into the room and screamed.

"I think he's had a heart attack," Darrow said. He shoved his palm into the general's chest and began counting out compressions. The secretary pulled the phone off the desk and dialed 911.

"Come on, *come on*," Darrow said, pushing against McQueen's rib cage. He wasn't the general's biggest fan, but he sure as hell didn't want him to die.

Out of nowhere, a hand reached up and gripped Darrow's shirt with such force he almost screamed. McQueen's eyes flew open and he stared at Darrow.

"Ad," *cough*. "Ee," *cough*. "She's sir," *cough choke*.

"What?" Darrow said. A strange wheeze came out of McQueen's throat. Darrow shook his head. "Stop. Don't try to talk."

McQueen's assistant began shouting into the phone.

"I'm in the office of General James McQueen, fourth floor of the Eisenhower Executive Office Building. He has an arrhythmia and appears to be having a heart attack," she said.

McQueen heaved another breath.

"Sir..." he sputtered again. And then the hand gripping Darrow's shirt released and fell to the ground. Darrow watched in horror as General McQueen's eyes stopped looking at him and rolled into the back of his head. He pushed a few more compressions, but it was pointless.

All the breath left Darrow's chest. McQueen was dead. The operator's voice drifted from the phone in the secretary's hand.

"Please remain where you are, ma'am. Help is on the way."

A tall, slim figure leaned against the cool granite of the EEOB's exterior wall, just out of sight of the main entrance, hunched beneath a black trench coat. From behind a pair of sunglasses he watched the stretcher carry away the corpse. He knew it was a corpse and not a patient because the sheet had been pulled over the large man's face. A crowd had gathered, including several who were covering their faces and sobbing, along with the typical curious onlookers who were snapping photos with their phones and whispering among themselves, hoping they'd witnessed the demise of someone important.

The legs of the stretcher screeched as the EMTs lifted it into the back of the ambulance. He watched as the rescue vehicle drove away. No lights flashing. No sirens for the dead.

It was done.

He turned and disappeared into a crowd of tourists and made his way down Pennsylvania Avenue. As he walked, he looked down at the phone in his hands, slick from his sweaty palms. He was still in shock. He had been worried the plan might not work. He almost wished it hadn't. He'd never helped kill someone before, and it left him with a strange feeling in his gut. Hollow. Like a different person. A weird shell of himself.

Sometimes he hated this world—a world where it was possible to kill so easily, without looking someone in the eye.

Today, an EEOB janitor had made sure of that. A quick swap of McQueen's normal daily heart medication for a lethal dosage while the general was away from his desk exercising, and a half hour later the general had unwittingly offed himself. Michael's body suddenly felt inexplicably light, as though he could no longer feel his arms and legs. What had he just done? And what did this make him? A terrorist? Was he no different than . . .

He couldn't think about it anymore. He tapped the phone's screen and typed a message. The answer came back almost immediately.

Good work, son. I'm proud of you.

I'm proud of you. It was all he'd ever wanted. He smiled and put the phone in his pocket, trying to forget about the man under the sheet. He wasn't a man. Just a threat. That was all.

A threat that had to be neutralized.

CHAPTER 36

Darrow stood outside Harper's "recording studio," tapping his foot and glancing furtively up and down the empty hall. When the red light flicked off he knocked and pushed the door open, not even waiting for an answer.

"Hey," Harper said with a jolt. She pulled her earphones off. "You scared me."

"Sorry." Darrow walked inside. The room was all of four feet by four feet, walls covered in thick black soundproofing foam. Harper sat in front of a small table that held a computer, a couple of speakers, and a notepad. A big silver microphone on a retractable metal arm stretched in front of her face. She pushed it away as Darrow pulled the door shut.

"What's up?" Harper said. "Want to be interviewed for my segment on the children of the rich and famous and how they manage to cope with driving ridiculously fancy cars and hanging out with beautiful people?"

"No," Darrow said, without even smiling at her lame recurring joke. He began pacing the small room. "Something's happened. I need your help." He'd come straight from McQueen's office. The whole thing had left him rattled, and not just because he'd never seen someone die before. What the hell had McQueen been trying to tell him? It was something . . . something about Addie.

"Whoa, deep breath," Harper said. "Have a seat and tell me what's going on."

Darrow sat in a metal folding chair tinged with rust and tapped his long fingers nervously on the desk. "I need a favor."

"Okay," she said slowly. "What?"

"Remember last year when you did that exposé on the football team selection?" Darrow said. "Recorded the coach taking bribes for the starting lineup?"

"Yeah," Harper said with a snort. "Shit really hit the fan on that one. But what does that have to do with you?"

"I was hoping I could borrow whatever you sent the assistant coach in to record them with," Darrow said, spitting the words out almost faster than he could properly pronounce them. They felt like little missiles shooting from his mouth. "You know, without anyone knowing."

"Come again?" Harper shook her head. "You want to record someone without anyone knowing? Who?"

Darrow didn't say anything.

"You're gonna have to do better than that," Harper said. "Addie."

"Addie?" Harper said. "What the hell for?"

Darrow's cheeks burned and he looked away. "It's complicated," he said.

"Yeah? Well I'm not giving you shit unless you tell me

what's going on," Harper said. "You can't just invade some-one's privacy for no reason. Sorry, D."

Darrow knew she was right. He'd made the same argument to McQueen just days ago. Right before the guy died in his arms, gasping Addie's name.

"Okay," he said. "You can't tell anyone, all right?"

"When have I ever told anyone anything?"

"I know," Darrow said. He trusted Harper. Right now, she was probably the only person he trusted. "Here's the deal. There's just something . . . off, you know what I mean?"

"She's been locked in a room with almost no human con-tact for eight years," Harper said. "Of course something's off."

"That's not it," Darrow said. "You know that whole thing with Elinor trying to expose you and Emma?"

Harper visibly cringed. "Someone really saved my ass on that," she said.

"I'm pretty sure that someone was Addie," Darrow said.

"Seriously? What makes you think that?"

"I just know the way she thinks," Darrow said. "And I'm pretty sure she did the same thing for me, too. Erased my juve-nile record before someone could use it against me."

"Okay, so she's some sort of high-tech vigilante. What's the big deal?"

"It makes no sense! How does someone learn how to do that when they've been locked up with no outside contact for half their life? And why hide it if you can?" Darrow said in a rush. It felt good to talk to someone about his fears, even if Harper was going to tell him he was nuts. In fact, he kind of hoped she would. Then maybe he could stop worrying about Addie and get on with his life.

"So, what, you think she has some kind of...agenda? Someone on the outside is controlling her?"

Darrow shook his head. "All I know is I'm scared. If there *is* someone controlling her, she could still be in danger, her whole family could be in danger."

"Then you've got to go to the Secret Service," Harper said. "Her father. Your mother. Someone."

"I can't," Darrow said. "They won't believe me."

"That's insane."

"Oh yeah? That guy I told you about?" Darrow said. "The one who was going to use my juvenile record against me? He's the only person in the administration who wasn't buying Addie's story. He was trying to blackmail me so I'd spy on her. Then he e-mailed me this morning to say something had changed and he needed to see me. Except when I got to his office this morning, he died. Right in front of me."

Harper's blue eyes were huge. "How?"

"It seemed like a heart attack. But...it's weird, right?"

"I don't know. Have you thought about just *talking* to Addie?"

He shook his head. "You don't get it. She's hiding something. Big. And she's scared, I can tell. This is the only way I can find out what it is."

Harper sighed, opening a desk drawer and shuffling its contents around until she pulled out a small silver disk, no bigger than an M&M. "I really hope you're wrong about this."

She handed him the recording device, then grabbed a larger black rectangle with an antenna that looked like a walkie-talkie and gave him that. "This is the receiver," she explained.

"So how does it work?" Darrow said.

"Like you think it would," Harper answered. "Place the recorder close to your subject—as close as possible. I have to warn you, the sound quality isn't great. It's not like I'm operating on a big budget around here. So it's critical you place it properly."

"Okay," Darrow said. "Then what?"

"You'll need to be within a mile to pick up the transmission," Harper said. "So plan accordingly."

"Thanks," Darrow said. He stood and twisted the doorknob, the light from the hallway hitting him square in the eyes. He squinted. "I owe you one."

"You owe me several," Harper said. "But who's counting?"

A small laugh escaped from Darrow's lips.

"You sure you know what you're doing?" Harper said.

"Not at all. But when did I ever let that stop me?"

Harper shook her head. Darrow closed the door, walked into the hall, and froze. Addie was standing directly across from him, leaning on a locker and scrolling through something on her phone. She glanced up.

"Hey," she said.

"Hey," Darrow answered, trying to hide the surprise on his face. "You're here. I'm glad you're okay."

"Why wouldn't I be?" Addie said.

"I heard about the drone from my mom," Darrow said, lowering his voice "I was worried about you. You didn't answer my text last night. . . ."

"It was pretty scary, but I'm okay," Addie said. "And I texted you back this morning. You didn't see it?"

"I guess not," Darrow said. "I was busy."

"I noticed you weren't in morning meeting," Addie said.

"Didn't feel like contemplating your inner light for an hour?"

"Overslept," Darrow said, beginning to feel uncomfortable.

"So what, you were busy or you were sleeping?" Addie said. "Or were you busy sleeping?"

Darrow gave what he hoped was a casual shrug. "I was busy oversleeping. Gotta run. Don't want to be late for History."

"Right," Addie said, squinting at him. "Well, guess you'd better hurry then."

"Yep," Darrow replied. "Catch you later."

"Yeah, if you can," Addie said, a smile tucked into the corners of her mouth.

The key to winning chess was to always stay at least three moves ahead of your opponent in your mind. Addie had learned that from Mikey. She remembered the first time they'd met. He'd knocked on her door one afternoon when she was eight, about three months after she'd been taken. It was a soft knock. Not the authoritative *rap-rap-rap* she was used to hearing. Instead, the key scraped gently in the lock and the door slid open slowly.

"Hello?" a soft voice said.

It wasn't a man but a boy; he was only a few inches taller than Addie. He was thin, with olive skin and wispy, light brown hair.

"I thought perhaps you'd like to play?" His speech was oddly formal, not like any other kid Addie had ever met. She wondered if he spent much time with other children. He held out a wooden box. "I have chess," he said. "It's all Father lets me play. Do you know how?"

She shook her head. "Maybe you could teach me?" She

was so excited to see another person after three months of near-isolation—another kid—she had to restrain herself from running over and pulling the boy into the room. There was something so cautious about him, the way his shoulders hunched and he kept his eyes cast downward, that she was afraid she'd scare him away if she did.

"Can you come in?" Addie said.

"If you'd like," the boy said.

"I would. What's your name?"

"Michael," he answered as he trod carefully across the carpet, barely making a sound. He set his box on the table where Addie ate her meals every day and began unpacking the pieces, placing them on the board. He held them up as he talked. "This is the king. This is the queen. These are the rooks, bishops, and knights. And, of course, the pawns. White always goes first."

"Why?" Addie said.

"I don't know," the boy answered. "Those are just the rules."

He had a sweet voice that he barely raised, and a kind smile. He didn't seem like a Michael, not at all. More like a Mikey. So Addie began calling him that. And he didn't object.

Addie began to watch the clock, waiting for his visits. And he came back, every day—box tucked under his arm, carefully setting up his pieces and patiently explaining the game. After the third day, Addie had already figured out how to beat her new friend. But as she cornered his king, preparing for checkmate, she saw the boy's face crumple in disappointment. Terrified to lose him, she let him win that day. On the fourth and fifth day, too.

And on the sixth day, the man finally let her come out of her room to join the family.

Addie craned her neck and watched Darrow disappear around the corner. She hadn't expected to see him come out of Harper's studio. And it was clear he hadn't expected to see her, either. She could tell by the look on his face. It reminded her of when they used to play Go Fish back in the governor's mansion. It was always obvious whenever Darrow drew the card Addie needed. He was totally incapable of holding anything in. Also, Darrow was never late. For anything.

So what was he trying to hide from her this time?

She didn't know, but she would find out. Because she was pretty sure it wasn't the ace of spades. And this wasn't a game of Go Fish anymore.

Darrow sat at his desk at home, the childish butterfly locket laid out in front of him. The glue Addie's nanny had used to fix it had long since given way, a single broken hinge barely holding the two halves of the wings together. Darrow flipped it open and pulled Harper's bug from his pocket. He licked his lips and carefully placed it in the center, breath held.

A perfect fit.

Darrow exhaled. He unscrewed the glue and squeezed a new coat around the edges. It wasn't pretty, but he hoped it would work. He closed the locket and held it tightly shut, the cool metal leaving wing imprints on his thumb and forefinger. In less than five minutes it was as good as new.

Or at least, as good as it had been nine years ago.

He gave it a shake. The glue held, and the secret inside barely rattled. Now to make sure it worked.

He turned on the black walkie-talkie, held it to his ear, and spoke into the locket.

"Testing, testing," echoed back at him.

Darrow switched off the receiver, shoved it all into his desk, and went to bed, even though he knew sleep would be almost impossible now.

CHAPTER 37

The wind from *Marine One*'s blades lifted Addie's hair and sent it whipping around her face. She should have followed her mother's lead and tucked it into a ponytail. Instead, she was now stuck pulling long black strands from her lip gloss while the White House press corps snapped photos. It was early Saturday morning and the president was returning from a two-day economic summit in Brazil, just in time for a huge reception tonight at the White House in Addie's honor.

The green-and-white helicopter lowered onto the South Lawn, not far from where the drone had landed next to Addie days earlier. Her stomach lurched. Something wasn't right. No one had come forward to take credit. And when she'd tried to make contact this morning, she discovered the secure chat room had been shut down with no warning.

The helicopter's rotor blades spun to a stop straight ahead and the door opened. The silver stairs dropped down and the president exited, flanked by white-gloved Marines and followed by staffers typing on their smartphones. The president stopped at the base of the stairs, saluted the Marines, and strode across the lawn to his family. He gathered Mackenzie in his arms and hugged Addie and her mother.

"I've missed you so much," he said, tightening his grip around Addie.

Click, click, click went the cameras in the background. Everything was a photo op. Never a private moment. Addie longed to go back to the shadows and be anonymous again.

"I missed you, too, Daddy," Mackenzie said, head buried in his shoulder. Liz Webster kissed her husband on the cheek.

"Welcome home, hon," she said.

"Hope you had a nice trip," Addie said.

"I did," the president said. "But it's good to be back."

He turned and waved at the photographers and led the family inside. They boarded the elevator and retreated to the relative quiet of the residence. Addie prepared to head back to her room, to try and untangle her hair along with her thoughts. But the president caught her gently by the arm.

"Ad, honey," he said. "Do you have a minute? I was hoping we could spend a little time together."

"Sure, Dad," she said, attempting a smile.

The president gave Liz a knowing nod, concern crinkling the edges of his eyes. Liz immediately took Mackenzie by the hand. "C'mon, Mackie monkey, let's go have a look at your dresses for the party tonight."

"I don't want to go to the party tonight," Mackenzie whined. "I want to stay here. And show Daddy my new blocks."

Addie didn't want to go to any party either. Blocks sounded much better.

"Tell you what, Mackie," Liz said. "Why don't we go build something together right now. And you can show Daddy later. Okay?"

"Okay," Mackenzie said with a sigh. "But I still don't want to go to any parties. There are too many people there."

"I know, honey," Liz said. "It's just for tonight. Then you won't have to go to another one for a long time. I promise."

Liz and Mackenzie headed to the playroom.

"Have you had breakfast yet?" the president asked.

"Just some coffee," Addie answered.

"I figured," the president said. "Me too. Let's go to the kitchen. I'll whip us up something to eat."

"You don't have to do that," Addie said.

"No," the president said, "I want to. I'm hungry. And they never let me cook around here. Crazy, right? I've literally got my finger on the nuclear button, but apparently I can't be trusted not to burn the house down. Come on. It'll be like the old days."

"Ha," Addie said. "Lead the way."

She followed him into the kitchen, where he hung his jacket on a chair before taking out containers of flour, milk, chocolate chips, and butter, and dumping everything into a mixing bowl. Flour puffed everywhere, coating the countertop, containers— even the president's shirt. He patted himself, spreading more white stuff around.

"Are you sure they just don't let you cook because you're a mess, not because they're afraid you'll start a fire?" Addie said with a small laugh.

"You know," the president said, "I think you may be right. Although I haven't started cooking yet. . . ."

He pulled out a skillet and set it on a burner, cranking up the gas. Addie watched the blue flames licking the bottom of the pan as the president poured in the batter. While it cooked, he pulled two plates from the cabinet and set them on the kitchen table, with forks and knives on either side.

"Have a seat, peanut," he said.

"Do you need some help?" Addie said.

"No, I've got it. Go on, sit down."

Addie pulled out a chair and sat in front of a place setting. A moment later, the president shuffled over, holding the steaming skillet. With a flick of the spatula, he slid a pancake onto Addie's plate, then one on his own.

"Well?" he asked, smiling. "What do you think? Do I still have my magic touch?"

Addie looked down at her plate. A chocolate-chip pancake shaped like a bear sat in the center. To her surprise, she choked up a little, a rush of memories overwhelming her all at once. Addie, kneeling on the barstool in their Clifton kitchen, pouring in the chocolate chips while her dad mixed the batter. Decorating her bear with little pats of butter and a syrup shirt.

"It's great," she said.

"Just how you like it?"

Addie nodded, even though she hadn't had a bear pancake since she was eight. Since before . . .

The president hurried to the refrigerator and grabbed syrup and butter, placing them on the table. "Can't forget the accoutrements," he said.

Addie smiled sadly. He was trying so hard. Why couldn't she at least pretend to be happy?

The president sat down in the chair next to her and dug

into his pancake. "Not too bad," he said. "And I didn't burn down the kitchen."

"No, you didn't," Addie said as she ate. "This was really sweet. Thanks, Dad."

She finished her pancake, wiped away the syrup from the edges of her mouth, and began to stand. The president placed his hand on hers.

"Hold on, peanut," he said. "Don't go just yet. I need to talk to you about something." The sickly taste of pancake rose up in Addie's throat. "Oh? What is it?"

Something about the way the president began to link and unlink his fingers made her uneasy. She wasn't sure she'd ever seen him this nervous. Even that night at the Richmond Hilton ten years ago, when the family had waited for the result of the gubernatorial election in the hotel's ballroom.

"There's something you need to know," he said. "I got a call today. From the director of the FBI."

Sweat began to form along Addie's hairline. The FBI? She was sure she'd been careful. Covering her tracks every time she went online. Had she made a mistake? Or was it that busboy? Addie knew something was off. She took a few shallow breaths, ready to fake a panic attack if she needed to. "Oh?"

"Yes. I'm not sure how to put this," the president said, "so I'm going to come right out and say it."

Addie blinked several times. "Okay."

The president put his hand on her knee. "They've found the people who held you captive. David and Helene."

"What?" The room began to spin. Addie's lungs momentarily forgot how to breathe. She put her hands on her knees and gasped for air. "I don't understand."

"I know, honey," the president said. "This is all just going down so quickly. I only got the call a half hour ago. I've barely had time to process it myself. But I wanted to make sure you heard it from me first, before it blows up all over the news."

"All over the news?" Addie repeated back.

"Yes, the FBI is preparing to move in, but they have to plan accordingly because, as you know, there are children in the house. And, they have reason to believe, a large stockpile of weapons."

"The children are in the house?" Addie said, voice quivering.

"Yes," the president said. "But don't worry, okay? The FBI is taking every precaution. They will not make a move unless it's safe."

"But how can they be sure they have the right people?" Addie said.

"The sketches you provided the Secret Service with are close matches," the president said. "Of course, I'm sure they will need you to make a positive identification. But they have other evidence."

"Like what?"

The president nodded. "E-mail communications between some of the remaining members of Judgment Day, from what I understand. The FBI and Secret Service are still very much in fact-gathering mode. But the real kicker is, it turns out Helene Brown has a brother. Half brother, actually. Guy by the name of Dawson Cooper, who just so happened to work at the governor's mansion as a groundskeeper at the time of your abduction."

"Whoa." Addie felt light-headed. She tried to fit the pieces together in her mind. But it was like they all came from different puzzles, locking together and forming a picture that made no sense.

The president exhaled. "Can't believe that slipped by us eight years ago. Every employee was grilled several times over, but no connection was ever made. Helene and Dawson had different mothers, different last names, and didn't grow up together. It wasn't even apparent that they knew each other at the time."

Addie sucked in a breath. "I can't believe it," she said. She rubbed her head and whispered, "I think I need to lie down for a little bit, if that's okay."

"Of course it is. I completely understand," the president said. He helped Addie to her feet. "This is all an awful lot to take in, I know. I'll walk you to your room."

"No, I'm okay," Addie said. "You can stay here. You just got back. I'm sure you have work to do."

The president hesitated.

"Okay," he said. "In the meantime, please keep this discussion between us. The investigation is ongoing."

"Of course, I understand," Addie said. "Thank you for confiding in me."

"You deserve to know. It's thanks to you that they even found them. I will keep you updated as soon as I know anything," he said.

"Thanks, Dad."

"You're welcome, Addie. We will get through this. Together. I love you more than anything."

"I love you, too," she said.

Addie hurried to her room at the end of the hall, and on

the way passed her mother and Mackenzie sorting blocks in the playroom. Mackenzie counted as she stacked. Liz's eyes darted in Addie's direction and she began to speak. But Addie kept staggering forward, afraid her feet would forget how to move again if she stopped.

She stumbled into her room, barely breathing, and slammed the door shut.

The Janie Liu gown was laid out on her bed, pressed and ready for her welcome-home reception tonight. It was almost more than Addie could take. The walls felt like they were starting to close in, crushing her from all sides.

She grabbed her computer. It was cool and slick beneath her sweaty fingers. She flipped it open and began to type a warning. But it was pointless.

She had nowhere to send it.

CHAPTER 38

The line of well-wishers had snaked all the way around the corner all night, out of the East Room and down the red carpet of the Cross Hall. Addie had been standing here for more than two hours with the president, the first lady, and her little sister. Her back hurt from wearing high heels, and every time a tray of shrimp passed by, the sickly ocean smell made her queasy. The gown she'd felt so beautiful in, just nights before, now felt like a straightjacket. Standing here, she was nothing more than a decoration. Like one of the gilded eagles that formed the base of the grand piano across the room.

Finally, the end of the line approached. Yet another D.C. power couple, subtly Botoxed faces displaying the requisite mix of relief and concern. Addie didn't recognize them, but she definitely knew the type: the tailored suit, the Louis Vuitton wingtips, the Hervé Leger dress with pearl choker. High-powered lobbyists. Lawyers. Maybe wealthy donors. It didn't really matter; they were all the same. All here for their two minutes of face time with the most powerful man in the world.

"Honey," the president said, wrapping an arm around Addie's waist, "I'd like to introduce you to Brad and Rebecca Martin. Rebecca was one of the primary fund-raisers on my presidential campaign."

"Nice to meet you," Addie said. Her cheeks hurt from smiling so much.

The woman grabbed Addie by both hands. "Oh, Addie," she said. "You don't know how hard we prayed for your return."

Addie's face started to burn. She couldn't help it. She was worn-out, rubbed raw by all the hugs, handshakes, and faux concern. If people had done all the praying they'd claimed to, there'd be a giant hole in heaven right now. Maybe they should have spent a little more time looking for her, and a little less time reading the polls and holding fund-raisers.

"Guess it must have paid off," Addie said, the fake smile pressed hard into her cheeks. "Here I am, just in time for campaign season."

The woman's perfectly tweezed eyebrow arched. "Excuse me?"

Addie just grinned wider and shrugged. Rebecca Donor, whatever-her-name-was, cleared her throat and moved on to Mackenzie.

"And how are you tonight, dear?" she said, kneeling.

Mackenzie, who had spent most of the night with her face hidden in the folds of Liz Webster's dress, peeked at the woman, eyes wide. It made Addie even more annoyed. What right did they have to drag a six-year-old out here? To make her meet and greet D.C.'s finest, when she clearly would rather be home with her books and building blocks? Addie felt like slapping someone on Mackenzie's behalf, like grabbing her sister and hiding her from the limelight.

"I think she would like to be left alone," Addie said. "Besides, she's too young to vote, you know."

Rebecca Donor's face blanched. "Well, I . . ." She put her hand to her neck and clutched the pearls that coiled three times around it like a snake.

"Rebecca, I'm very sorry," the First Lady cut in. "It's been a long night for Addie. She's not herself."

Not herself? What did they expect? She'd been gone eight years. And right now, two innocent people were about to be arrested because of her. Nothing made sense anymore. Her fists clenched so tightly her fingernails dug into her palms. She was about to open her mouth again when Darrow came walking briskly across the room, eyes trained on her. He was wearing a black tuxedo and an easy smile. The heat rose in Addie's face. She couldn't decide whether she was happy he was headed her way, or if she wanted to take off her shoe and throw it at him.

"Hi, Addie." Darrow sidestepped Rebecca Donor and took Addie by the elbow. "Mr. President, Mrs. Webster, sorry for interrupting. Can I borrow Addie for a minute? The band is playing my favorite song, and the only way she'll dance with me is if I publicly embarrass her."

Addie definitely should have thrown her shoe at him.

President Webster laughed, clearly relieved that the awkward conversation had been broken up. "I'm sure we could all use a quick dance break. Rebecca?" He held out his hand and Rebecca Donor beamed. Addie tried not to gag as Darrow pulled her away.

"I'm not interested in dancing," she said.

"Me neither," Darrow said. "I don't even know what that song is. You just looked like you could use a break."

Darrow pulled Addie around the corner, into the appropriately named Green Room. She squinted, taking in the green Oriental carpet, green chairs, and green walls.

"It looks like someone puked in here," she said.

Darrow laughed. But Addie didn't. Her nostrils flared.

"Are you okay?" Darrow said. He'd been watching her the whole evening, as more than a hundred of President Webster's donors, friends, and colleagues lined up for their chance to welcome Addie back. With each hug and handshake, she'd seemed like a flower whose petals were being pulled off one by one. All that remained were the thorns.

"Am I okay?" Addie said. "God, I wish people would stop asking me that! I'm not okay. I just got home and they're already parading me around like a trophy. Like *they* had anything to do with me being found. I wouldn't even be here if *I* hadn't escaped myself. Was anyone even looking for me anymore? I mean, my mom was back at work right after I disappeared."

"Whoa, Addie. Slow down," Darrow said. "That's not true...."

"It's entirely true," Addie said. "But I guess billions of dollars can take your mind off your missing kid, right? Like nothing ever happened. Actually, more like the best thing that ever happened. You can't tell me my disappearance didn't help Mark Webster become one of the youngest presidents in United States history."

"No..." Darrow began.

Addie scowled.

"Okay," he said. "Even if it did, I know your father was heartbroken when you vanished. *Everyone* was heartbroken. Believe me, I was there."

"Right," Addie said, her voice growing louder. Her hands were clenched in fists at her sides. "The only person Mark Webster cares about is himself. And the only security he cares about is his own. Think about it. If he cared so much about safety, why wasn't he protecting me that day? How was someone able to snatch me away from right under his nose? In a building full of security guards and cameras?"

In that instant, Darrow saw himself running through the halls of the governor's mansion, heart racing, searching in vain all the places Addie should have been. He could see the slant of light that illuminated her empty beanbag chair in the tree house. He could hear the creak of the empty swings. He remembered all too well the checkers strewn across the floor.

"I don't know how it happened," he said. "But I've never forgiven myself for it."

"What?" Addie said. "You were nine years old. What were *you* supposed to do?"

Darrow bit his trembling bottom lip. Everything he'd kept bottled up for the last eight years came bubbling to the surface. All the feelings he had tried to push away, first by making the wrong decisions, then by becoming a classic overachiever— everything he'd done to forget and move on.

"Save you," he whispered.

"Dare," Addie said, her voice softening. "You couldn't save me then." She looked away and spoke quietly, but Darrow could still hear her when she said, "You can't save me now."

"What do you mean?" he said. "What do you need saving from?"

Addie didn't say anything.

"Ad, you can tell me. Please, let me help you."

"Nothing," she said. "I meant rhetorically. See? SAT word. I can fit right in." She sounded slightly hysterical.

"Addie, listen." He took a deep breath. "When I was fourteen, I got picked up drinking with a bunch of guys from Southeast. There was a fight with the cops. My mother, she—she made it go away. Everyone else went to juvie." Lance, Daniel, and Nick. Their faces, scared and defiant as the police handcuffed them, loomed in his memory. They were probably still living the aftermath of that night. While he ate caviar in a Versace tux. He wondered if they ever thought of him: the rich kid who'd used them to stage his pathetic little rebellion.

"Why are you telling me this?" Addie said softly.

"Because I know what it's like to hide something from the world that you carry with you every day. And what it's like when there's someone holding it over your head to try to control you." He watched Addie's face for a flicker of recognition, but it stayed still as stone.

It was now or never. Darrow sucked in a breath and dug in his tuxedo pocket, wrapping his fingers around a small velvet box. He pulled it out, stretching his hand to Addie.

"What's that?" she said.

"Open it," he said.

Addie took the box, eyebrows arched, and creaked it open. Her mouth dropped.

"My locket?" she said, blinking in surprise. "How? Where did you get this?"

224

"I found it the day you . . ." Darrow cut himself short.

"And you kept it all these years?"

"Of course I did. I know it might not exactly be your style anymore, but I thought you might want it back," Darrow said, heart beating wildly against his chest.

"Dare. Thank you. Help me put it on?" Addie held the silver chain out and turned her back toward him, lifting the hair off her neck. Darrow fumbled the clasp open and hooked the necklace in place. Addie turned around.

"What do you think?" she said.

"Very becoming," he replied. "Takes almost a decade off you."

Addie tried to smile, but quickly looked away. Darrow's breath caught in his chest as he saw a tear roll down her cheek. How could she be so open and vulnerable one moment, and like a stranger the next? But the real Addie was in there—he'd seen her. And she was scared. Of what, he had no idea. All he knew was that he wanted to punch everyone that had ever hurt her, to build a wall around her and stand guard day and night. With a trembling hand, he reached over and touched her face, wiping away the tear. Her breath hitched as he stroked her feather-soft skin. He leaned into her, his heart pounding, and her green eyes fluttered shut.

Just as Darrow's lips grazed Addie's, a voice floated across the room.

"Well, there's the guest of honor."

The swell of shock was like an electric jolt. Darrow jerked up straight, gazing at the tall, light-haired man approaching. Darrow recognized him as Karl something-or-other, a Swedish national who ran a cybersecurity firm that occasionally did business with the White House. In fact, Darrow remembered the guy coming around the governor's mansion, too. He was sort of hard to forget, with that smooth Scandinavian accent that made him sound like he should be narrating commercials for luxury cars. But from what Darrow could recall, the guy was a former classmate of Liz Webster's during graduate school at MIT. Computer geek, like Liz.

Karl extended a hand to Darrow. "Karl Erlander," he said. "Global Security Solutions. Nice to see you again, young man. I was just chatting with your mother. I don't think a woman could ever be more proud of her son. White House intern. Early acceptance to Georgetown, she tells me. Impressive."

"Thank you, sir," Darrow said. His cheeks burned hot. He wasn't sure if it was from the man's compliment, the fact that he had just tried to kiss Addie, or both.

"And you, dear Adele." Karl kissed both of her cheeks. "I'm sure you don't remember me. It's been many years. But oh, how I enjoyed watching you and your mother play when you were just a little thing. I know she is simply overjoyed to have you home. As we all are."

Darrow's back stiffened. He waited for Addie to hurl another round of insults at her latest faux admirer. But the look on her face had changed, like a mask had slipped over it. The warm smile and nod she returned to the man were sweet and unassuming. Darrow's skin prickled.

"Thank you," she said shyly. "It means so much to me that you and everyone else came tonight. I don't even know what to say, except I'm grateful."

"I wouldn't miss it," Karl said. "And I am honored to be

your parents' guest this evening. Shall we return to the party?" He extended an elbow to Addie. She looped her arm through it.

"Sounds great," she said.

Darrow followed them back through the Cross Hall and to the reception in the East Room, trying to get a bead on Addie's sudden change in demeanor. She walked with her head held high, gliding through the crowd effortlessly, smiling and nodding at men in tuxedos and women in cocktail dresses as she passed. It was the exact opposite of the girl with the rigid shoulders and pained expression in the receiving line, the girl who had just exploded like a grenade in front of him moments earlier.

Darrow tried to tell himself that she had just been tired, but the voice in his head wouldn't shut up. Something about Addie wasn't right.

The party guests now sat in gold chairs at round tables draped with blue-and-white tablecloths while the quartet played. Karl, Addie, and Darrow passed the dance floor, where a small group was moving to the music. Karl stopped and twirled Addie. Her dress spun in a perfect, shimmering arc, and she laughed.

A chill went up Darrow's spine.

They reached the president's table, where Addie's family was seated with his mother. As Karl, Addie, and Darrow approached, the group stood, trading handshakes and hugs. But Darrow noticed the president was somewhat stiffer than usual as he sat back down.

"Please, have a seat," President Webster said in his official voice, the one he used for speeches and greeting foreign prime ministers. "So glad you could make it tonight, Karl. It has been a while."

"Thank you," Karl answered. "I'm delighted to join you. And thank you for having me as your guest this evening. I am so thrilled to see Addie home. I'm sure I don't need to tell you that." He smiled warmly.

As the small talk continued, Darrow watched as Addie kept up the act, smiling and nodding like a wind-up doll. He felt like poking her. Maybe kicking her beneath the table. Instead, he kept his hands in his lap and cracked his knuckles.

"So, little one," Karl said, turning his attention to Addie's younger sister. "Would you like to hear a riddle?"

"Yes, Mr. Karl!" Mackenzie sat up straight.

"That's my girl," he said. "Now, listen carefully. Two fathers and two sons each had an egg for breakfast. They ate a total of three eggs. How is that possible?"

Mackenzie grinned. "Because one of the fathers is the grandfather, too."

"You didn't even have to think about that," Karl said. "A genius, just like your sister."

"How do you know my sister's a genius?"

Karl chuckled. "Because, dear." He patted Mackenzie's head. "I knew your sister even before you were born. And I knew your mother even before that. The genius gene runs long in the Chan—or should I say, Webster—family."

"Oh," Mackenzie said, looking back and forth between Addie and Karl. "I guess that makes sense."

Karl raised his glass. "To Adele," he said.

"To Adele." A round of glasses met in the center of the table and clinked. Servers came by with silver trays of foie gras on toast, shrimp skewers, and exotic cheeses.

"And where is your son this evening?" Darrow's mother asked Karl.

"With his mother in New York," he answered. The mood at the table grew strangely somber. Addie, who had been smiling that weird plastic smile, cast her eyes down as her face dropped. The cracks in the facade began to appear again. What the hell was going on?

Darrow nudged Addie. "Want to dance for real this time?" he murmured.

Addie blinked, looking momentarily startled. As though she'd almost forgotten that he was there. That anyone was even there. Like she was a robot that had been briefly unplugged.

"Sure." She stood and took Darrow's hand. He led her to the dance floor, keeping her right hand in his left and wrapping his other hand around her waist. They spun, cheek to cheek. Addie glided effortlessly to the music.

"How did you learn to dance?" Darrow said.

Addie pulled her head back so they were looking straight at each other. "With you, silly," she said. "Don't you remember?"

"Oh yeah," Darrow said as it came back to him. The two of them in Addie's playroom while some boy-band song streamed from her MP3 speakers, Elinor sulking in the corner, watching. "Pretty sure you always had to be the one in the lead, though."

Addie laughed. "Like this?" she said, forcing Darrow to spin around.

"It's all rushing back now," Darrow said, pretending to shudder.

A flicker of something flashed across Addie's eyes. Darrow wasn't sure what—something bittersweet, sad but beautiful.

"Ad," Darrow said, pulling her closer and lowering his voice to a whisper. "About what happened back there . . ."

"Oh, Dare," Addie said, that plastic smile falling back into place. "I was just tired. And overwhelmed. I didn't mean to snap like that."

"No? It seemed pretty real to me." Darrow's hands felt clammy and he misstepped, stumbling onto Addie's foot. Addie spun him again.

"Think you'd better let me lead," she said, and tucked her head against his chest.

CHAPTER 39

Addie tried to keep her breathing quiet. The hallways were dark, the rest of the family sound asleep. She walked awkwardly, feet still sore from a night in high heels, and crept past her sister's suite. Something clattered inside. A light flicked on, sending a shaft of light under the closed door that cut across Addie's slippers like a knife. She stopped, pressed her back to the wall, and waited. After a moment the light went back off, and Addie quickly made her way to the back staircase and took the steps two at a time.

When she got to the game room, he was already there, leaning against the pool table with a red pool cue in his hand.

"Lilla," he said with a smile. His real smile, the one that felt like it was just for her. It was somehow both reassuring and disconcerting to see him, now that they were both no longer playing their roles. *Lilla*. "Little one" in Swedish. After only a couple of weeks of not hearing it, the nickname already sounded strange in Addie's ears. She folded her arms across her chest. The pajamas she wore suddenly felt too thin, the chilly air blowing right through them.

"Father," she said. "It's good to see you."

"It's good to see you, too, dear." He folded her into a hug, and she allowed herself to sink into his warmth for a moment before letting go. He handed her a cue. "Care for a game?"

Addie nodded. She wasn't exactly in the mood, but she'd learned long ago it was never a wise idea to tell Karl Erlander no.

"Great." Karl racked the balls. "You break," he said.

Addie steadied her hand. It was hard to keep the pool cue from vibrating. She loved her father, but sometimes he scared her. There was something cold and calculating in his blue eyes that could chill Addie to her core. Sometimes she wondered how Karl and her mother had ever gotten together in the first place. Liz might be brilliant, but she was Karl's exact opposite when it came to the courage of her convictions. And Addie knew Karl's love for his wife was all-consuming. But maybe, like Father had always said, he and Liz Webster had just happened to collide at a time when they'd both needed something only the other could give. And while he'd regretted the affair, he didn't regret what had come from it: Addie. Addie's only wish was that her mother had been brave enough to tell her the truth.

Addie leaned over the table, stick nestled between her fingers, and hit the white cue ball. The colored balls scattered, and the red three-ball fell into a side pocket.

"Nice," Karl said. "I see you haven't lost your touch."

"Thanks," Addie said, feeling pleased despite her nerves. She leaned in for another shot.

Karl rubbed chalk on the end of his cue stick and blew the fine powder away. "So tell me then, what happened to you tonight?"

Addie straightened and looked at Karl. "What do you mean?" she said.

"I think you know what I mean." Karl took a step closer. "You lost your cool. You should know better, after everything I've taught you. You can't go around insulting people, drawing attention to yourself. You'll make people suspicious."

Addie shrugged. "What? I was just tired. And my feet hurt. People would get suspicious if I *was* calm all the time. I'm traumatized, remember?" She returned his cold smile, daring him to question her further. After a moment she turned back around and aimed at the white cue ball again.

But this time, her shaking fingers slipped. The white ball skidded sideways, barely nipping the blue. Karl grabbed her stick and held it tightly. Addie stood and faced him. She had to bite her bottom lip to keep it from trembling.

The world is a threatening place, little one. The things I teach you here may seem harsh, but they're to keep you safe. Out there.

Addie shivered.

"Look, Lilla," Karl said, his voice dangerously soft. "I know this is stressful. But I don't think I need to remind you what's at stake, do I? We're almost there. You need to stay focused."

"Yes, Father," Addie said. She hesitated, trying to form the words to ask about what the president had told her earlier. But her voice caught in her throat.

"Good," Karl said. "It's just easy to get lulled into this . . . lifestyle." He waved his cue stick around the room. "You start to believe you're untouchable. Like the president. But the same isn't true for the rest of the world. For people who don't have your level of protection. People like Mikey."

Karl took his shot, knocking two striped balls into the pockets. His next shot missed.

"Mikey," Addie said. "How is he?" She pulled back her cue and sank the one, the two, and the five in rapid succession.

"He's doing well," Karl answered. "Sends his regards. He misses you."

"I miss him, too," Addie said. *Mikey.* Her half brother and only friend these last eight years. The boy she had let hide under her bed when Father was angry. The boy she'd tried to protect the only way she knew how—by always thinking one step ahead. The boy she'd laughed with over silly jokes, who'd been her partner in late-night cookie-stealing missions after Father was asleep.

"Good," Karl said.

"Good?"

"Yes, good," Karl repeated. "It's important you don't forget your family. Or why you're here."

"I haven't forgotten anything," she said. She leaned over and tapped the cue ball with her stick, knocking the four-ball into the corner pocket. The six and seven followed. She wasn't going to let her father rattle her again. She was going to win this game.

"I'm glad to hear that," Karl said. "Sometimes we can play a part so well, we forget which side we're on."

"I know which side I'm on," Addie snapped. "Eight-ball, left corner pocket." She knocked the eight-ball in.

"How is the progress with Shi?" Karl said.

"I'm still searching for it," Addie said. "But I'll have it," she added quickly. "By the end of the week. I promise. It's just been a little more difficult than I expected." Her voice wobbled.

"I know you can do it," Karl said, and gently touched her arm. "Is something else bothering you?"

Addie set her cue stick across the felt of the table. "Yes," she said. "They say they actually found David and Helene? I don't understand. . . ."

"I know," Karl said. "The FBI worked faster than I expected. There's nothing to worry about, though."

"What do you mean?" Addie said, her voice betraying her again with its quiver.

"Just trust me," Karl said. "I've taken care of things."

"How?"

"It's probably better that you don't know," Karl said. "Sometimes too much knowledge is a dangerous thing."

Addie was well aware of that fact. A noise came from somewhere outside the room. Addie had to steady her legs, keep herself from running.

"We've closed down the chat room," Karl continued. "I'm concerned there may have been a breach." Karl watched Addie, as if gauging her reaction.

"Oh?" she said as nonchalantly as possible, legs still shaking.

"I've set up a Burnchat account instead." He reached into his pocket and handed Addie a small piece of paper. "Contact me through this as soon as you've found Shi."

"Okay," Addie said.

"And have you forgotten the reason for this reunion?" Karl asked. Addie flushed as Karl pulled something else from his pocket. A digital camera—what she would have received in Virginia if she hadn't missed the handoff. He gave it to Addie as well. "For prom. You know what to do."

"Take pictures?" Addie said, raising an eyebrow.

Karl didn't laugh. "It's a diversion," he said. "The device inside will cause a small explosion, but it won't be lethal. It will just appear that way. Like the one in the Reagan Building. We'll extract you right before it goes off. And . . ."

Addie nodded, her lips pressed together. She didn't need him to say the words. She knew what was supposed to happen. "I'd better get back to my room now," Addie said, finding it difficult to talk. "I don't need anyone to get up and notice I'm gone."

"Very good," Karl said. But as Addie began to walk away, he caught her by the arm. "Just one more thing, little one," he said. "That boy you were with in the Green Room?"

"Darrow?" Addie said, heartbeat accelerating.

"Yes, Darrow," Karl said. "I suggest you keep your distance. I know he seems nice. But he's an ambitious young man. Don't let yourself be a means to an end."

"That won't be a problem," Addie said as she slipped from Karl's grasp.

She headed toward the door.

"I wish you could have known her, Lilla," Karl said.

Addie slowed, turning back to Karl. Her heart ached at the haunted look in his eyes. "So do I, Father."

"Nothing can undo the past, little one. All we can do is learn from it." His gaze turned hard. "I know you won't let her down."

Darrow sat in his car on G Street, a block from the White House, exactly half a mile away. The reception had ended an hour earlier, but he'd made up an excuse—he needed to stick around and finish a project before he went home. Instead, he'd driven around the corner and parked alongside the Old Ebbitt Grill, where a few late-night diners were still filtering in and out of the popular restaurant.

Darrow slinked in his seat as a couple passed, peering into his car. The black receiver on the center console next to him was in plain view. Darrow covered it with a file folder and chastised himself for being stupid. In fact, it was starting to feel like bugging Addie may have been one of his all-time stupidest moves. All he'd heard so far was his friend saying good night to her parents, water running, feet shuffling. She was probably asleep now and not even wearing the necklace anymore. He should just go home.

Suddenly, the receiver crackled to life. Darrow heard something again. A door opening and closing. Light footsteps. Raspy breathing. Darrow sat at attention and cranked the volume. But the sound quality was terrible. Harper hadn't been kidding. He closed his eyes, as if that might somehow improve his hearing, and listened as voices broke through the static.

"Hello,—" *crackle, crackle.*

It was Addie. But what had she just said? It had sounded like "Peter." Who was that? And why was Addie talking to him? Someone outside the car laughed loudly, and Darrow couldn't hear the response of whoever Addie was talking to. He held the receiver directly to his ear and heard a man's voice, but the man was clearly farther away from the bug, and harder to understand. Addie's and his words were also punctuated by a strange sound—a clacking, crashing noise that happened in small bursts. Between the sounds, Darrow picked up that the man wanted to know if Addie had something yet. More clacking noises; the receiver sputtered.

Darrow pulled it from his ear and fiddled with the dials. It sputtered a few more times and went silent. Finally, after several minutes Darrow got it working again, and the man's voice broke through. He said something about prom. *Prom?* The receiver crackled and popped, the sound fading in and out. Darrow banged it, hard, trying to process what he'd been hearing. Something was going to go down at the Cabot prom?

A thump on the side of his car jolted him out of his thoughts. Darrow looked to his left, just in time to see a girl with a long blonde ponytail on a Vespa skidding sideways away from his door. The scooter wobbled and the girl put down a foot, stopping a few yards ahead. Darrow leapt from his car, concerned.

"Hey!" he yelled. "Are you okay?"

The girl glanced over her shoulder at Darrow. He could barely make out a set of big brown eyes beneath the rim of her black helmet. She studied him a moment, then sat upright and sped off. Darrow spun around and looked at his car—a huge scratch ran along the driver's side door.

"Hey!" he yelled again. "Come back here. You hit my car!"

Straight ahead, the girl on the Vespa accelerated, taking a sharp right into an underground parking garage on the corner of 14th Street. *Seriously?* Darrow balled his hands into fists and gave chase. She'd probably just done a couple thousand dollars' worth of damage to his custom paint job. His mom would have his head. No way could he let that girl just ride away.

Darrow raced down the sidewalk into the garage, and came to a dead stop. It was dark, lit by a half-dozen fluorescent tube lights that flickered and buzzed, the only sound in the near-empty place. Darrow scanned the dim garage and shivered. It was about ten degrees colder in here than outside. A single row of delivery trucks sat parked against the far wall. The rest of the concrete structure was empty. The Vespa was nowhere in sight.

Suddenly, Darrow heard the echo of screeching tires. He took a step toward the sound, only realizing a moment too late the foolishness of running blindly into an abandoned parking garage in downtown D.C. at night.

A hand clamped over Darrow's mouth and nose, cutting off his breathing. Darrow swallowed a scream, hands reflexively balling into fists. But before he could put up a fight, the cool blade of a knife pressed against his neck.

"Don't even think about it," a man's voice said.

The hand over Darrow's face released its grip slightly, and Darrow gasped for air. His heart raced, along with his thoughts. He was about to become one of the city's grimmer statistics. Mugged in a dark garage. Or worse. What the hell had he been thinking?

"Hey, I don't want any trouble," Darrow said. "Wallet's in my right front pocket. Take it. It's yours."

The man let out a laugh, low and sinister.

"I don't want your wallet."

Darrow began to lose sensation in his legs. What *did* this guy want, then? To kill him and leave him on the floor of this garage? His body kicked into fight-or-flight mode, muscles twitching. His senses went into overdrive; he became acutely aware of his own heartbeat pounding in his ears, the man's jagged breath on the back of his neck. Darrow only had one shot to get away. He'd go for a stomp on the foot, coupled with a well-placed elbow to the ribs. Buy himself enough time to make it back onto the sidewalk up ahead. Darrow willed his body to relax and prepare to attack.

Suddenly, the point of the knife pricked his skin. A warm trickle of blood ran down Darrow's neck, staining the crisp white collar of his tuxedo shirt. He jerked up straight and let out an involuntary gasp. The man leaned forward and whispered in Darrow's ear.

"Stay away from Addie Webster," he hissed.

With that, he pulled the knife away and sucker punched Darrow in the side, knocking him to the ground. Darrow stayed frozen there on the cold concrete, hyperventilating, listening as the man's footsteps receded into the bowels of the garage. Darrow pulled himself shakily to his feet and stumbled out to the sidewalk. He pressed his fingers to his neck and drew them back, staring in shock at the smudges of blood across the tips. He wanted to scream, but couldn't.

Instead, he stood there, trapped by his own racing thoughts. What was Addie involved in? Even worse, what could *he* possibly do about it? He reached for his phone to call for help, and realized in his haste he'd left it in his car. He took an unsteady step down the sidewalk. He'd never felt so alone as he did in that moment, staggering down G Street, blood congealing on his neck. Not even the night he'd sat in a cold jail cell, waiting for his mother to bail him out. At least then, he'd known someone had his back. Now, all he could feel was the burn of unseen eyes watching his every move. They'd found him here; they could find him anywhere.

He walked faster, slid back into his car, and slammed the door shut. As he hit the lock, the phone he'd left sitting on his center console buzzed. Darrow glanced down. An anonymous message flashed across the screen and Darrow recoiled, swallowing the scream welling up in his throat.

It was a picture of his mother, looking elegant in her deep blue gown from tonight's reception, walking up the brick steps to the front door of their Georgetown row house. A simple message was typed beneath:

We won't warn you twice.

CHAPTER 40

It was late and Michael was tired, but he couldn't sleep. Besides, he preferred to avoid the crazy Manhattan crowds. During the day, this place would be crawling with people: tour groups, curious passersby, sometimes even people like him. It was better now, without the clicking cameras. The obnoxious chatter. He preferred the peace and stillness of nighttime. He sat quietly, hands folded in his lap, on a wooden bench just across from her.

Sometimes, Michael felt like talking to his mother. But not tonight. He wasn't sure he needed to, anyway. Ever since he was a little boy, Michael had been convinced his mother could hear his thoughts. That's what mothers did—they comforted without words. They loved unconditionally. Michael ran his fingers through his thick brown hair—his mother's hair—and thought about what he would say.

I'm scared, Mother. We're so close to reaching our goals. But I've had to do some things that frighten me. I can live with what happened to the man. I think. But not what might happen to her . . . if she doesn't fix things. I'm afraid of what Father will ask me to do. I'm afraid of losing . . .

Michael was interrupted by someone stumbling up the sidewalk. He turned to see a drunk guy tripping over his own feet, a near-empty bottle clutched in his hands. As he passed Michael's bench, the guy teetered sideways. The bottle fell, rolling to a stop in front of Michael. The guy staggered on, oblivious, talking to himself.

Michael leaned over, picked up the bottle, and chucked it in the trash. This was no place to be littering. People could be so disrespectful.

"I'm sorry, Mother," he said.

Michael leaned back and closed his eyes, pulling his trench coat around himself. When he was young, he used to imagine how she'd answer. But somewhere through the years, he'd lost the sound of her voice. He wasn't even sure he'd ever known it at all. The only thing that remained in Michael's memory was a melancholy tune, the dark outline of a face humming over his crib when he couldn't sleep.

You are my sunshine, my only sunshine. You make me happy when skies are gray . . .

A siren wailed on some distant street. A dog barked and a cat screeched. The plaintive sounds of the city at night. A crowded yet lonely and empty place.

You'll never know, dear, how much I love you . . .

Michael stood, eyes filled with tears, and approached the slick marble wall. Just beyond, the crater that had once been a busy subway station had been turned into a park, the train long ago rerouted. But this place would never be anything other than a mass graveyard in Michael's mind. More than a thousand innocent people were buried under the newly planted grass and sapling trees. The sprouting daffodil bulbs couldn't mask the fact that this was the site of one of the worst terrorist attacks on American soil. It was hallowed ground, and Michael would never set foot on it.

He reached his hand out and ran his fingers across the letters engraved in the black marble of the sprawling monument before him:

SUSAN ERLANDER

Michael blinked back his tears and stood tall.

"I wish I could have known you, Mother," he said. "But I will make things right. You know I will. For you."

He glanced higher up the wall to the inscription that ran across the top, along with the date nearly fifteen years ago that he was too young to remember, but would be seared in his mind forever. The anniversary was coming up. April fifteenth.

WE HOLD YOU IN OUR HEARTS. WE WILL NEVER FORGET.

CHAPTER 41

Voices echoing in the hallway outside Addie's room awakened her from a deep sleep. The shades were still drawn, but Addie could see pale light slanting in from the tall windows. It must be morning. Early. She heard a soft rap on her bedroom door, and the handle twisted slowly open.

"Addie?" her mother whispered. "Are you awake?"

Addie stayed still, pretending to be asleep. Her head was pounding and she didn't feel like getting up. She listened as her mother clicked the door shut and started talking to someone just outside.

"No," she said. "She's not up. Do you think I should wake her?"

A slight pause. The president's voice answered. "No, let her sleep. But make sure to get her as soon as she wakes up. I want to make sure we see her first, before the news. . . ."

Addie's heart began to thump, and her palms grew cold and clammy. Had someone heard her sneak up to the game room? She thought she'd been so careful . . . Wait, news? Addie held her breath and listened, but the hallway had grown quiet.

She waited a beat, then crept from bed, grabbed her computer, and slipped back under the covers. She flipped the screen open and with trembling fingers launched the browser, hoping to figure out what her parents were talking about. What she found made her heart seize up in her chest. A breaking-news item flashed red across her home page:

Alert: Standoff at West Virginia compound of David and Helene Brown enters fifth hour.

Addie clicked on the link and a video screen popped open. A young reporter, blonde hair in a ponytail, stood at the edge of a dirt road holding a microphone. Helicopters circled above her head, causing her blue Windbreaker to ripple. It was barely daylight, the sky an eerie blue-gray. Addie notched up the volume.

"We're here live at the West Virginia compound owned by David and Helene Brown, where an intense standoff has been under way since just after midnight. According to our sources, the Browns are believed to be affiliated with a fringe neoconservative political group known as Judgment Day. No official word yet why the FBI descended on this remote property in the middle of the night, but anonymous sources have told CNN that the raid may be connected to the Adele Webster kidnapping."

Addie's head went from pounding to dizzy. She gripped the edges of the computer and took small, shallow breaths. The reporter continued.

"While we wait for new developments, let's go back to Brian in the studio for a look at what Judgment Day is and why its members may have drawn federal interest."

The reporter's face shrank to a small rectangle in the corner of the screen, which was then filled by a dark-haired man sitting at an anchor's desk.

"Thank you, Amy," he said. He turned and looked directly into the camera. A graphic appeared behind him: the scales of justice. But in place of a blindfold, Lady Justice had a tattered American flag wrapped around her eyes. In place of a sword, she gripped an automatic rifle. The words JUDGMENT DAY were scrawled in blood red across the image.

"Here's what we know," the news anchor continued. *"This is a radical conservative group that traces its origins to the aftermath of the 1995 Oklahoma City bombings. The group formed in response to what it saw as a conspiracy to cover up what they believed was the true mastermind behind the attack: the U.S. government itself."*

The image behind the anchor switched to side-by-side pictures of a middle-aged man and woman. The man's head was shaved, but he had a long beard. The woman had dirty-blonde hair pulled into a severe ponytail. She wore no makeup and had a stern look on her face. Addie recoiled from the screen, heart racing. The anchor continued.

"Formerly led by David and Helene Brown, Judgment Day garnered a hundred or so followers in its early years, but dwindled to just a handful of widely distributed supporters in the last decade. The Browns live here with their three children...."

The image switched again to a live aerial shot of a secluded compound surrounded by trees and a tall metal fence. Addie began to grow nauseous.

"They are living almost entirely off the grid here," the anchor said. *"No connection to municipal water, sewage, or electric utilities. They raise their own livestock, grow their own produce. Sources say they are believed to be stockpiling weapons and survival gear. But no one really knows the Browns. Even in this rural town, where people pride themselves on their live-and-let-live attitude, the Browns are seen*

as loners and outsiders, only coming out of their compound to stock up on supplies at the local feed and grain store."

The news anchor's face froze and he put his hand to his ear. "We have a breaking situation at the Brown compound," he said. "We have reports of shots fired. The FBI is moving in. Let's return to Amy on the scene."

The corner screen enlarged and the blonde reporter returned, glancing behind her shoulder and back at the camera, hand on her earpiece. "That's right, Brian," she said. "We are hearing shots fired from somewhere in the compound. No word if it's the Browns or the FBI."

A flurry of activity erupted somewhere off camera. The reporter began to run, still talking and breathing heavily into her microphone.

"We're being asked to push back," she said. "Brian, can you switch to the chopper for a better view of what's happening on the ground?"

Once again, the screen changed: an aerial view of the compound. In the center was the rectangular shape of a house, surrounded by a field and fence. Black figures moved in from the edges, so small they looked like toy soldiers.

Suddenly, the flash of a muzzle lit up from the house, followed by another. Brian began to narrate breathlessly.

"Confirmed. We do have shots fired," he said. "They appear to be coming from inside the house. I repeat, shots are being fired from inside the house."

"That's right," Amy's voice interjected. "We can hear the FBI. They are yelling over their loudspeakers for the Browns to drop their weapons and surrender."

There was a moment of silence. A smoky substance billowed from the house.

"It appears the FBI has shot tear gas into the building," Brian said. *"But they are approaching with caution as there are reports of children in the house."*

The chopper circled back for a tighter shot. On-screen, the house's front door swung open. Two figures ran out into the front yard, guns blazing.

The surrounding black figures' weapons lit up like a string of flashing Christmas lights.

The couple at the center fell to the ground.

And the news feed cut out.

CHAPTER 42

Addie pulled the covers to her chest, trying to hold back tears, trying to process what she'd just seen. David and Helene Brown were people. Real people. And they were dead. Because of her. None of it made sense. They were supposed to be just a story, something to lead the FBI astray.

Addie tried to push the horrible scene she'd just witnessed from her mind, desperate to replace it with a happier thought. A memory washed over her. She was thirteen, strolling with Father and Mikey down the Avenue des Champs-Élysées in Paris. Father had swept the family away on the surprise trip as a reward after Addie successfully hacked into a jihadist Web site and shut it down—but not before alerting French authorities about their plans to bomb a nightclub.

Addie was in heaven. She loved everything about Paris—the French Baroque architecture, the sounds of street musicians mingling with car horns honking and people chatting, the style and grace of the city's people. But most of all, Addie loved the feeling of freedom she had in the City of Lights. Here, she was just another teenage girl—Lilla Erlander—strolling the boulevards with her father and brother. She wasn't Addie Webster, the terrified child who'd been stolen from the Virginia governor's mansion five years earlier. Here she could simply be herself without constantly needing to look over her shoulder, mindful that someone might recognize her.

As the family meandered down the sidewalk, they peered in the windows of the upscale boutiques that lined the avenue, admiring the fashionable displays: sleek fitted dresses with wide leather belts, tailored suits, sparkling jewels. A street vendor caught Addie's eye. She stopped at the wooden cart, shelves crammed with miniature Eiffel Tower replicas, postcards, and colorful silk scarves. With a grin, she grabbed the tackiest thing she could find: a black beret with PARIS written in bright yellow script across the front. She turned to Father, stood on her tiptoes, and placed the hat squarely on his head. She stepped back and giggled, hand over her mouth, as his eyebrows shot up. Michael shook his head and tried to hide his smile.

Father leaned forward and inspected his reflection in the small rectangular mirror hanging from the vendor's cart. He looked ridiculous, like an oversized kid on a class trip. Addie waited for him to fling the hat off, but instead, he gave an exaggerated gasp.

"Très magnifique!" he said, and pulled a wad of crumpled Euros from his pocket and gave them to the vendor.

They all laughed, continuing down the avenue. They stopped at a small outdoor café and sat down at a black wrought-iron table beneath a yellow umbrella. Addie couldn't help but feel sophisticated as she tore off pieces of warm croissant and popped them in her mouth, followed by sips of espresso from a white demitasse cup. She leaned back and closed her eyes, sucking in a breath of the sweet-smelling air, tinged with the scent of sugar and roasted coffee beans. She smiled as the late afternoon sun warmed her cheeks.

As the sun crept lower on the horizon, the family headed back toward their rented apartment. Along the way, they passed a small jewelry shop tucked into a large brick building. Addie came to a sudden stop, transfixed by a display on the other side of the store's window: a glittering hair clip shaped like a butterfly, but elegant, not childish. Dozens of sparkling red and blue gems decorated the wings. Addie reached up to her own hair, finally growing back out after having been cut short and bleached blonde for so many years to disguise her looks. She didn't even notice Father slip in the store's front door. A moment later, a hand reached over the display and retrieved the clip. Father emerged a few moments after that, carrying a small velvet box.

Addie's eyes widened. "You got it for me?"

Father smiled and creaked the box open. He pulled out the delicate clip. "May I?" he said. Addie nodded and he gently secured it in her hair. Father caught his breath. "You look lovely, Lilla," he said. "So grown-up."

Addie glanced at her reflection in the store window. She did look grown-up, barely a trace of the scared child left in her strong, confident gaze. She threw her arms around him.

"Thank you," she whispered. "I love you, Father."

"I love you, too, Lilla," he said. "And I'm so proud of the person you've become. The world will be a better place thanks to you."

Addie pulled the covers tighter to her chest. How could someone who cared so much about the safety of others purposely lure two innocent people to their deaths? She couldn't wrap her mind around it. It was like discovering two plus two equaled three.

The image of David and Helene Brown crumpling to the ground—dead—flashed through Addie's mind again. *They were just supposed to be a story.* Something to fool investigators. But as she listened to the voices in the hallway start up again, growing louder and closer, heading her way, Addie wasn't sure who she was trying to fool anymore. Her mother. The president. Darrow . . .

Or herself.

CHAPTER 43

Darrow's biceps flexed as he pulled the oars across the glassy surface of the Potomac. It was Monday, after school—a perfect spring afternoon for the first regatta of the rowing season. The sky was a brilliant blue, dotted with puffy white clouds that looked like a child's finger paintings. A crowd of Darrow's classmates had assembled on the riverbank to cheer Cabot on as they faced off against three rival high schools. Archer Prep was in the lead, with Cabot a close second. Saint Paul Academy and Riverside High came in at a distant third and fourth.

The coxswain at the front of Darrow's boat shouted out a new command. "Power ten!"

Darrow gritted his teeth and dragged his oars hard through the water, hands tightly gripping the smooth wooden handles. The eight-man shell pulled forward, just inching ahead of Archer. Darrow heard a cheer rise up from the crowd. He exhaled, and even though he was trying to focus, his mind wandered right back to where it had been all day—Addie.

She hadn't been at school, and he was worried. For her. For

his mother. For himself. The news yesterday that her kidnappers were dead should have come as a relief. Instead, Darrow was filled with dread. If Addie's kidnappers had been killed, who was the man that had attacked him in the parking garage? And why? Darrow felt like he was contemplating a trick SAT question, one with an obvious false answer. Or maybe one that had no answer at all.

Out of the corner of his eye, Darrow could see the Archer team gaining speed. He gripped his oars so tightly his knuckles strained against his skin. He couldn't let himself get distracted. That was all he'd been doing lately, and it was going to cost him this race. Maybe more. Darrow grunted, dropping his oars in the water. Sweat rolled down his cheeks as he pulled the handles. The finish line was straight ahead. Cabot and Archer were now neck and neck.

"Power twenty!" the coxswain called out.

Darrow's muscles strained, but he rowed as hard as he could, keeping pace with his seven teammates. Sweat burned his eyes and he could barely see anymore—just the outline of the rower in front of him, silhouetted by the late afternoon sun. More cheers rose up from the crowd, but Darrow tuned it all out, focusing only on the rhythm of his oars dipping into the water, the smooth glide of the shell, the sound of his own heavy breathing.

One, two, three, four...

The Cabot boat pulled into the lead again as they rapidly approached the finish. Darrow put everything he had into his last strokes, letting himself be one with the rhythmic motion of the oars. But just then, the Archer boat sped forward, crossing the finish line a nose ahead of Cabot.

"Check it down," the coxswain said as Cabot finished in second place.

"Damn it!" Darrow let out a loud grunt and dropped his oars squarely in the water. The boat came to a stop. Saint Paul and Riverside crossed the finish line in third and fourth. Darrow put his face in his hands, still breathing heavily. So. Damn. Close.

The teams rowed their boats to the dock and Darrow climbed out. His muscles ached and he dripped with sweat. He wiped his face on the back of his forearm and shook the perspiration from his hair, splattering droplets all over the wood by his feet. As he walked toward the boathouse, someone called his name. It was Harper, blonde hair glittering in the sunlight as she ran down the steps toward him.

"Dare," she said, panting. "We need to talk."

Darrow kept walking. "Not really in the mood right now," he said.

"I know. Tough race. But it's important," Harper said. "I wouldn't bother you otherwise."

Darrow sucked in a breath full of air and stopped, sweat still burning his eyes. "Okay," he said as his teammates streamed past. "What is it?"

Harper shook her head. "Not here. Too many people. I need to talk to you alone."

"Yeah, all right. Just let me get my things from . . ." He stopped short, glancing over Harper's shoulder at the familiar motorcade parked on the street. His heart strained against his rib cage, even harder than it had moments ago when he was trying to bring his boat home.

"Ad . . . ?" he began.

The back door of the Town Car opened. A set of long, slender legs in black leather leggings swung out and a pair of high heels hit the ground. A girl emerged, wearing round sunglasses that covered half of her face. She leaned casually on the car, scanning the crowd. The heat rose in Darrow's cheeks. It couldn't be...

The girl lifted her sunglasses. She briefly caught Darrow's eye, biting her lip, and smiled ever so slightly. Then, with a flip of her golden-brown hair, she slipped back into the car. A moment later it pulled away.

CHAPTER 44

Addie and Liz sat beneath a big blue umbrella on the patio of the Café du Parc. The French bistro was located on the ground floor of D.C.'s Willard Intercontinental Hotel. A low wrought-iron fence was all that separated their table from the bustle of Pennsylvania Avenue on the other side. But for a brief moment, as Addie took in the aged facade of the Treasury Building across the street, she almost could imagine she was back in Paris.

A waiter approached, said *"Bonjour,"* and placed a basket of warm baguette on the table.

"Some fresh bread," he said.

"Thank you." Liz inhaled deeply. "It smells wonderful."

"Just out of the oven," the waiter said. "Do you require more time with the menu?"

"Yes, please," Liz answered. "We haven't even looked yet."

"Very well." The waiter bowed his head. "I will check back on you."

Addie tore off a piece of bread, thinking suddenly of the quaint little café on the Avenue des Champs-Élysées. It made Addie's heart ache a little. Especially after this afternoon, which Addie had spent at the FBI, answering follow-up questions about the Browns. But she couldn't really tell them any more. Not any more than she already had. Up until a few days ago, she hadn't even known they were real.

Liz placed her hand on Addie's.

"I know this has been a rough day," she said. "But I'm proud of you."

"Thanks, Mom," Addie said.

"And I have a surprise for you," her mother continued. "After we eat, I'm taking you to Janie's studio. We're going to find you something spectacular for prom on Saturday."

Addie smiled, but she knew it looked forced. "Great," she said and glanced away. A family was coming up the sidewalk, pushing twin babies in a double stroller. An older child walked alongside. Three children. Addie felt a painful swell in her chest. The Browns had three children. And now those children didn't have any parents. Addie didn't know what to do to make things right. She only knew the hole in her heart couldn't be patched with designer dresses, no matter how good her mother's intentions were.

Liz picked up a menu. "Do you know what you want to eat, Ad?"

Addie glanced at the menu and felt her throat tightening. The last time she'd been in Paris, she'd had an amazing *coq au vin*, the most delicious chicken she'd ever tasted. "I'm not sure. I—I don't really know what any of this is."

Her mother was silent for a moment. When Addie glanced up at her, there were tears sparkling in Liz's dark eyes.

"Mom?" Addie said.

"God. Of course you don't. I'm sorry, baby. You've been so

strong all day, and now I'm the one who's a mess." She wiped her eyes with the back of her hands. "Sometimes it just hits me when I don't expect it."

"Don't be sorry," Addie said, not really knowing what else to say.

"I can't help it," Liz said. "I know you want to move forward, and I think that's the bravest thing in the world. But sometimes I think I'm still stuck in the past. After you were taken, Addie, it was like time stopped. I threw myself into work. I didn't know how else to cope."

"I'm sure you did the best you could," Addie said.

"Yeah? I'm not sure," Liz said. "I think I'll always wonder. I can't help it. Like, maybe I should have just shut myself away after you were taken, like all the critics and pundits said." Liz let out a sad laugh. "Maybe it's appropriate that the best program I ever created was during that time—and that it will never see the light of day."

Addie's hand twitched, making the silverware clink. "Best program? What was it?"

"Something called Shi," Liz said.

"Shi?" Addie's heart began to thump wildly.

"Means 'guardian,' " Liz said. "Or 'lion,' technically, in Chinese. I started developing it shortly after your disappearance."

"So what does it do?" Addie asked, even though she knew exactly what it did. There was a reason Father wanted it so badly.

Their conversation was interrupted by the waiter's return. Addie listened impatiently as her mother ordered for both of them. When he finally left, Liz raised an eyebrow.

"Where was I?" she said.

"You were telling me something about a program you created," Addie said. "What it did, I think?"

"Right. Shi. It's basically a very sophisticated electronic surveillance program," Liz said.

"Some kind of spyware?"

"Yes," Liz answered. "But it's not like anything else out there on the market today. The best way I can describe it is that it operates like a skilled hacker. You know what a 'zero-day flaw' is?"

"No."

"It's a flaw in an operating system that isn't discovered until it's too late. And by the time it's found, you have—"

"Zero days to fix it."

"Yes, exactly," Liz said. "Well, Shi seeks out those flaws and corrupts them, exploits them to gain access to a user's system, then installs itself and runs virtually undetectably in the background, collecting information and transmitting it back to the host computer. It can be programmed to find any type of data the user is seeking."

"That sounds . . ." Addie struggled for the right words. "Scary."

"It is scary," Liz said, "because I programmed Shi using artificial intelligence. It learns from its mistakes, with the primary goals of preserving itself, spreading across systems, and collecting data. So even if one flaw is found and fixed, Shi just looks for another. And once it gains a foothold in a system, it spreads exponentially, like a virus. There's almost no stopping it once it starts. I'm sure you understand why it couldn't be let loose in the world."

"Dad," Addie answered. Everyone knew Mark Webster had

run on an anti-spying platform, and had spoken out against the NSA-sponsored cyber-surveillance programs long before he ran for president.

Liz sighed. "No. Of course, your father would never have approved of something like this for domestic use once he became president, but he couldn't have prevented me from selling it at the time. *I* was the one who pulled the plug. The NSA was all ready to snap it up, but when it came down to it, I just couldn't do it. I think all along I'd never really planned to actually let it be put into use."

"Why?"

"It's too dangerous, Addie," Liz said. "Just think about it. You'd have one user with unfettered access to all that data— every single person with a computer, smartphone, you name it. It's terrifying. What if the program ended up in the hands of a dictator or a tyrant?"

"So what did you do with it?" Addie said, voice shaking. "Destroy it?"

"No," Liz said. "The only copy is on my development computer in my home office. It's not networked, so no one can access it. But I couldn't get rid of it—partly out of pride, I guess. But also because it's only a matter of time before someone else begins to develop the same type of software, and I have to be ready if Nova is going to stay competitive."

Addie's ears began to ring. So that's why she couldn't find Shi in any of her mother's directories. It was on a stand-alone.

The waiter came and placed two steaming bowls of soup in front of Addie and her mother. The pungent smell of fish made her queasy.

"I'm sorry, Ad," Liz said. "Am I boring you with all this

work talk? Sometimes I can get off on a tangent, and forget everyone isn't as interested in programming as me."

"No," Addie said. "I feel like I'm learning a lot." She tried a small sip of soup. It tasted better than it smelled. "I'm curious about something, though," she said. "If you never really planned on letting Shi see the light of day, why spend all those years creating it in the first place?"

"Like I said," Liz sighed. "It was how I coped. A part of me believed that if I could just make the world more secure, you never would have been taken in the first place."

CHAPTER 45

Darrow found himself momentarily speechless as a group of students passed him on their way off the dock. What in the hell was *she* doing here? Harper waved a hand in front of his face.

"Um, Darrow?" she said. "You look like you just saw a ghost."

Darrow snapped back to reality. "Not a ghost. *Elinor*," he said, a knot forming in his stomach. "I just saw Elinor. I had no idea she was coming back so soon. Is that what you wanted to talk to me about?"

"I didn't think she was coming home until summer break either," Harper said. "That's crazy. But no, it's not what I want to talk to you about. So can we go somewhere else?" she said, stuffing her hands in her pockets and glancing around anxiously.

"Sure," Darrow said, even though he wanted nothing more than to go home, shower, and forget this day ever happened. "I'm parked behind the boathouse. Let me grab my things and I'll meet you at my car."

Darrow picked up his stuff, avoiding the post-race recap

with his teammates. He found Harper in the parking lot, leaning on his scratched driver's side door.

"What happened here?" she said. "You piss someone off?"

"Long story," Darrow said. He pushed his key fob and the car doors unlocked with a beep. Darrow climbed in the driver's seat and Harper slid into the passenger side.

"So what is it?" Darrow said. He rolled down the window to let in some fresh air and shifted on the hot leather seat, facing Harper.

"It's McQueen," she said in a rush.

"McQueen?" Darrow repeated, confused. "What about him?"

Harper took a breath. "So you know how it looked like he had a heart attack? Well, his toxicology report just came back..."

"Whoa. Wait a minute," Darrow interrupted. "His toxicology report? How did you get your hands on that?"

"A source," Harper said, shortly. "Sorry, can't say."

"Fair enough," Darrow said. The halls of Cabot were filled with the children of high-level players from all over the world. It wasn't hard to imagine Harper would find several solid sources among them. And Darrow knew she'd never give them up.

"Here's the thing," Harper said. "According to the toxicology report, McQueen had ten times the normal dosage of Ramipril—that's an ACE inhibitor, lowers the blood pressure—in his system. More than enough to kill him."

Darrow sat there a moment, letting Harper's words sink in. "What? How does something like that happen?" he said shakily.

"Autopsy is calling it suicide."

"Suicide?" Darrow said. "That doesn't make sense." McQueen was the last person on earth Darrow would peg as suicidal. "Exactly," Harper said. "That's what my source said, too. And with that kind of overdose, it couldn't have been accidental."

If it wasn't suicide, or an accident... "So what you're saying..." Darrow began in a low whisper, then stopped and shivered. "Why would someone tell you all of this?"

"Because not everyone in the family is buying the official version," Harper said. "They don't have anything to go on, and they're afraid to go public with it. But they're not getting anywhere with the administration, either. They say President Webster's advisors just want to sweep the whole thing under the rug because either way they spin it, an overdose makes the administration look bad. If McQueen killed himself because he was stressed about the attacks, they're afraid it hands Cerberus a win; and if he was murdered, well..."

"Holy shit," Darrow said, understanding now why he hadn't heard his mother mention anything about this at home. She confided in Darrow a lot, but not about everything—especially when it involved things that might paint the administration in a bad light.

A group of students crunched across the gravel in front of Darrow's car, startling him. He was reminded of how vulnerable and exposed they were sitting out here. D.C. had been under attack. Darrow himself had been threatened in a dark parking garage on Saturday night. And now someone might have tampered with McQueen's medication. But who? And *why*? What had McQueen wanted to talk to him about? What about the situation had changed?

His thoughts raced back to the morning when he'd found the general. He pictured McQueen, sprawled on the floor, fingers clutching Darrow's shirt. He'd been choking out words, trying to tell him something. But what? Darrow replayed the scene over and over in his head.

She's sir... She's sir... She's...

What did that mean? Cheshire? She's sure. She's sir...

All the blood drained from Darrow's face and he gripped the steering wheel, knuckles white.

She's Cerberus.

Addie, McQueen had said. *She's Cerberus.*

CHAPTER 46

It was early October, six months ago, and a chill had already settled into the air. Addie sat at the computer in her bedroom of the New York farmhouse. She and Michael were home alone on the sprawling estate just south of Penn Yan and the Finger Lakes. The compound, complete with its own private airstrip, had been in Susan Erlander's family for generations. As Susan was an only child, it was bequeathed to Karl and Michael upon her death. At first, Karl had left it mothballed, too plagued with memories of his dead wife to return. When Addie had joined the family he'd gone back, merely seeking a remote place to hide at first. But as he'd uncovered the antique sofas and chairs, dusted off the tables and pictures, he'd discovered it made the perfect home base. A place to go when they weren't busy traveling the world for Karl's many meetings. A place where the many images of Susan's smiling face were a comfort—and a reminder of why they needed to take action.

On this particular night, Father was en route to Milan on a business trip. He'd left Addie and Michael behind. There was no longer any fear that Addie would try to run. She had long since accepted her place in the family. Her rightful place. She, Michael, and Karl. *Cerberus.* The three-headed beast that oversaw a legion of loyal followers, tasked with keeping a watchful eye on the underworld while everyone else slept. Addie alone didn't have the tattoo—too risky, if anyone saw it.

Addie's palms were sticky with sweat. She'd been monitoring the chat room of an obscure terrorist group based in Yemen that Karl had tipped her off about right before he left. They were chattering about something big going down. Tonight. She wasn't sure if what she was seeing now was true, but she hoped like hell it wasn't. She called for her brother.

"Hey, Mikey! Come here. Quick."

Michael came in from the kitchen, sidestepping the jeans she'd left all over the floor, and stood behind her. Addie pointed at the computer screen.

"Is this what I think it is?" Addie said shakily.

Michael read. "Someone's hacked into the power grid. Why? They looking to cause a major outage?"

"No," Addie said. "It's worse. Look closer. At what they're targeting."

Michael leaned in. "Calvert Cliffs ... Three Mile Island ... Diablo Canyon ..." He stopped and let out a horrified gasp. "Nuclear power stations?"

"Yeah," Addie said. "And if I'm reading this right, they're not just planning to cause outages. They're going to cause simultaneous meltdowns."

"Oh my God," Michael said. "Meltdowns?"

Addie nodded, too horrified to speak. "Call Father."

Mikey pulled his phone from his back pocket, dialed and waited. "I can't reach him," he said, his voice high with anxiety.

"He must not have service. I don't know when we'll be able to get through." He dropped the phone on the desk. "What about..." Mikey trailed off. No one was allowed to contact Cerberus's followers besides Karl unless he gave explicit permission. Only he knew the true scope of the network—and the identities of all its members.

"You know I don't have the access codes—or the time," Addie said. "This is happening *now*."

"So what do we do?"

Addie thought about trying to alert the authorities. But the clock was ticking, and she realized by the time she reached the right person, it might be too late. They might not even believe her—whoever had hacked the grid was covering their tracks well, using dummy pages to make it appear that operations were normal.

"We have to stop it ourselves," Addie said. But she knew that "we" meant Addie. Mikey was by no means useless with a computer, but Addie had left him in the dust years ago. Unfortunately, Father never let him forget it. But there was no time to think about that now.

Addie cracked her neck and started to type. Sweat formed on her brow. Whoever had hacked into the grid had also set up a wall of security to keep anyone from shutting their operation down. Addie couldn't get in with any of her usual methods. She kept sucking in short breaths, but couldn't seem to fill her lungs.

"Whoever did this is good," she said. "I'm not getting in."

"You can do it, Lilla. I know you can. Like you did that time Father took us to Paris, remember?" Michael said. He'd been pacing back and forth behind her, leaving a groove in the carpet. "Father said that hack was nearly impossible."

Addie cracked her knuckles. She remembered the SQL injection she'd used to get into that jihadist site. It was worth a try. Frantically watching the clock, she typed. The screen switched over—she was in. But there were still lines of complicated code to sort through, and time was ticking away.

There was a buzzing in her ears. "I don't think I can do it," she said, the words coming out flat and toneless. Ninety-nine reactors scattered across thirty states, and they were poised to melt down in minutes. Addie tried not to consider what would happen if she failed: immediate death for hundreds of thousands; radiation poisoning and slow, agonizing deaths for millions more.

Hands shaking, she tried a simple system reset. It immediately failed. Not that she had expected anything different. It was going to take too long to rewrite the code. But she had to keep looking for a solution. Suddenly, her screen flashed. It was an alert. The core temperature at Turkey Point was rising rapidly, five minutes ahead of schedule.

Addie blinked back tears. Turkey Point was just south of Miami, Florida, one of the most highly populated areas near any nuclear plant. In desperation, Addie inserted a quick line of code into the script running in front of her—a virus she and Father had designed together but hadn't tested yet. Something that would disrupt a system and allow her to take control.

She held her breath as the screen flashed again. Addie let out a small cry as she continued typing.

"What is it?" Michael gasped. There were red marks all over his face from where he'd been clutching it. "Is it too late?"

"No," she said, breathlessly. "I'm in. The core temperature at Turkey Point is dropping. I'm resetting the grid."

She kept typing frantically until, several minutes later, she was done. She stood and faced Michael.

"I knew you could do it, Lilla," he said.

She choked back a sob, then collapsed into his arms, crying with relief.

"Maybe," she said. "But I couldn't have done it without you."

CHAPTER 47

When Addie and Liz returned to the West Wing after dress shopping, Liz broke away to meet with her chief of staff about an upcoming "Twitter town hall" with the First Lady. It amazed Addie how quickly the White House had returned to normal, how quickly the entire country seemed to have reverted to the status quo, now that Cerberus had apparently been stopped in its tracks. The president's press office was riding a wave of sudden popularity, touting how swiftly the administration had shut down the attacks and brought Addie's kidnappers to justice. Their naiveté blew Addie's mind; it was a constant reminder of why her mission wasn't complete. Not yet.

She rode the elevator to the residence, where she was greeted with silence. It was almost 6 P.M. Mackenzie was in her playroom with the nanny; the staff was in the kitchen preparing for dinner. Addie stepped into the foyer, waving good-bye to the Secret Service agent manning the elevator.

When the door slid shut, Addie entered the Center Hall. But instead of returning to her room like normal, she went the other way, straight for her mother's study. She paused at the door and caught her breath, hesitating. For years, Addie had been plagued by the idea of her own mother forgetting about her. But it was a lot easier to believe it when Liz was a distant figure on the news. Now that she'd seen the lines on her mother's face, felt the way Liz trembled when her slender fingers wrapped around Addie's, she knew it wasn't true. Her mother had never gotten over Addie's disappearance. And she'd created Shi to try to save her. She might have been too late, but at least she had tried. How could Addie steal it from her, knowing what she knew now?

Except she wasn't stealing it. She was making sure Liz's technology was put to use. So no other child had to face what Addie and Michael had faced. So that attacks like the nuclear meltdown she'd stopped at the very last minute never had a chance of happening again. Millions of lives meant more than Addie's guilty conscience.

She pushed open the door and slipped inside. It was still the cluttered mess she remembered, the desk with a computer and papers in toppling stacks. And there was the second computer, by itself on a side desk. Addie couldn't believe she hadn't thought of that earlier. Of course her mother would keep important development work on a stand-alone. She was way too careful to leave her work accessible to hackers. She didn't make herself vulnerable to things like zero-day flaws. Liz Webster's only flaw was her love for her daughter, Addie realized as guilt stabbed again at her heart. And she'd never realize what had happened until it was too late.

Addie exhaled, sat in front of the computer, and powered it up. It didn't take long to find Shi. In fact, after all her searching, it almost felt too easy. Addie pulled the blank thumb drive from her pocket—she'd been carrying it around for days, just in case—and jammed it into the USB port.

She dragged the Shi icon to the drive, taking short breaths, trying to keep herself from hyperventilating as the program transferred. She sat still as a stone, acutely aware of every sound in the hallway outside.

She checked the progress bar: fifty percent complete. She clenched and unclenched her fists, wishing this thing would just. Hurry. Up.

Status: 64%

Addie heard voices echoing from somewhere else in the residence. Someone was getting off the elevator. Her mother? Addie began to sweat. She heard the elevator door ding.

75%

85%

Footsteps, headed her way.

92%

Addie swallowed a scream as the tapping of feet grew closer. And closer.

97%

Almost to the door.

100%

Addie yanked the drive out and jammed it into her pocket just as someone spoke.

"There you are."

Addie spun around.

A girl was standing at the door. She was a few inches taller than Addie, with golden-brown hair cut in an asymmetrical bob. Her oversized sweater hung off one shoulder, showing off a hot-pink bra strap, and her calculating gray eyes took Addie in, lingering on her face.

"Ellie," Addie breathed. "Oh my God, no one told me you were—"

She broke off as her sister collided with her, wrapping Addie in a tight hug. Elinor was slight, like Addie, but she felt more jagged somehow—all angles, no curves.

"I can't believe it's really you," Elinor said into her shoulder. "I'm so glad you're home."

"Yeah, you too," Addie said, pulling back and looking at her sister. "Are you back for good?"

Elinor flopped into a chair and began picking at her chipped fingernail polish, the same shade of pink as her bra. "No," she said. "I'm just here for a few days. Got a weekend pass. Part of my 'rehabilitation.' " She made air quotes with her fingers and rolled her eyes. "Have to make sure I can be trusted not to do something stupid on my own. Down a bottle of pills or slash my own wrists or something."

"Oh," Addie said, at a loss for words. "Ellie," she began awkwardly, "I just wanted to say, I'm sorry about everything that happened after . . . you know. It can't have been easy."

Ellie just looked at her. "Seriously, Addie? You were freaking *kidnapped* and you're saying sorry to me?"

"No, I just mean—about the pills, and . . ." Addie trailed off. This was going all wrong.

Ellie reached up to brush a lock of hair from her face. Addie noticed her hand shaking.

"I've been fine, Ad," she said, her voice cool and distant.

Addie nodded and decided to change the subject. "I met one of your friends at Cabot. Olivia, I think it was."

"Oh yeah. She just sent me a picture of the dress she got for prom. Did you and Mom find something awesome? A Janie Liu original, right? Jealous. I've been begging Mom to let her design something for me for years. Guess I'll just have to live with off-the-rack."

"Does that mean you're coming Saturday?" Addie said, voice cracking. She didn't know if she could deal with having her sister at her side, when . . .

"Don't worry," Elinor said, standing up. "I won't be there. Shrinks won't let me near any sort of party yet. You'll have Darrow all to yourself."

"What?" The heat rose in Addie's cheeks.

"Seriously, it's *fine*," Elinor said as she walked toward the door. "I'm over him anyway."

Addie did a double take as her little sister spun around and regarded Addie, head cocked to the side.

"Oh, he didn't tell you?" Elinor said. Her eyes softened, and for a moment Addie could see Ellie as she once was, the little girl who had cried when Addie killed a spider in the playroom. Then the spite returned to her sister's eyes.

"Tell me what?" Addie said, mouth dry.

"About us," Elinor said, watching Addie's face for a reaction. Addie pushed her lips together, refusing to give her one. "Eh," Elinor continued. "It was only a couple months. Not like it's sloppy seconds or anything."

Before Addie could come back with any sort of retort, Elinor was at the door. "See you at dinner, Ad."

CHAPTER 48

The next morning, Darrow sat in Harper's studio, drumming his fingers on the table and watching the door. Where was Addie? She'd ignored all his texts and calls yesterday. Having Harper pretend to want to see her was the only way he could think of to talk to Addie alone. Darrow chewed on his bottom lip, checking the time again. Five more minutes and he'd be late to class.

A light knock snapped Darrow from his thoughts. The door in front of him opened.

"Harper?" Addie said softly. She walked into the room. Darrow stood and caught her gently by the arm, pushing the door shut. Addie's eyes went wide and she recoiled from his touch.

"What are *you* doing here?" she said.

"I needed to talk to you," Darrow said. "And you won't return any of my calls."

"Maybe that's because I don't want to talk to you," Addie said, turning toward the door. Darrow quickly slid in front of it.

He shook his head. Addie glared at him. "I'm serious, Darrow," she said. "Get out of my way."

"No," he said. "Not until I get some answers."

"Really? *You* want answers?" she retorted.

Darrow didn't know what that was supposed to mean. He pressed on. "Yes, I want answers," he said. "For starters, what do you know about General McQueen?"

A flicker of something—recognition, guilt?—crossed Addie's face. She glanced away, staring at the unlit red "on air" light above Darrow's head. "I have no idea what you're talking about," she said flatly. "I've never met the guy."

"Really?" Darrow said. "Because he sure seemed to know you. In fact, when he died—right in front of me—the only name to come out of his mouth was *yours*." Addie shifted her gaze back to Darrow. "Weird, right?" he said. "You'd think a dying guy's last words would be for his wife. Or kids. Or maybe God or something."

"What?" she said. "Why would he say something about me?"

"Good question," Darrow said, not taking his eyes off Addie. "Because word is, McQueen didn't have a heart attack, or some sort of overdose, or commit suicide . . . someone killed him." Addie began to back up slowly, bumping into the table. Darrow could see her lower lip quivering.

"I swear, I don't know what you're talking about," she said. "Maybe you misunderstood. . . ."

"Maybe. But I definitely didn't misunderstand *this*," Darrow said. He pulled down the collar of his shirt, exposing the small, scabbed-over spot where the knife had pricked his skin Saturday night. Addie gasped. "This is what some guy did to me. Right after he told me to stay away from *you*. Seems you're pretty popular these days...."

"You're starting to scare me, Dare," she said.

"You should be scared, Ad," he said, voice growing louder.

"I'm scared. I don't know what you're involved in, but it's not too late. Whatever it is, you can get out.... Prom isn't until this weekend. Whatever you're planning..." Darrow stopped short as Addie's back straightened, her trembling lip suddenly stiff.

"You think I'm planning something?" she said coolly.

Darrow hesitated. He hadn't meant to let that slip.

"Yes—I heard you," Darrow said, trying to regain his composure. "Talking to that man after the reception..."

Addie's face turned bright red and she breathed loudly through her nose. "You were *spying* on me?" she said, voice rising. *"How?"* Darrow didn't respond, but his eyes flicked reflexively to the locket around her neck. Addie's lips parted and she glanced down in shock.

She yanked the silver chain from her neck and threw it to the ground. The butterfly clattered across the floor and cracked in half. The bug fell out. Addie pressed her lips together, blinking back tears. "I can't believe I ever trusted you. My sister was right...."

"Elinor..." Darrow said under his breath, putting it together.

"Yeah, Elinor. Were you ever going to tell me?" Addie said. "Or did you just think I'd never find out? What was I, your backup plan until she got out of rehab?"

"No," Darrow said vehemently. "I swear it wasn't like that. Elinor..." He balled his hands into fists and released them.

"There are a million reasons why we never . . . that doesn't matter right now." He took a shaky breath. "What matters is you. Please, let me help you."

"Help me?" Addie said with a snort. "If you wanted to help me, you wouldn't have lied to me."

"You're calling me a liar?" Darrow said. "All you've done is lie to me since the moment you got home! And get me to lie *for* you. Maybe start with what you were really doing out in the woods that night in Virginia!"

Addie stepped in front of Darrow, so close he could feel the heat of her breath on his face. She was shaking with anger, and something else. There was a wildness in her eyes that he'd never seen before, a desperation that had been simmering below the surface and was finally out in the open. She closed the distance between them, and her body was suddenly pressed against his, her chin tilting up as his lips found hers. He deepened the kiss, feeling her lips parting as his hands traveled down to her waist. He slipped one under her thin T-shirt and felt the warm skin of her back. Her fingers were tangled in his hair and they tightened as he pulled her closer, his tongue exploring her mouth. Every nerve ending in his body was on fire. Suddenly she broke away from him, gasping.

"Darrow—" Her cheeks were flushed, and there were wisps of dark hair all around her face.

He tried to catch his breath. He couldn't look away from those green eyes, blazing with a furious kind of energy that he never wanted to see snuffed out.

"Darrow," she whispered again. "I can't."

"Why? Why can't you?" he said.

"Because you'll only get hurt." She whirled around, flung

the door open, and raced into the hall. He heard Alvarez's alarmed questions on the opposite side, and their voices faded into the din of the hallway.

Darrow slid to the ground, his back against the wall, breathing like he'd run a marathon. *Because you'll only get hurt. . . .* How could Addie hurt him any more than she already had? It wasn't possible. Nothing could hurt worse than the guilt he'd felt over her kidnapping, the years he'd let himself veer off-track, the emptiness of her absence. Even a knife-prick to the neck didn't compare.

Except . . . he'd seen Addie's eyes flashing wildly just before she kissed him, and he knew it was possible. She could hurt him. The only way to protect himself was the one thing it killed him to do—stay away from Addie Webster.

CHAPTER 49

Addie could barely focus for the rest of the day. She and Darrow avoided each other, but all she could think about was the lingering warmth of his lips on hers, even as fear gnawed away at her. Someone had gone after Darrow, because of *Addie*. She knew about McQueen's blackmail attempts. But McQueen was dead. So who? And what the hell was Darrow talking about anyway, that someone might have killed McQueen?

The questions dogged her all afternoon. The only explanation Addie could come to—the most frightening one of all— was that McQueen must have found something. Something big.

When Addie got home from school, she went straight to her room. She opened her computer and headed for McQueen's directory.

She searched for half an hour through every single one of his files, but came up empty. Definitely nothing in there that would have gotten him killed. Most of the guy's time seemed to have been dedicated to researching security protocols, terror groups, and cyber threats. None of that was out of the ordinary. That was his job. She must be missing something.

She read through McQueen's file directories, then his e-mail folder and calendar for a second and third time.

That's when it hit her. Something *was* missing...

Cerberus.

McQueen had been hired directly in response to the Cerberus scandal, yet there wasn't a single file on his computer related to it. Not a single e-mail. Not one word. Addie knew the White House had kept McQueen on a short leash, but it wasn't plausible that there would be *nothing* to show for his six months in office. Someone had wiped all traces of Cerberus away.

Addie knew only one person who would have the skill—or the motive—to scrub McQueen's computer of everything Cerberus-related. Her father. But why hide it from her? Unless ... he was only giving her half the story, only telling her what he thought she needed to hear in order to get the job done.

The back of Addie's neck began to sweat; she could almost feel him there, leaning over her, whispering in her ear.

Don't do it, Lilla. You can't hide anything from me. I know your every step, before you even take it....

Addie wiped the cold sweat from her neck and started typing anyway. He hadn't changed her password in the home network, which came as a surprise, given his paranoia. Maybe it was just because he knew she'd be back. Or maybe it was something worse ... like a trap he knew he could catch her with. Like all those times she'd run out the unlocked front door, only to find him waiting on the other side.

She covered her tracks as best she could as she read through Karl's directories. He was meticulous, every operation—the

Republican fund-raiser, the Metro attack, the hijacked car, even the drone flying over the White House gates—all carefully documented with e-mails, screenshots of chat rooms and text messages that showed their planning. She'd never dug deeply into her father's files, and part of her wanted to scroll through every bit, find out what else he was hiding. But she knew every minute she spent hacking his system was one minute closer to exposing herself.

She opened another directory and searched for the most recent files, finding a folder simply labeled *GJM*. General James McQueen. She clicked it open. Everything was there— frustrated e-mails between McQueen and the NSA director, spreadsheets charting the location of Cerberus's messages, IP addresses, lists of suspected Cerberus members throughout the world. A final note to himself:

Believe to have isolated Cerberus IP address. Traced communication between Cerberus chat room IP and computer on White House network. Need AW computer for confirmation.

The last file was a message to Darrow, requesting a meeting.

An hour later, McQueen was dead.

So that was it. McQueen had connected her to Cerberus. But it didn't appear he'd had a chance to share what he'd found with anyone. Except maybe Darrow. Addie tapped the trackpad and shakily moved the cursor to exit Karl's computer. She'd already spent too long on here. But something caught her eye. A folder labeled *Turkey Point*.

Despite her fears, Addie clicked it open. The file contained the evidence Karl had sent to the press—screenshots Addie had taken of the chat room where the terrorists had planned their attack that proved the administration had missed critical intelligence.

But that wasn't all. Karl's file also contained several screenshots of the main power grid, as well as Turkey Point's core monitor with its temperature rising. A wave of nausea washed over Addie before her eyes could even fully accept what she was seeing. Addie hadn't taken any screenshots of the power grid or the Turkey Point page before shutting the reactor down. Just the chat room. There hadn't been time for anything more. And no one else knew about the attack, no one else had been watching, it had all been up to her to stop it . . . so how did Karl have these images? The answer hit her like a ton of bricks.

Addie stood so quickly her chair toppled backward, hitting the hardwood floor with a thud. Karl had known about the attack on the nuclear power stations *beforehand*. Suddenly the timing, the fact that Karl had been so conveniently unreachable right when the attack was under way, made her wonder . . . what if the Yemeni terrorists *hadn't* been pulling the strings? What if it was just . . . Karl? Her head was swimming, and for a moment she thought she might pass out. She knew the attack had been real. And she knew if she hadn't stopped it, millions would have died. Just so Karl could prove a point. Just so he could manipulate Addie into carrying out the next phase of his plan—infiltrating the White House.

Addie reached over and pressed the power button on her computer, holding it until the screen went dark. Tears clouded her vision. She grabbed her phone. She needed answers. She typed a Burnchat message.

Father. Have acquired Shi. Need to meet.

The response came back almost immediately.

Excellent work, Lilla. Handoff tomorrow. Will message later with details.

After suffering through the world's longest dinner, barely able to look Elinor in the eye, Addie returned to her computer and inserted the thumb drive holding Shi into her USB port. She spent the next several hours reading through layers of code. Her mother had been right; the program was brilliant.

But . . . Addie hadn't been lying at lunch the day before. It was also terrifying. She hesitated. There were no take-backs for something like this. She needed more time to think. So she cloned the program and removed the original drive.

Then she set about making an inverted program. One that wouldn't seek out and exploit the flaws in operating systems, but one that would do something else entirely with them.

It was well after 2 A.M. when Addie was finally finished. She copied the program to a new thumb drive, marked it with a tiny red dot, and stuck it in her desk.

Exhausted, she collapsed into bed.

She was nearly asleep when the phone next to her bed buzzed. A follow-up Burnchat with the rendezvous point. She quickly read and committed the details of the plan to memory, just before the message self-destructed.

CHAPTER 50

Addie's limo rolled up to the side entrance of Cabot. Addie leaned on the door, her breath fogging the window. She wiped it away and watched her classmates milling about the entrance. She'd barely slept last night. And when she had, all she could dream of were hands. Hands grabbing her. Hands pulling her deep into a pit of darkness. When she woke up she felt like she was covered in palm prints, a million fingers pressed into her raw skin.

"You okay?" Agent Alvarez asked. "You don't look like you're feeling too hot."

"Yeah," Addie said. "I'm all right. Just a little stressed."

"I know the feeling," Alvarez said.

"You know what would help, though?" Addie said. "A run. A real one. I'm sick of the track. Think maybe we could do the National Mall? Reflecting pool? Something like that?" Addie held her breath.

"That's gonna take some time to coordinate."

"I know," Addie said. "I was thinking after school. Three, three thirty or so?"

The car rolled to a stop. Addie waited for Alvarez to come around to her side and let her out.

"Three, three thirty..." Alvarez said. "Sounds doable. I should be able to pull together a team by this afternoon."

"A team?" Addie said, swallowing hard. She thought she could outrun Alvarez if necessary, but she wasn't too sure about an entire team. "I'd rather just run with you. Those guys you work with make me self-conscious."

"I hear you," Alvarez said. "Don't worry. I'll be the one to run with you. The rest of the team will be positioned in vehicles in advance of us and behind us, okay? I'll do my best to keep them low profile."

"You're the best," Addie said.

"Yeah, yeah, flattery will get you everywhere," Alvarez said. "Just make sure to give me a nice review on Yelp."

Addie laughed. She liked Alvarez. She really liked her.

Which made what Addie was about to do even harder.

It was a perfect afternoon for a run. Seventy degrees and sunny. Barely a cloud in the sky.

Addie and Alvarez jogged along the path that ran parallel to Jefferson Drive on the National Mall, the Washington Monument looming large behind them. Tourists clogged the green, flying kites, sitting on picnic blankets, and wandering from museum to monument. Nobody paid any notice to the pair of runners in their midst—one famous, one lethal. In their athletic shorts and T-shirts, MP3 players strapped to their arms, Addie and Alvarez blended right in with the rest of the joggers and cyclists circling the Mall.

Alvarez tapped Addie's arm. Addie pulled out an earbud and listened.

"Here's the deal," Alvarez said. "We're going to follow the path here all the way around. Twice is four miles. Sound good?"

"Perfect," Addie said. She popped her earbud back in and pretended to turn on her music. Alvarez scanned the crowd for threats. Addie looked for an opening. It was already three forty-five. They'd gotten a late start. Addie would need to find an out— quickly. Timeliness was nearly as important as security to him.

Addie and Alvarez passed the main Smithsonian Institution on the right, a large red sandstone building known locally as "The Castle." From the left, Addie heard the sound of old-fashioned carnival music and squealing children as the Mall's carousel spun, a blur of blue and gold, painted horses and dragons, and brass poles bedecked with American flags. A hollowness tugged at Addie's core.

She blinked and saw herself—small feet tucked in metal stirrups, hands wrapped around the cool pole, face upturned, wind lifting the hair from her neck. She could hear her own laughter, riding on the breeze like the peal of wind chimes, while her mother stood next to her holding a camera in the air. It felt like a dream. A long-forgotten dream.

Addie cracked her neck and refocused. Time was running out.

Straight ahead, a huge school group exited the Air and Space Museum, chaotic and disorganized, and made their way across the road onto the Mall. Addie's heart rate accelerated. This was her chance. She watched as a harried teacher tried to rein in the wandering middle-schoolers bouncing around like pinballs, doing cartwheels on the grass and taking selfies with their phones.

Addie glanced over her shoulder. The car trailing their jog was stationed at the corner of Independence and 7th, and she knew the advance car was up ahead at the junction of 3rd.

If she was going to make her move, it had to be now.

The voices of the schoolkids grew closer and louder. Agent Alvarez tapped Addie's arm and pointed to the left.

"Let's go around this way," she said.

But Addie just nodded her head to the music she was pretending to listen to in her earbuds, even though they'd been turned off for the entire run. Without looking at Alvarez, she picked up her pace and jogged straight into the crowd of kids. She could hear Alvarez's shouts as she charged behind her. Addie spun around, catching the agent with a well-placed foot and a quick shove to the shoulder. Before she had a chance to catch herself, Alvarez tumbled sideways between dozens of shuffling sneakers.

And Addie was gone.

Addie scrambled through the group of kids, threw her sweatshirt to the ground, and sprinted across the Mall. She pulled a hat from her pocket, tucked her hair beneath it, and quickly yanked the sides over her ears. Straight ahead she saw her destination—a Capital Bikeshare kiosk on Madison.

She reached the row of bikes and leaned on the rack to catch her breath. But there was no time to waste. Alvarez was probably already on her feet by now, wondering what had just happened, where Addie had gone. Addie counted down three bikes—okay, this should be the one. She pulled on the bicycle with sweaty fingers.

It was stuck.

Addie's sweat turned cold and she looked left and right. She was sure this was the right spot. It was the only stand not in clear view of her Secret Service motor detail. It was the only stand on the whole damn block. She wiped her palms on her shorts and yanked again.

Locked tight.

Across the Mall, sirens blared.

Addie's fingers clenched into fists. They were coming for her. She was almost out of time. She furiously pulled the bike to no avail, then steadied her breath and counted the bikes again. She was sure he'd said number three.

One, two . . .

Hold on. Now that she looked at it, the second bike was actually missing from the rack. So that meant she hadn't been pulling the third, but the fourth.

She backed up one bicycle and gave it a yank.

It slipped easily from the rack.

Addie hopped on and sped off. The sound of sirens faded away, replaced by the noise of everyday life. People shouting, horns honking, music pulsing from passing cars.

For a brief moment, Addie remembered what it felt like to be free—truly free. The wind rushing through her hair. The bright sun in her eyes. And for once, nobody watching. She thought about just riding away. Pumping her legs until she reached the end of the earth, where no one could touch her.

But she knew there was no such place.

She turned the bike and raced down Constitution, the White House looming large to her right, and pedaled away.

CHAPTER 51

Addie pumped her legs, muscles twitching, and reached the entrance of Kogan Plaza at three minutes past four. She hopped off, steadied the bike against the wrought-iron fence, and ran inside. The university campus was crammed with students. They sat on benches, clustered around the fountain and beneath the flowering cherry blossoms. At the domed gazebo ahead, Addie caught a glimpse of pale blond hair peeking out from beneath a blue-and-gold GWU baseball cap. She almost didn't recognize him. He never wore hats. Or cheap Windbreakers like the one zipped over his polo shirt.

Addie steadied her breath and walked toward the stone structure. She went up the small steps to where he stood, leaning against a column.

"Lilla," he said. He reached out to hug her, but Addie stayed stiff.

"Is something wrong, little one?" he asked.

"I didn't expect anyone to die," she said.

Karl's stern face softened. "I know," he answered. "But

sometimes in war there are casualties. Sometimes we have to tell a lie so the truth can be exposed."

Like the nuclear attack?

"But the Browns were innocent," she said.

"And they chose their own fate," Karl answered. "No one made them run into a hail of bullets. They could have surrendered."

Addie breathed deeply. *But you knew they wouldn't.* That nagging doubt began to creep back up in Addie's brain. *And that's exactly why you chose them.*

"What about McQueen? Did he choose his own fate?"

"Lilla," Karl said, "you need to trust me. You're aware that General McQueen was about to expose you. Aren't you? He was gathering evidence." He stared intently at her face, as if daring her to say more, maybe expose herself. Did he know . . . ?

Addie looked away.

"Listen to me," Karl said. "I did it to protect you."

"What if someone figures it out?"

"They won't figure it out," Karl said. "And if they do, who will they suspect, anyway? The first person they'll look to is the last one who was with him. Someone with a motive. Especially if there's evidence McQueen was threatening him."

Karl let the words hang there. He didn't say more. But Addie understood. If she dared make an issue out of McQueen's death—if anyone did—all the clues would lead straight back to Darrow. She couldn't meet Karl's eyes.

"Look at me, Lilla," he said.

She did.

"The world is a dangerous place," he said. "And I am the

only one who can protect you. Everyone else has failed. Do you understand?"

"Yes."

Karl raised an eyebrow and cocked his head to the side.

"Yes, Father."

"Good. Have you brought the program?" Karl said.

Addie nodded. Karl held out his hand. Addie fingered the thumb drive in her pocket. She needed to know, once and for all: Was she a rook, or just a pawn? Was he willing to sacrifice her too? Just like the Browns, and McQueen. Just like all those people who lived near Turkey Point.

"Let me come with you," she said.

"Excuse me?"

"I have the program. All you need to do is get into the network and run it remotely. I've already created a hole for you to do it." She had, too. It was ready and waiting. "Please, let me come with you. I'm scared. I want to come home." She looked at him, eyes pleading. "You can make it look like something happened to me here. Now. We don't have to wait until prom."

Karl's face turned cold. "No, you know that isn't possible. We do have to wait. The final attack must occur on April fifteenth. For Susan. No other day is acceptable. I've waited fifteen years for this. You, little one, can stand to wait three more days. Understand?"

It felt like her chest was caving in. She thought of the butterfly clip, Father's gentle hands as he'd placed it in her hair. If he loved her so much, how could he just leave her here?

"Yes, Father," Addie said, gaze falling to the ground.

"The program?"

Addie hesitated, then pulled a thumb drive from her pocket and pressed it into Karl's hand. He deposited it into his jacket pocket and smoothed his khaki pants, edging his shoulder away from her as he talked. "I'd like to stay and catch up, Lilla. But it's best that we're not seen together. I'll be in touch. Good-bye for now."

"Good-bye," Addie said.

She started to turn away; then Karl spoke again. "Lilla." His voice was gentle, and there was a tinge of sadness in his blue eyes. "This will be over soon, and we will have a better world. Because of you. I'm very proud." Addie nodded, throat tight, as Karl pulled his GWU cap over his eyes and walked down the steps, disappearing into the crowd of students.

Addie sat on a cool marble bench and tried to collect herself. She knew the Secret Service had to be going crazy by now. Helicopters circled in the distance. She wondered if they were looking for her. Addie pulled out her phone and hit Alvarez's number on speed dial. The agent answered on the first ring.

"*Addie!* Christ, are you okay? Where are you?"

Addie faked a sob. "I'm sorry, Christina," she said, sniffling. "I lost you and then I thought someone was following me and I freaked out. I panicked and just started running."

"Why didn't you hit the emergency button on your phone?" Alvarez said.

"I don't know." Addie fake-cried even harder. "I got confused. Can someone please come get me?"

"Where are you?"

"Someplace called Kogan Plaza, I don't know where..."

"I got it," Alvarez said. "You're at George Washington

University. Just stay where you are. And dammit, hit the button on your phone so we can track you to an exact location."

"I will," Addie said. She disconnected and hit the button, making sure to re-engage the GPS she'd turned off before she began her run.

Within moments, the sound of helicopters got closer until they were hovering directly overhead. Sirens blared. A fleet of black vehicles screeched down H Street and skidded to a stop in front of the plaza entrance. Half a dozen agents leapt from the cars, guns drawn, with someone in a navy suit between them.

Addie froze at the sight of President Webster racing toward her.

"Addie," he said, scooping her up in an embrace. His entire body was shaking. "Thank God you're okay."

"What?" Addie blinked over and over. She'd been gone all of twenty minutes. She didn't even think he'd notice between meetings and power lunches. The president squeezed her tightly again. "I was so afraid I'd lost you," he said.

"Mr. President," one of the Secret Service agents said, scanning the tall buildings that surrounded the park. "This area has not been cleared. You're too exposed, I need you to—"

"In a moment," President Webster interrupted, his voice brusque. He turned back to Addie. "You're sure you're okay? What happened? Did something scare you?"

"Sir, please!" the agent said, his voice urgent. "We need to get you both back to the vehicles. *Now*—"

But before he could finish, a shot rang out, and the calm of the park was broken by screams.

CHAPTER 52

The next few moments were a blur. The sound of more shots. The shouts of students as they covered their heads and hit the ground. Spilled coffee cups. Books and papers scattering. The flurry of Secret Service agents rushing toward the president and Addie, guns drawn.

And then the horror as Addie realized President Webster lay crumpled on the ground, bright red blood staining his crisp white shirt. The last thing Addie remembered before collapsing beside him was screaming a single word: *Dad.*

Addie sat on a paper-covered exam table while a doctor shone a flashlight in her eyes. Addie didn't even have any awareness of blinking in response. Her body felt numb, like she wasn't even in it.

"Adele," the doctor said. "Can you talk to me?"

Addie squeezed her eyes shut. All she could picture were the president's legs twisted at an odd angle beneath him. All she could hear was the sound of his head as it hit the ground.

The crack of the gun. *Bam-bam-bam*. It replayed in her mind over and over in slow motion.

"Adele," the doctor said again. "You are okay. You weren't hurt. Your body is just reacting to the stress of the situation. Do you understand?"

Addie blinked and nodded.

"Good," the doctor said. "Do you need to lie down?"

Addie shook her head. "No," she whispered. "I just need to know if he's okay. Is the president okay?"

"Yes," the doctor said. "It was a superficial wound. Grazed his arm. Thankfully, it missed the brachial artery. He's fine. And he's been asking the same thing about you. If you feel okay, I can take you to see him."

"Yes, please," Addie said. She stood and her legs wobbled. The doctor shook his head and pointed to a wheelchair pushed against the far wall.

"No walking for you," he said. "Stay put and I'll have a nurse come in and help you."

"Okay," Addie said, leaning back on the table. The doctor pulled back the curtain and left the room, passing the pair of Secret Service agents who were standing guard. Addie made another attempt to stand, but her legs faltered. She sat back down. The smell of the hospital made her feel sick: a combination of rubbing alcohol and air freshener. The same scent that rushed into her nose when she tore open an antiseptic wipe. The kind she'd used to dab on the angry red welts across Mikey's back.

Addie shifted on the table. The paper cover crinkled. The clipboard at the end turned sideways. She picked it up, thumbing through her medical chart on top. Pretty standard hospital stuff. Her name, address, date of birth. She reached the fourth line and her heart caught in her throat.

Blood type: AB

Addie read it again. She re-checked her name at the top of the page. She inspected the blood type again.

AB AB AB AB AB AB AB

Addie's ears started to ring so loudly she was afraid it was like a siren going off in her head that the whole hospital could hear. A nurse walked into the room, thick-soled sneakers squeaking across the tile floor. Addie's chart fell from her hand and hit the ground.

"You doing all right, young lady?" the nurse said, retrieving the file and setting it on the table. Addie nodded. But she was far from all right. They'd just covered this in biology class: type AB blood was the rarest of all. And it could only come from a person whose parents were type A or B.

Addie knew Karl's blood type. He'd needed a transfusion once. It was O.

The nurse rolled the wheelchair to Addie's side. "You ready to go, young lady?"

Addie was grateful now that she didn't have to walk. She wasn't sure her legs would carry her anymore. She lowered herself shakily into the wheelchair and gripped the sides. Stars flashed in her eyes. The nurse put a hand on Addie's shoulder.

"Let me take you to your father," she said with a smile.

Agent Murawczyk and another Secret Service agent Addie didn't recognize stood outside the president's hospital room door. They nodded at Addie as she was wheeled past.

"Miss Webster," Murawczyk said.

"Hello, Agent Murawczyk."

The nurse pushed Addie into the room. The president—no, her *father*—was propped up in a hospital bed, watching television and eating Jell-O. He held up the cup and spoon.

"Your mother never puts this stuff on the menu," he said. "Too plain. I think it's delicious, though. Want some?" He held out the spoon.

"No thanks," she said, afraid she might throw it right back up.

The nurse wheeled her next to President Webster. "I'll leave you two alone," she said.

"Thanks," President Webster said. He tapped the edge of his bed. "Come, sit with me."

Addie lifted herself from the chair and sat next to her father. A small television on a metal arm extended over the bed, tuned to a twenty-four-hour news channel with the volume off. Addie immediately recognized the scene: Kogan Plaza and the surrounding GWU campus. Secret Service and FBI agents were swarming the grounds. The view shifted to a nearby dorm, where a young man was being led out the front door in handcuffs. The script beneath read:

SUSPECTED SHOOTER DETAINED

Addie stared at the screen in disbelief.

"They've already arrested someone?" she said. "How?"

"Anonymous tip to the FBI," the president answered. "Another student said a classmate was plotting a shooting spree. Looks like we just got caught in the cross fire. FBI found the kid in his dorm room right after, the gun tossed in the Dumpster next to it."

Addie looked back at the television screen, watching the boy as he was led down the sidewalk toward an awaiting patrol car. He had dirty-blond hair and his eyes were wide with fear. Even without the volume on, Addie could tell by the way his mouth was moving as the agents pushed him into the back of the car that he was shouting the same thing over and over:

It wasn't me.

Addie's breath grew stuttered. The president flicked off the television.

"We don't need to watch this," he said.

Addie struggled to regain control of herself, something that was getting harder and harder to do with each passing moment.

"Are you okay?" the president asked.

Addie didn't have an answer for that. "Are you?" she said.

President Webster glanced down at the bandage wrapped around his left arm. "Only a graze," he said. "Got lucky."

"Yeah. Lucky," Addie said. And that was the other thing that kept gnawing at her brain. The president had been standing next to her on the plaza—until the shot rang out. Then he'd jumped in front of Addie, shielding her with his own body.

"That bullet would have hit me," Addie said in barely a whisper. "If you hadn't moved the way you did."

"Like I said, Ad, got lucky," the president said.

"No," Addie said. "That wasn't luck. You saved me. Why?"

The president's gray eyes held hers for a moment. "Addie, sweetie, are you sure you're okay? There's nothing scarier in the world to me than something happening to you. You'll understand if you have kids one day."

Addie felt her eyes fill up. How could she have asked him *why*? He would die for her. She knew that now. It was instinct—a parent's instinct. She inspected his face, for the first time really seeing him since she'd gotten home—the flecks of gray at his temples, the lines around his eyes, the ready smile. Not a caricature, but a person. A man she had more in common with than she cared to admit: a man who was willing to risk himself for the people he loved.

She looked away, her lips trembling.

"Oh, honey." He put his uninjured arm around her and pulled her against his broad shoulder. It had been Addie's favorite place to rest her head when she was little, and she'd forgotten how good it felt. A safe place. She hadn't even thought such a thing existed anymore.

"Dad . . ." she said, choking back a sob.

"It's okay, peanut," her father said. "I'd take a thousand bullets before I let anyone hurt you ever again."

CHAPTER 53

Agent Alvarez paced the reception area of the Secret Service director's office. She'd been called here precisely two times in her career: once when she was offered the Adele Webster detail, and now, when she was pretty sure she was about to lose it. In fact, she'd be lucky if she was even sent back to ATM wire fraud. It was more likely she would be suspended while they investigated, then fired with cause. Number one rule in the protective services: never lose your charge.

Alvarez tried to distract herself by looking at the photos and memorabilia that lined the room. Pictures of past directors. Iconic photographs of black-clad agents guarding presidents throughout history. It only made Alvarez feel worse, seeing her lifelong dream displayed on someone else's shelf. A dream she knew was about to be shattered.

She stopped in front of the framed blue-and-gold Secret Service flag, staring at the agency's logo imprinted on the left side. It was a five-star gold badge, reminiscent of something pinned on the vest of an Old West sheriff. It reminded Alvarez of her favorite Halloween costume when she was a kid, the one she'd worn for three years straight. Alvarez was a grown woman now. But she really hadn't changed. That badge meant everything in the world to her. She told herself it was okay: she could lose it and move on. But she knew she was full of shit.

The director's administrative assistant entered the room, startling Alvarez from her thoughts. She stood at attention.

"Agent Alvarez," the man said. "Director Wilson will see you now."

"Thank you, sir," Alvarez said, following the man into a large office with windows overlooking the busy downtown traffic. Director Robert Wilson stood from behind his desk and motioned toward the chairs in front.

"Agent Alvarez," he said. "Please, have a seat."

"Thank you, Director Wilson." Alvarez lowered herself into a chair, willing herself to keep her composure. It wasn't easy. The cars passing on the street outside began to blur in Alvarez's vision. She had to blink several times to focus.

"I'm sure I don't need to explain why I asked to see you," Wilson said.

"No, sir."

"Good," Wilson said. "I know you've spoken with investigators, but I want to hear it straight from you. What the hell happened out there this afternoon?"

Agent Alvarez drew in a breath and clasped her fingers together on her lap. The holster tucked beneath her jacket suddenly felt too tight, like it was squeezing against her chest, making it difficult to breathe. In a minute she'd have to take it off. Turn in her gun. She exhaled slowly.

"Yes, sir," Alvarez said. "I was jogging on the National Mall with Ms. Webster. At her request." Alvarez paused. "As we took the path by the Air and Space Museum, a large group exited, blocking our way. I tapped Ms. Webster and told her to go around. But she didn't appear to hear me, and ran straight into the crowd."

"Hold up," Wilson said. "Didn't appear to hear you?"

"That's correct," Alvarez said. It was something that had been bothering the agent from the moment she'd lost the girl. "She didn't appear to hear me, but I can't imagine she didn't know why I was signaling her. It was an obvious shitshow straight ahead. Pardon my French, sir."

"No offense taken," Wilson said. "So if she did hear you, why do you think she ignored you?"

"I can't say for certain, sir," Alvarez said. "But it was almost as if she was trying to get lost."

Director Wilson nodded. "Okay, continue."

"So I chased after her, but got caught in the crowd," Alvarez said. "And then someone tripped me."

"You're certain you didn't just accidentally stumble over someone's foot and fall down?" Wilson said.

"I'm positive," Alvarez said. "I was tripped..." That was the other thing nagging at Alvarez's brain. "And I'm pretty sure it was Addie Webster that tripped me."

"What makes you think that?" Wilson said.

"Because I could have sworn I heard her say 'sorry' as I fell." Alvarez shifted in her seat. She'd replayed the whole scene in her mind a thousand times, and it always came back to that one detail—Addie Webster had pushed her. And she felt bad about it. "I just don't know why," Alvarez said.

"You're not the only one," Director Wilson said.

"What?"

"Look, Alvarez," Wilson said. "I know you're a good agent. A competent one. But given any other circumstances, you'd be getting your ass handed to you right now."

Alvarez nodded, head feeling like it was stuffed with cotton.

"And we—you, me, the entire Secret Service—are under serious scrutiny right now. Just a few inches to the right and the president would likely have bled out before we ever got him to the hospital today. The *Post* is going to have a field day with this, you know what I'm saying? And congressional inquiries can't be far behind."

"Yes, sir," Alvarez said, attempting to calm her voice. This was torture. She wished the director would just fire her and get it over with.

"So here's the deal, Agent Alvarez," he said. Alvarez sucked in a breath. Here it came. "You're staying on Addie Webster's detail."

"What?" Alvarez said, barely able to hide her shock.

"It's not the call I would have made," Wilson said. "And I voiced my objections. You should know that. I don't care if you're friggin' Superman and Lex Luthor just spiked your drink with Kryptonite. It just doesn't look good, no matter how you slice it. But the president insisted. Seems the Webster girl has grown pretty attached to you, and refuses to let anyone else near her."

"I see," Alvarez said. "I like the kid, too."

"That's the other thing," Wilson said. "I don't care how much you like that kid. I want you to watch her like a hawk. Everything you see, hear ... every time that girl so much as sneezes, I want it documented. I don't care how inconsequential it seems."

"Yes, sir," Alvarez said. "But why?"

"I'm sure you have an idea," Wilson said. "The president refuses to see it, but I agree with you. I don't think she just got lost today. And it was no accident that she ended up at Kogan Plaza. Which leads me to believe the shooter might have been expecting her."

Alvarez's eyes widened with shock. "You think she was trying to draw the president out?"

Wilson shook his head. "Doesn't fit. From what we can tell by the angle of the shot, the girl was the target. Not the president. He jumped in front of her and took the bullet."

"Jesus," Alvarez said. She tried to wrap her mind around the implications. "I thought her kidnappers were dead."

"We all did," Wilson said.

"So she could be in danger," Alvarez said.

"She could be in danger. She could be complicit," Wilson said. "Maybe both. Which is why you don't let her out of your sight. If she's communicating with someone, figure it out. Got it? You have one chance to redeem yourself for today's fiasco. Don't mess it up." Wilson stood, extending his right hand. Alvarez rose to her feet, meeting his firm handshake.

"Yes, sir," she said. "I won't disappoint you."

CHAPTER 54

The ticking clock had become Darrow's enemy. He glanced at it again. Four minutes past ten. He'd been sitting here in his mother's office since just after four. Since Addie had disappeared from her jog and the president had been shot. He'd refused to go home until he saw her. She might never speak to him again, but he could live with that as long as she was okay. It didn't matter how hard she pushed him away. How much she tried to block him out. He would never turn his back on her.

Cheryl Fergusson sat at her desk, fielding phone calls and trying to hold off the press. She had taken out her contacts and replaced them with glasses, something his image-conscious mother was loath to do. Darrow watched her click the phone back into its cradle, only to have it light up again. She ran her thumb and forefinger over her eyebrows, sighing, and let the call roll into voice mail.

The loud whir of helicopter rotor blades snapped her back to attention. She spun around in her chair. The helicopter's searchlight flashed outside the window across the South Lawn.

"They're back?" Darrow rose to his feet.

"Yes," Cheryl said. She stood and pulled her suit jacket from the back of her chair, slipping it over her shoulders. She smoothed her frazzled hair. "I have to meet them. Wait here."

"I want to come with you," Darrow said.

"Sweetie..." his mother began. "I'm not sure that's such a great idea."

"Please, Mom," he said.

Cheryl exhaled. "Okay," she said. "Just please stay in the background."

He followed his mother through the corridor and out to the South Lawn. *Marine One* lowered to the ground. The *thwap-thwap-thwap* of the rotors ground to a halt and the Marines exited. Next came President Webster, his right arm wrapped around Addie. The left was bound to his chest in a blue sling. Darrow's mother rushed to the president's side, but Darrow stayed in the shadows, leaning against the column of the portico.

Addie walked carefully, almost unsteadily, and for a moment Darrow wondered if she'd actually been hurt. But he couldn't see any bandages or visible signs of injury. She looked so small next to the president, taking measured steps, as though she might detonate a land mine each time her foot hit the ground. Her head hung down, hair covering her face so Darrow couldn't see her eyes.

They drew closer, walking up the portico steps. Just as they were about to turn the other way and enter the building, Addie's head tilted up and she glanced to the left. Right at Darrow. He caught his breath as she met his eyes, just for a moment, before quickly looking away. Darrow exhaled. At least she was okay....

He suddenly heard quiet footsteps approaching. Darrow

spun around, startled, to see Elinor standing behind him. She wore plaid pajama bottoms and a pale yellow camisole, and there were tears shimmering on her face. He moved toward her, but she shook her head sharply, brushing the wetness from her face. They stood there for a moment, watching as Addie's mother embraced her.

Darrow spoke softly. "It's okay, Ellie. I'm scared, too." He hesitated, then wrapped an arm around her slender shoulders. They stayed like that as Addie disappeared inside with her parents.

Finally, Elinor glanced up at him, locking her gray eyes on his. "What happens now?" she said.

Darrow shook his head. He had no answer. He'd never been less certain of anything than he was now—about himself, about Addie, about what the future held.

CHAPTER 55

Addie didn't even remember falling asleep. She was so tired after riding the elevator up to the residence—her mother's arm around her waist, the image of Darrow and Elinor on the portico burned into her mind—that she'd just flopped into bed without even changing or brushing her teeth. When she awoke the next morning, she was still in her jogging clothes. They smelled like sweat and something else Addie couldn't identify. Dirt, maybe, from when she'd been shoved to the ground. Hospital antiseptic. Or maybe fear.

Addie pulled herself from bed, showered, and headed to the kitchen. Her mother and Elinor were seated at the table, drinking coffee and finishing breakfast.

"Well, look who's up," her mother said, eyes laced with concern. "How are you this morning?"

"I'm fine," Addie said in a hurry. "But I'm late for school."

"School?" Liz said, setting down her mug. "Oh, honey, you don't need to go to school. In fact, I think it's best you don't go anywhere right now. Not after what happened . . ."

"Oh," Addie started, "I . . ."

"If I get shot at, can I skip going back to rehab?" Elinor said, smirking.

"Elinor!" Liz said.

"I'm just kidding, Mom," Elinor said. "You know that, don't you, Ad?"

"Sure," Addie said. She didn't look directly at her sister. The image of Ellie and Darrow—together—was still almost more than Addie could stand. She filled a coffee cup and sat next to her mother.

"I'm really okay," she said. "And I have a test in History today."

"Honey," her mother said. "I know your teacher isn't going to expect you there. And everyone will understand if you spend the next week or two at home. . . ."

"What?" Addie said, taking a hard sip of coffee. It burned her throat and Addie coughed. "The next week or two? What about prom?"

"I don't think so," Liz said, slowly shaking her head. "There's always next year though, hon."

Not for me, there won't be. . . .

Addie tried to think of a good argument, but words failed her. Elinor's sharp voice cut through the silence.

"Wasn't the shooter arrested?" she said.

"Yes, that's right," Liz answered. "He's in custody."

"So what's the problem?" Elinor said. "Let her go to prom."

Liz's eyes flitted back and forth between both of her daughters. "I don't know. It just makes me nervous," she said. "Something could happen."

"Well, *your* nerves are no reason to make Addie stay home," Elinor said. "It won't help. I should know. You and Dad kept me under lock and key for the last eight years, and look how well *that* worked out." Elinor got up, dropped her coffee cup in the sink, and walked away without saying another word.

Tears began to form in the corners of Liz's eyes. She wiped them away and wrapped her hands around her coffee cup, staring straight ahead.

"I'm sorry, Addie," she said softly. "It seems like I just can't get it right."

"That's not true, Mom. . . ." Addie said.

Liz sucked in a breath, placed a hand over Addie's, and looked her in the eye. "I don't know, maybe it is. I'll talk to your father about prom, okay? See what we can do. But no school today. Or tomorrow. Deal? I just want to keep you here with me."

"Deal," Addie squeaked out, a terrible heaviness weighing on her. And it only got worse as the hours ticked by. Addie spent the day fumbling through the motions of normal life—stacking Legos with Mackenzie, making small talk over dinner. But as she moved from room to room in the grand residence, taking in the high ceilings and chandeliers and glossy furniture, Addie's entire world began to feel like a mirage. She could almost see it shimmering into thin air before her eyes.

By the time night fell, Addie was exhausted. She climbed into bed, quickly drifting into a deep, dark, and dreamless sleep.

Hours later, Addie felt someone's warm breath against her neck. She bolted upright, a scream catching in her throat. She clutched the blanket to her chest and looked down. A familiar tangle of honey-brown hair fanned across her pillow.

Elinor.

Her sister muttered something in her sleep and rolled in

Addie's direction, eyes still closed. Catching her own breath, Addie watched her sister, chest rising and falling beneath the sheets. Ellie had become someone Addie barely recognized. Someone whose blunt words cut at the people around her. Someone who exacted revenge out of malice, not to right a wrong.

But right now, curled in a ball, she was the same Ellie who used to sneak into Addie's bed at night when she had a nightmare, one small hand holding Addie's, the other stroking Mr. Fluff.

Addie slid back down next to her sister and tucked an arm around her narrow waist. Elinor moved closer, still asleep, and buried her head in Addie's shoulder. Addie breathed in the strawberry scent of Elinor's hair, so familiar and sweet. All these years and Ellie hadn't changed her favorite shampoo.

Addie closed her eyes and all the anger and frustration, all the fear and confusion she'd felt began to melt away. She couldn't be mad. At Elinor. At Darrow. At any of the people who'd been left behind when Addie had been taken. They'd been through hell, too. And she finally understood—they'd all coped the only way they knew how.

She only hoped they wouldn't blame her, either. That maybe, when all was said and done, they'd find it in their hearts to understand. And move on.

CHAPTER 56

Agent Alvarez did one more walk around the perimeter. She had agents stationed at every entrance, two in each corner of the room, as well as three on the balcony overhead. She'd done a half-dozen checks of the facility to ensure it was clear, and then ordered her staff to do three more.

Still, this whole thing made Alvarez extremely nervous. She glanced at the vintage TWA propeller plane hanging from the ceiling and the American jet that extended to the dance floor, the nose of the 747 jutting from the wall, with an open catwalk leading to the cockpit. Alvarez paced back and forth. She didn't like it. Not at all. There were just too many places to hide, too much obstructing her view.

She'd strongly advised that the kid not be allowed to attend prom. But the president had insisted—he wasn't going to keep his daughter under lock and key, not after everything she'd been through. Besides, there hadn't been a Cerberus attack since the busboy had started giving up names. And the FBI had the alleged shooter from Kogan Plaza in custody. Despite the student's continued denials, the ballistics on the gun matched up, and his DNA had been found on the handle. The case was air-tight. For all practical purposes, it was just a coincidence that Addie and the president had turned up in the plaza that day.

Except Alvarez didn't believe in coincidences anymore.

Her earpiece buzzed. It was Agent Devers, stationed out front.

"Speak to me," Alvarez said.

"Guests are beginning to arrive."

"Roger that." Alvarez said. "Positions, people. We're in play."

Addie's limo pulled up to the front entrance of the National Air and Space Museum. The concrete-and-glass building stood silhouetted against the night sky, lights twinkling atop the tall metal spire out front. Dozens of Cabot students gathered on the stairs, chatting and snapping photos. Addie hesitated. She considered tapping the driver on the shoulder and asking him to take her home.

But then she pictured Mackenzie, tiny arms wrapped around her tonight before she left, telling her she was beautiful. She saw her parents, beaming as they took her picture. She even saw Elinor, watching her from the hallway with her arms folded across her chest, an unreadable look on her face.

Addie steeled herself, willing away the tears that were burn-ing the corners of her eyes. She had to see this through to the end. It was the only way to save the people she loved, even if it meant she might destroy them in the process.

Her door swung open. Agent Alvarez stood on the other side.

"You ready?" Addie glanced toward the steps, and up at

the top she saw a familiar swing of blue-tipped hair among the crowd forming at the door. She swallowed down the anxiety rising in her throat.

"I'm ready," she said, and stepped from the limo. Her strapless, wine-colored dress swept to the ground. It was Italian silk with a delicate lace pattern swirling up her bare back. She wore a pink freshwater pearl necklace set that her mother had given her that evening. Alvarez let out a low whistle.

"Look at you," she said. "That poor boy is going to eat his heart out."

Addie didn't know whether to laugh or cry. Alvarez hadn't pressed Addie for answers after she had rushed out of Harper's studio in tears, but given that Addie and Darrow hadn't spoken since, Alvarez clearly thought they'd broken up. Addie hadn't bothered to correct that assumption. And even though she'd forgiven Darrow, Addie had let that wall between them stand. It was better that way. For everyone.

Addie gathered the front of her dress in her hands and climbed the steps toward where Harper stood waving. When Addie reached the top, Harper embraced her in a warm hug.

"You look ah-may-zing!" she said. Addie pulled back, running her eyes over Harper's short, sequined halter dress, topped with a leather biker jacket.

"So do you," she said. "Where's everyone else?"

"Inside. Except Darrow. I, um, don't know if he's coming tonight."

"He's not?" Addie hadn't expected that. Not after what Darrow had said he'd overheard. But it would make everything easier.

Addie and Harper went inside and hung a right into Gallery 102, the America by Air exhibit. Alvarez followed close behind. Round tables decorated with red-and-gold linens were scattered among the exhibits, surrounded by gilt-backed chairs. A two-story wall of windows overlooked the National Mall, the lit columns of the National Gallery of Art shimmering across the green. Dozen of airplanes hung overhead, suspended by giant cables, and the nose of a 747 jutted out over the dance floor. Addie glanced up at it and shuddered.

They found Keagan, Luke, and Connor staked out at a table beneath an old plane. As the others chatted and laughed, Addie grew more and more aware of the passing seconds. Her palms started to sweat. She pulled her phone from her handbag and checked the time: eight thirty. Three and a half hours until everything changed. . . . She chewed her lip and put the phone away, catching Keagan staring at her.

"What's going on?" she said. "Limo turn into a pumpkin at midnight?"

Addie swallowed hard. "Yeah, something like that," she said. She stood up. "I'm going to have a look around," she said, waving to the rest of the table. "Be back in a bit."

Addie walked along the edges of the room, pausing and pretending to check out the exhibits. Just past the dance floor, she climbed a set of stairs, crossing a catwalk to the 747 at the end. A couple other students were in the cockpit, so Addie paused and waited at the door. She glanced over her shoulder and waved at Alvarez, who had followed her, of course, and was lurking at the other end of the catwalk. The other students walked out. Addie slipped inside. Barely breathing, she pulled the camera from her handbag and tucked it on the floor out of sight, beneath the plane's control panel. Then she hurried back out, nearly colliding with Alvarez.

"Not into planes?" the agent said.

"Too small in there," Addie said, face pale. "Made me claustrophobic."

"I can see that." Alvarez looked at her closely.

"Think I'll stick with open spaces," Addie said. She walked past Alvarez and back to the table. She sat down, just as Connor and Harper got up to dance. Luke and Keagan had already wandered off, so she sat by herself, sipping a San Pellegrino soda.

The band struck up another song, something achingly familiar, the opening chords reaching deep into Addie's memory. She suddenly felt someone's presence behind her.

"Remember this one?"

Addie swung around and saw Darrow standing there, tall and graceful, in a tux that fit him like a glove. Addie's voice failed her. She remembered. It was the song she had played over and over in the playroom, back when she'd made Darrow dance with her. She glanced up at him, and realized her mistake the moment she met his eyes. They weren't angry like she had expected—they were calm and open, like the night when he'd found her in the woods. Like he was just trying to understand.

"I thought you weren't coming," she said.

"Changed my mind. Dance with me?"

She found herself standing, and let him take her hand. It fit perfectly in his. Darrow deserved so much more than her. But if she was what he wanted after all of this, the least she could give him was a good-bye. Darrow led her to the dance floor and wrapped his arm around her waist as they swayed to the music. Addie rested her head on his chest, breathing in deeply. This was enough. All she wanted, in this moment, was to rest in his arms; to pretend that she was just another girl at the prom, falling for the perfect guy. She wanted to hold on to the fairy tale, act like the clock wasn't ever going to strike midnight. Because she knew eventually it would. Then she'd have to face the consequences of her actions. The nose of the 747 jutted overhead, a constant reminder that in a few short hours, Addie would be dead to everyone who cared about her.

Darrow pulled back slightly, looking down at Addie.

"I just wish you could trust me," he murmured.

"Why?" Addie gazed straight at him. "Why should I trust anyone?"

"Because I trust you. I know you don't want to do whatever you're planning tonight."

Addie started to reply, but her voice caught in her throat.

Suddenly, she was hit by the memory of Darrow's lips on hers. His back, pressed up against the door to Harper's studio. His hand, smooth and warm, running along her bare skin.

"You shouldn't trust me. You don't understand."

"Then make me understand." Darrow gripped her tighter around the waist.

"This isn't real," Addie whispered.

"It sure feels real to me," Darrow said. "You, me. Here. Together."

"That's not what I'm talking about," Addie said, more forcefully now. "This. None of this is real. None of what is going to happen is real, okay? Just remember that—when I'm gone. None of this was real!"

"What do you mean, *gone*?" Darrow began.

But Addie had already broken away from Darrow's grasp, leaving him standing there, bewildered and alone. She ran, eyes clouded with tears, into the bathroom. Alvarez stayed right on her tail, but Addie ignored her, going straight into a stall and closing the door. She sat on the toilet, covering her eyes, and held back sobs, her chest heaving. After a few minutes, there was a light rap on the stall door.

"You okay in there, Songbird?" Alvarez said.

"Yeah, I just need a minute," Addie answered.

There was a pause and Alvarez started talking again.

"Look, I know I'm not much help when it comes to fashion choices," she said. "But I've been where you are before, crying over some guy in the bathroom."

Addie didn't answer.

"And the good news," Alvarez continued, "is that maybe it sucks now, but it's not forever, okay?"

Addie grabbed a handful of tissues and wiped her eyes. The phone in her purse buzzed against her thigh. Addie pulled it out with shaking hands and read the message. One by one, the hairs on the back of her neck stood on end.

This wasn't right . . . it was too soon. What was going on? She needed more time.

Shakily, Addie stood and opened the door, where Alvarez was waiting.

"Should I call the driver and have him bring you home?" Alvarez said.

"No," she said. "I'm ready to go back. Just needed a little break." She splashed some water on her face and returned to the prom, Alvarez following. Addie scanned the room for an out. Connor, Luke, Keagan, and Harper were back at the table. She didn't spot Darrow anywhere.

Addie walked to her friends and tapped Connor on the shoulder. He put down his drink and turned around.

"Hey," Addie said. "Want to dance?"

Connor smirked. "Thought you'd never ask," he said.

There was no time for charm. "Well, I am now." She grabbed his hand and pulled him toward the dance floor, still clutching her handbag.

She checked Christina's location as Connor grinned at her, his hand on her waist. The agent had moved to the edge of the dance floor and was bobbing her head back and forth to see Addie. Addie spun around and pulled Connor deeper into the crowd.

They finally stopped in the middle of the floor and began dancing. Addie moved closer to Connor, pressing her hips against his.

His eyes widened. "Not bad, Webster."

"Yeah?" Addie leaned in, her lips at his ear. "You'll like this even more.... Close your eyes."

"What?"

"You heard me," Addie whispered. "Close your eyes. And don't open them until I say so."

Agent Alvarez craned her neck, trying to get a better view of Addie. She could see her lanky dance partner, but it was hard to see the girl. She was short—almost as short as Alvarez—and the agent couldn't see her over all the bobbing heads. They pushed deeper into the swell of students.

Alvarez moved around to the other side of the dance floor.

She caught a flicker of burgundy dress, and could just make out the boy's Converses. A head of long, black hair whipped around. Finally, the song wrapped up and the crowd began to thin. Alvarez could see the boy still there, swaying back and forth. But...

She pushed her way through the students, colliding with Connor.

The boy opened his eyes, stunned.

Addie was gone.

CHAPTER 57

Addie ran as fast as her feet would take her, to the entrance of the IMAX theater on the other side of the building. The first two doors she pulled were locked, but when she reached the third it swung open. Addie slipped inside, closing the door behind her.

"Father?" Addie said into the darkness. "I'm here. Are you taking me home?"

There was no answer. Addie blinked, trying to adjust her eyes to the dim room. Finally, she could make out the large screen straight ahead, the rows of theater seats . . . and the outline of two heads. Addie's heart began to pound wildly. What was happening? She made her way down the aisle, trying to control her shaking knees. When she got closer, an involuntary gasp escaped her lips.

Just to her left sat Darrow, still as a stone. Michael sat on his other side, holding a gun to his head.

"Hello, Lilla," Michael said, turning to face Addie. Darrow began to turn, too, but Michael pushed the gun into his temple.

"Don't even think about it," he said.

Darrow froze.

"Michael?" Addie said, trying to tamp down the shock in her voice. "What are you doing?"

"What does it look like I'm doing?" Michael said.

"I don't know," Addie said. "I got a message from Father saying something had come up and we needed to move earlier. . . ."

Michael pulled a thumb drive from his pocket and held it up. Addie's skin went cold.

"What?" she said. "What does that have to do with—"

"Oh shut up, Lilla," Michael said. "And quit playing stupid. It doesn't suit you, you know."

Addie tried to speak, but her voice seized up.

"We know you gave us the wrong program," Michael said. "And don't even try to tell me you didn't. Father and I tested it. Instead of exploiting the flaws in our system, it *fixed* them. Clever, I'll give you that. But I don't know what you're trying to pull."

"I'm not trying to pull anything," Addie said.

"Fine," Michael said. He chucked the thumb drive onto the floor. "Then here's the deal. You give me the real program, or you can say good-bye to your boyfriend here." He pushed the gun against Darrow's head again, hard enough this time that it tilted in Addie's direction. She willed herself to stay calm.

"He's not my boyfriend," she said coolly. "Go ahead and shoot him for all I care."

She stared at Michael, watching out of the corner of her eye as a bead of sweat sprang up on Darrow's forehead and rolled down his cheek. Michael considered her words for a moment.

"Think you can call my bluff? Really?" he said. "Don't be a

fool. I wasn't afraid to shoot you that day in Kogan Plaza. I'm not afraid to shoot him now."

Addie was knocked off-balance. "Wait, that was you?" Tears burned at the edges of Addie's eyes. Mikey, the boy who had been her brother these last eight years. Her best friend; her only friend; the one she'd always done anything to protect. He had tried to shoot her? "Why?" she stammered.

"You hacked into Father's computer," Michael said plainly. "You overstepped your bounds. So Father said you needed to be reminded of your vulnerability. But maybe it would've been better if I'd just killed you that day. All you've ever done, since the day you came home, is get me in trouble." His voice faltered.

"That's not true," Addie said. "It's not me. Or you. It's Father. Don't you see? He's always tried to play us off each other. But we don't have to let him do that anymore."

"What the hell do you mean by that?" Michael said. Addie watched as the gun in his hand began to wobble. Darrow took a deep breath. Addie started talking faster.

"Mikey," she said, locking eyes with him. "Don't go back. Let's get out of here together. Now. I'll help you, I promise. We have each other. We don't need Father to protect us."

Michael took several deep breaths and Addie locked eyes with him. "Please," she said.

Suddenly his face turned cold. "Forget it, Lilla," he said. "I trusted you before. And all it did was get me hurt." He instinctively ran his fingers across his back. "I have the scars to prove it. I'm not nine years old anymore. You can't make me do what you want for a chocolate bar."

"I'm not trying to make you do anything," Addie said. "Just listen—"

"Stop it," Michael cut her off. "Father's not stupid. You don't think there isn't a backup plan? If I don't come back with the program, that entire dance out there, all your friends, will blow sky-high."

Darrow gasped.

"What?" Addie said, recoiling. "How?"

"You should know," Michael said with a cold smile. "You're the one who planted the explosive."

Addie's head began to spin. The camera she'd left sitting in the 747. The device she'd been told was just a diversion, a fake bomb that would make it look like she'd been killed when she had actually escaped. Karl had lied to her. Again. Her worst fears were true. She was a pawn. Nothing more.

"Mikey, no . . ." Addie said. "Please don't do this. I'm your sister, and I . . ."

"No, you're not," Michael said flatly.

"What?" Addie stammered. "You know? How?"

"The FBI verified your identity using paternal DNA," he said. "Father hacked in and read the report."

"Why didn't he tell me . . . ?" Addie started, knees buckling. Why *would* Karl tell her? Had he done so, she might not have followed through with his plan. "It doesn't matter," she said, blinking back tears. "You're still my best friend, Mikey."

"Everything matters," Michael answered. He grabbed Darrow by the arm and forced him to stand, pressing the barrel of the gun against his side. Keeping his gaze on Addie, Michael pushed Darrow into the aisle and stood beside him, facing her. She took a step back as he held out his free hand. "I'm done talking. Now give me the program," he said.

"But I can't. I don't have it with me," Addie said, taking

another step away and clutching her purse to her chest. Michael's eyes flitted from Addie's face to the purse, her fingers wrapped around it in a white-knuckled grip. A small laugh escaped from his lips.

"Sure you don't," he said, yanking the purse from her hand. Addie watched as Michael flipped it over, shaking the contents loose. Her phone and a pack of gum fell to the ground.

"What?" Michael said.

"I told you," Addie said, glancing at the floor. "I don't have it with me. It's in my room. If you want it, I'll have to go back and get it." She nodded toward Darrow. "But I'm not doing that until you let him go."

Michael narrowed his eyes.

"Enough with the games," he said in a low growl. "I know you. And I know you'd never leave something like that just lying around where anyone could find it. Not tonight of all nights. Now hand it over. I'm not going to ask you again!" He raised the gun, pointed it directly at Darrow's temple, and cocked the hammer. Darrow's mouth pressed into a thin line, hands balled into fists at his side.

"Don't give it to him," Darrow said, voice rough.

Addie glanced quickly at her old friend, heart filling with so much pain she thought it might explode. She couldn't let him die for her. She already had too much blood on her hands. She turned her gaze back to Michael.

"Fine," Addie said. "You want it?" Slowly, without taking her eyes off Michael, she reached down into the top of her dress and pulled out the thumb drive. She held it in front of her with one hand. She pressed the other hand against her thigh, counting down . . . *3, 2, 1.* She could only hope Darrow was watching.

That he'd remember their secret signal. The one they'd used on the playground when they were trying to outwit an opponent in freeze tag.

"If this is what you're looking for," she said, "then you're gonna have to go and get it." She tossed the drive into the air. As Michael's eyes followed its arc, Addie turned her gaze on Darrow and balled her hand into a fist.

Zero, she mouthed.

In that instant, Darrow jerked his elbow into Michael's arm. The gun flew from his hand and skidded beneath a seat. Addie dove after it, while Darrow tackled Michael to the ground. She could see them out of the corner of her eye, struggling over the thumb drive on the floor. Addie pressed herself against the ground, extended her arm, and reached for the gun. Her fingers wrapped around the barrel. But just as she stumbled to her knees with the gun, a hand reached out.

"Give me that," Michael said, grabbing the blunt end. Addie held on tight, feeling Michael's body jerk back and forth as Darrow tried to pull him off her.

"Let go!" she screamed.

Michael yanked the butt of the gun so hard it twisted Addie's arm unnaturally behind her back. She whimpered in pain. A loud bang suddenly filled the air. Smoke twisted from the barrel of the gun. Addie let go, hand burning, and turned— just in time to see Darrow collapse to the floor.

"No!" she yelled, tears clouding her vision. "Darrow..." She crawled toward him, the glint of her cell phone catching her eye, just ahead on the floor. She began to breathe rapidly. If she could reach it and push the panic button, she could get help. There was still hope....

She extended a hand, only to have Michael's foot land on top of it, crushing her fingers.

She cried out in pain.

"Forget it, Lilla," Michael said, slowly lifting his shoe. He scooped up the phone, tucked it in his pocket, and aimed the gun at Addie. "Now get up and come with me."

"Where?" Addie said, barely able to contain the tears welling up in her eyes.

"You know where," Michael said. "You've got a mission to complete."

CHAPTER 58

Agent Alvarez frantically searched the dance floor. She checked the bathroom. She went from table to table. No sign of Addie. She lifted her wrist to her mouth and spoke into the microphone tucked beneath her shirtsleeve.

"What's the status?"

"No sign of Songbird in the lobby," a member of the detail answered.

"We're combing the main floor now," another said.

Alvarez's earpiece buzzed.

"Hold on! I've got a visual. Songbird has left the building, heading north on the Mall."

"Shit!" Alvarez spun toward the tall windows, just in time to see Addie sprinting toward the National Gallery of Art in her dark red dress, black hair flying behind her, heels in hand. "Dammit!" She radioed the rest of the detail.

"Songbird on foot," she said. "Just passed the carousel, headed north. All units respond immediately."

Alvarez dashed from the room out the front door of the museum and down the steps. She still had a visual of the girl straight ahead. Agent Devers and the other agents who had been monitoring the exits and searching the museum joined in to give chase. The girl slowed as she neared the opposite side of the Mall and looked left and right, as though lost. Alvarez ran faster.

"We've got the perimeter cars coming down Madison and 7th," Devers panted, just as two Secret Service vehicles closed in from opposite directions, blocking the road.

The agents driving them flung the doors open and leapt from their cars. "Stop right where you are!" they yelled, guns drawn.

The girl stopped running and fell into a crouch, hands over her head.

Alvarez caught up with her, breathing heavily.

"Addie," she said. "Enough. Running. Okay?"

The girl didn't respond, but Alvarez could see her trembling with sobs. She nodded toward the agents with their guns still drawn. "Lower your weapons," she said. "She's not a threat. She's not going anywhere." Alvarez kneeled, putting her hand on the girl's back.

"Let's go, Addie. You're going to be all right." The girl had caused Alvarez more stress than she'd imagined possible, but she couldn't help but feel sorry for her, curled on the ground, vibrating with fear. "Come on, Songbird. I'm taking you home."

Slowly, the girl turned her head. As she did, her dark hair slipped to the side, revealing the three-headed beast tattooed on the back of her neck. Alvarez recoiled as she found herself staring into the eyes of a stranger.

"Who the hell are you?" she said in shock. "And where is Addie Webster?"

The girl simply shook her head.

Alvarez stood and turned back toward the museum. From across the Mall, she could see the outlines of students dancing in front of the tall glass windows. She looked back at Devers and the rest of the detail.

"Which one of you called me to report seeing Addie Webster running this way?" she said.

No one answered.

"Which one of you made the call?" she shouted even louder.

The agents looked back and forth at each other, shaking their heads. Fear gripped Alvarez by the throat as the terrifying realization washed over her: they'd been duped. They'd left the prom—they'd left the president's daughter—unsecured and completely unprotected.

CHAPTER 59

Addie struggled to remain calm as Michael led her across the museum and back toward the America by Air exhibit. As they got closer, she could hear the rhythmic pulsing of dance music and the laughter of her classmates. She sucked in a breath, the barrel of the gun hidden in Michael's trench coat pressing firmly into her side.

"You don't have to do this," she said again.

"Just shut up," Michael said.

As they entered the main hall, Addie frantically searched the crowd for Alvarez. But the agent was nowhere to be seen. Nor were the other agents on her detail. Just like before, the very people who were supposed to protect Addie had vanished. Karl might have lied about a lot of things, but he was right about one: Addie would never be safe.

"Where are we going?" Addie asked, trying to buy herself time. Michael didn't answer, but only kept his grip on Addie and pulled her past the dance floor.

He pointed at the 747. With a shove, he pushed Addie up

the stairs and across the catwalk that led to the plane. Addie hesitated at the door.

"Go on," Michael said. "Go inside."

Addie stepped across the threshold. Michael followed and stretched a red velvet rope across the entrance. An "exhibit closed" sign hung from it. He motioned Addie toward the front.

"Turn around," he said.

Addie slowly turned, facing Michael. He pulled a pair of handcuffs from his inside jacket pocket. "Now put your hands together and hold them out in front of you."

Addie choked back a sob, lifted her arms, and gave Michael one last pleading look. She watched as the corner of his eyelid twitched.

"I know you don't want to do this, Mikey," Addie said. "I know you. You don't kill people! Please . . ."

He moved toward her, clumsily trying to balance the gun in one hand while getting out the handcuffs with the other. Addie watched him, her leg muscles twitching at the ready. With each step he took closer, Addie focused her breathing.

Michael stopped in front of her and leaned forward, handcuffs at the ready. But before he could lock them to Addie's wrists, she raised her knee, slamming it hard between Michael's legs. He doubled over in pain. As his hands flew down to protect himself, Addie made a grab for the gun. But she had forgotten just how strong Michael was now. He jerked his hand back, stood tall, and swung his arm.

"I'm sorry, Lilla," she heard him say—just as the butt of the gun collided with the side of her head. Stars flashed in her eyes, and her ears began to ring.

The next thing she knew, her world went black.

CHAPTER 60

Alvarez clicked handcuffs onto the girl and pulled her to her feet. She shoved her toward one of the other agents.

"Take this girl into custody," she said. "Find out what she knows. The rest of you, come with me." She began to sprint toward the museum. But before Alvarez and the detail had made it even ten feet, Alvarez's earpiece screeched loudly and she winced in pain. She reached a hand to her ear and slowed. A strange computer-generated voice came over the speaker.

"*Special Agent Christina Alvarez,*" it said. "*This is Cerberus. And if you don't want hundreds of innocent children to die, I suggest you stop where you are, call your detail back, and listen very carefully.*"

"Excuse me, what?" Alvarez said.

"*I said, stop where you are, call the detail back, and then we will talk.*"

Alvarez's heart raced. *Cerberus?* She came to a dead stop.

"*That's more like it,*" the voice said. "*Now call the rest of the detail back.*" Alvarez hesitated. "*I said, call the rest of the detail back. Now!*" the voice repeated.

"Hey!" Alvarez shouted. "Hold up!" The other agents

slowed and looked back at Alvarez, confused. "I'm getting some information," she said, pointing at her earpiece. "Just a minute." The detail slowly walked back toward Alvarez.

"Thank you," the voice said.

Alvarez scanned her surroundings. Whoever was talking to her was obviously close by. She made note of a young couple, seemingly out for a walk; a homeless man in a pea-green jacket asleep on a bench; a middle-aged woman, jogging her way along the dirt path, MP3 player strapped to her upper arm. Still, there were several dozen more people out for strolls, enjoying the night air. It could be anyone.

"I suggest you stop trying to figure out where I am, and listen carefully...."

Alvarez stiffened and she held her hand to her ear. Agent Devers tapped her arm. "What's going on?" he said. "We're wasting time here. We need to get back to the prom."

The voice spoke before Alvarez could answer. Alvarez held up a hand to Devers and strained to listen. *"Tell the rest of the detail there's been a misunderstanding,"* the voice said. *"Addie Webster had a fight with her boyfriend and went home without your knowledge. The girl you have in custody has done nothing wrong and is free to go."*

Alvarez brought her wrist to her mouth, turned her head away from Devers, and whispered under her breath. "That's insane. Why should I?"

"Because if you don't, we will blow Addie Webster and the Cabot prom sky-high. We have complete control of the building and everyone in it. Just watch."

Alvarez glanced toward the museum, throat constricting,

338

as the entire building pitched into darkness. A split second later, the lights came back on and Alvarez could once again see the faint outlines of students dancing.

"Don't make me do something more drastic," the voice said. *"Now, release the girl; tell the detail to go. And you—stay right where you are."*

Alvarez turned to Devers, who was still watching her with an eyebrow raised. She tapped her earpiece. "I'm sorry," she said. "Just got word from the White House. Appears I jumped the gun. Songbird is at home. Had a fight with her boyfriend, called her mother, and left without my knowledge. We're no longer needed here." She motioned to the agents on the street, lowering the girl into the back of a patrol car.

"I made a mistake," Alvarez shouted to them. "Songbird is at home. You can let the girl go."

The agent holding her by the wrists did a double take.

"I said," Alvarez repeated, "uncuff the girl and let her go."

"You're in charge," the agent answered. "But I want it on the record that this was your call."

"Noted," Alvarez said. "Now let her go. And the rest of you, you're done for the night. Go on. Go home."

As the detail began to disperse, Devers hung back. Alvarez regarded him anxiously.

"Do you want something?" she said.

"Yeah," he answered. "You just let some girl running around in an Addie Webster dress go without further questioning? What the hell was that?"

"I told you," Alvarez said. "I made a mistake. So get out of here." She lowered her voice and spoke through gritted teeth.

"You can probably still catch the last quarter of the game. You don't want to miss the Buckeyes dominating, do you?" Devers stared at her.

"You're hilarious," he said. Alvarez shot him a look. He shook his head and walked away, joining up with the rest of the detail and speeding off. Alvarez spoke into her mouthpiece.

"Satisfied?" she said.

"We'll see," the voice said. *"It depends how good you are at following the rest of our instructions."*

"What do you want?" Alvarez said.

The voice on the other end laughed, an eerie robotic sound. *"You have to ask? We want what we've always wanted. For the administration to take the threats against this country—against the free world—seriously."*

"And you hope to achieve this how?" Alvarez said, unable to help herself. "By threatening to kill a bunch of innocent kids? Do you think that makes you any better than the people you say you want to protect this country from?"

The voice didn't answer immediately. Alvarez began to worry she'd crossed a line.

"Do we want to kill anyone?" the voice came back. *"No. But if we have to, we will. Sometimes it's necessary to make sacrifices for the greater good."*

Alvarez shifted her weight, leaning momentarily on her right foot.

"I told you!" the voice said. *"Stay where you are!"*

Alvarez froze.

"Now listen carefully," the voice said, *"because we're only going to tell you once. We want you to deliver a message. Tell President Webster we are done firing warning shots. This time, we're playing for*

real. He has failed to recognize the dangers in our world, and we will no longer sit on the sidelines. If he doesn't want to be responsible for the deaths of hundreds of children—the death of his own daughter—he will hold a press conference by midnight tonight, publicly acknowledging his failures and offering us a seat at the table."

"Wait, a seat at the table?" Alvarez said, incredulous. "You're kidding, right? There's no way President Webster is going to make a terrorist organization part of his administration. You must know that."

"We are not a terrorist organization. And we are done playing games. Tell President Webster that we have Shi...."

"Excuse me, what?" Alvarez broke in.

"He'll know what we mean," the voice said. *"Just convey this to the president: We have Shi. We have his daughter. If he doesn't renounce his failed policies and meet our demands—by midnight—we kill Addie Webster and anyone else who happens to be nearby. And when we're done with that, we'll set Shi loose on the White House. Every classified document, every e-mail, every intelligence briefing will be released indiscriminately online. There's no way to stop it; just ask Liz Webster. And if President Webster thinks the United States doesn't have a security problem now, he won't be singing the same tune tomorrow when terrorists worldwide have access to every state secret, the names of covert agents, the locations of secret weapons programs. It will all be out there for the taking."*

Alvarez had to bite her tongue. If she'd needed any more confirmation that she wasn't dealing with a rational person, she had it now. Only someone truly unhinged would believe they could make threats like this and expect the president to comply. The best Alvarez could do was to try to buy herself—and the kids at that prom—more time.

"Okay," she said. "I will deliver your message. But it's already past nine o'clock. These things take time. I can't promise results by midnight."

"That's too bad," the voice said. *"Because if you don't, you'll go down in history as the first agent with the blood of a First Kid on her hands. Good-bye—"*

"Wait!" Alvarez said. "Let's just say the president does agree. How am I supposed to make contact with you?"

"That won't be necessary," the voice said. *"We will contact you. We have control of all Secret Service communications. And we have our eyes on you. So if you're thinking about calling in a rescue team, or attempting to contact any of those students in there to tell them to evacuate, think again. You have one call to make. To the president."*

And with that, the transmission cut out. Alvarez radioed the dispatcher at headquarters.

"This is Alvarez with an urgent matter," she said, throat dry. "Put me through to Spider."

CHAPTER 61

Darrow's right leg throbbed as he lay on the floor. It was dark. And as far as he could tell, he was alone.

"Addie?" he said, voice hoarse.

There was no answer. Darrow sat up, gripped a nearby armrest, and tried to pull himself to his feet. The pain in his leg stabbed all the way from his thigh to his ankle. Darrow stumbled into a seat and looked down, shocked to see a circle of blood staining the front of his pant leg. The fabric was torn, his raw skin exposed underneath. He remembered the pop of the gun, the burn of the bullet as it hit, falling to the ground as Addie screamed. Darrow realized he must have passed out, but he didn't know for how long. Time had taken on a strange shape, measured only in staggered breaths and pounding heartbeats. In the distance, he could hear the sound of music pulsing. Prom must still be under way.

Prom. It all came back to Darrow in a rush. Michael—the bomb. Darrow's friends and classmates were in there. *Addie.*

He had to do something before it was too late. He grabbed the phone from his pocket, but there was no signal. So he pulled himself unsteadily to his feet and staggered up the aisle, leg dragging, drops of blood trailing behind. He hadn't made it ten steps before the room started to spin and he collapsed again.

When Addie came to, her vision was foggy and she couldn't get her bearings. Her head felt wobbly, like a balloon that had been cut loose from its string. For a moment, her body seized up with terror. It was happening. Again. The hands that had dragged her away when she was eight. They'd returned to steal her. Her greatest fear. Her worst nightmare. It just kept repeating like a string of code programmed to run forever. *:a (nightmare) goto :a (nightmare).* An infinite loop. Never-ending.

But as she strained against the handcuffs pinning her to the pilot's seat in the old 747, she realized the situation was far, far worse. This wasn't a nightmare. It was real. Straight ahead, she could see the camera she'd hidden in here earlier, now perched ominously against the window.

Down below, she could hear voices chattering, music, the laughter of her friends. All the sounds of normal life that she'd been denied the last eight years—all the things that had come to mean something to her again in the last few weeks. And it was about to end. She pulled at her restraints, the metal cutting into the soft skin of her wrists. She cried out, but the sound was muffled by the gag in her mouth.

At that moment, she knew the truth, the whole truth: Karl didn't have any intention of bringing her home. Maybe he'd always planned to let her die in here. After all, what better way to prove to the president that his stance on security was wrong, than to actually kill his oldest daughter? Kidnapping her obviously hadn't done the trick. Nor had hacking nuclear power stations, or planting fake bombs at fund-raisers and on Metro trains. Addie briefly wondered why he had even bothered sending her back to the White House in the first place. Why not just send her body floating down the Potomac with a note attached? But she knew the reason—Shi.

Addie shivered. *Shi.* That's what he had been after all along. Karl wouldn't be satisfied by simply proving a point. He wanted control—of everything. Every last bit of information in cyberspace.

Now he had it.

And Addie was the one who'd handed it to him. She hated herself for believing that he only intended to use it as a bargaining tool to force the president to change his policies. Karl knew that would never happen. She had been so, so stupid. Hot tears began to stream down her cheeks.

Her muffled sobs were interrupted by the sudden disappearance of the music down below. The room went silent, save for the whispers that swept across the crowd.

Down below, the students began to gasp.

"Oh my God!" someone yelled.

"What's going on?" another said. Addie strained against the handcuffs, ignoring the pain, trying to break free. But it was no use.

Someone tapped the microphone and Addie heard a woman's voice, speaking rapidly. "Students," she said. "Please remain calm. I have just been informed that there is a gas leak in the building. Everyone exit in an orderly fashion. Do not stop to collect your belongings."

Addie heard the shuffle of feet, chairs toppling, people shouting as they hurried toward the door. The room went eerily quiet.

Until something beeped.

Addie's gaze went toward the sound. The camera in front of her. Her heart pounded wildly against her chest as the timer lit up: ten minutes.

And it began counting down.

CHAPTER 62

Alvarez couldn't believe what she was seeing. Straight ahead, students in elegant gowns and tuxedos were streaming out the glass doors of the Air and Space Museum and down the front steps. Alvarez broke into a sprint, shouting into her mouthpiece, but she got no response—until another screech sounded and the voice from earlier returned.

"It's a shame you don't know how to listen, Agent Alvarez," it said. *"You can't say you weren't warned. Now the president's daughter dies."*

"Wait, no!" Alvarez screamed. "I did listen. I don't know what's going on. Please, you can't hurt her! I'm begging you. Give me a minute to figure this out."

"Sorry, too late." The transmission cut out. Alvarez tried to switch channels, radio for help, but it was useless. She pulled out her cell phone. No signal. Her only hope now was that Devers had understood the message.

Alvarez ran to the doors of the museum as the students pushed through, scattering in every direction. She searched the crowd for a familiar burgundy dress, but couldn't find it. There was no sign of Addie Webster. Anywhere.

The final student limped through the door, face pale, barely able to stand. Alvarez immediately recognized him—Cheryl Fergusson's kid, Darrow. Addie's friend. He was breathing heavily, a visible gunshot wound to his right thigh. Alvarez grabbed him around the waist and helped lower him to the steps. She removed her jacket and pressed it to the wound. Darrow flinched.

"You're going to be okay," Alvarez said. "Doesn't look deep. We'll get you help. But right now I need to know, where is Addie? Have you seen her?"

"No," he said. "I was hoping she was with you. That she made it out. Before I warned them about the bomb..." He began to breathe heavily. "Oh my God, that means he has her. He must have her...."

"Who?" Alvarez asked.

"That guy, Michael," Darrow said. "The one who shot me...."

"Any idea where he might have taken her?" Alvarez said.

"I don't know, I'm sorry." Darrow put his face in his hands.

"It's okay," she said. "I'm going to find her."

Alvarez stood, racking her brain. This Michael guy could've taken Addie anywhere by now. They could be miles away. But ...the threat had been very specific. They were going to blow up the Cabot prom *and* Addie Webster. Alvarez's gut told her it was ninety-nine to one that Addie was still in that building. And right now, a gut feeling was all Alvarez had to go on.

There was no time to hang around hoping for backup. Alvarez turned and ran into the cavernous museum.

Addie's entire body shook as she yanked against the handcuffs. The timer on the camera read three minutes, fourteen seconds.

348

Her arms fell limp. It was hopeless. This was where she was going to die. She wondered if dying hurt. But the thought of her own pain wasn't nearly as horrible as the thought of the pain her death would cause the people around her. They'd suffered through losing her once; now they would lose her for good.

A shout down below made her jolt forward. Someone was screaming her name.

"Addie! Addie, where are you?"

Alvarez. Her voice echoed from somewhere in the room below. Addie struggled against her restraints again, twisting her head and trying to loosen the gag in her mouth, her will to live rising furiously back up. She couldn't surrender. She couldn't let him win. She took a deep breath and scanned the cockpit, looking for something—anything—she could use to free herself from her restraints, make some noise.

The agent's shouts grew closer. Desperate, Addie tried to shout back through the gag, but the sound came out garbled and faint. Alvarez's voice began to move farther away. Addie was losing her chance. She tried to make noise some other way, pounding her head against the controls in front of her and stomping her feet on the floor. Alvarez's voice continued to grow fainter. But as Addie stomped, she heard something else, something rattling by her foot.

She looked down, catching sight of something shiny and gold on the floor. Her heart leapt. Mikey. She knew he wouldn't just let her die. Not without giving her a fighting chance. Carefully, she slid the black pumps from her feet and extended her leg, straining to reach the thing on the floor. Her toes hit the edge, pushing it just slightly farther away. *Shit.* Addie drew her foot back and took a few measured breaths. She only had one shot at this. She couldn't mess up. She shifted in her seat and extended her leg again.

This time, her foot landed on top of the cool glass face. Addie slid it over until it was directly beneath her and, with the other foot, pressed her phone's panic button. Nothing happened. Addie squinted at the screen. No signal?

She looked at the camera's timer—one minute, twelve seconds. She frantically jammed the button again, holding it down the way Alvarez had showed her to sound an audible alarm. After five seconds, a high-pitched wail filled the air, loud enough that Addie's eardrums felt like they might pop. She jolted and the phone slid out from beneath her foot. She tried to get it back, but this time, it was too far out of reach.

Alvarez was just exiting the room when she heard the unmistakable screech of Addie's alarm. She stopped short and spun around, trying to pinpoint its location. But no sooner had she taken a step forward than the sound came to an abrupt halt.

"Addie?" Alvarez said.

No response.

Alvarez searched the room—there was still nothing in here, save for the empty tables, toppled chairs, and random jackets people had left behind in their rush to flee. Maybe it was coming from somewhere else?

"Addie?" Alvarez said again, louder this time. She held still, listening for any sort of response.

Just then, Alvarez heard a faint thumping. She tilted her head toward the noise. It was coming from the nose of the 747 that jutted out over the dance floor.

"Hold on!" Alvarez shouted. "I'm coming."

Alvarez raced up the steps, across the catwalk, into the cockpit, and stopped short. Straight ahead, Addie sat in the pilot's seat with her back to the door, hands cuffed behind her. She made a muffled noise. Alvarez hurried over and pulled the gag from her mouth. The girl gasped for air.

"Christina," she choked out. "There's a bomb. . . ."

"Don't worry," Alvarez said. "I'm gonna get you out of here." She fumbled for her handcuff key, realizing that in her haste she'd left it in the jacket she'd pressed onto Darrow's leg.

"Damn it," she said, fiddling with the cuffs. "I'm just going to have to see if I can get these off some other way. . . ."

"Don't bother," Addie said, head dropping in defeat. "I've already tried. It's too late."

Alvarez stopped and looked at the girl. Her face was streaked with tears and an angry bump had risen up on her forehead.

"There's no time," Addie said frantically. "It's a bomb." She nodded toward the camera. The timer now read fifty-one seconds. "You should get out of here or you're going to die, too."

"No way, Songbird," Alvarez said. "I'm not leaving you behind."

Alvarez reached over Addie's shoulder. Sweat beading on her forehead, she carefully lifted the camera.

"Any idea what kind of explosives are in here?" Alvarez asked. She considered racing outside the cockpit and chucking it as far away as possible—but only if she could be certain what she was dealing with. A dirty bomb could still kill them, even at a hundred feet away.

"No," Addie said. "I'm sorry."

The timer read thirty seconds.

In that case, Alvarez would have to defuse it. "Well, here goes nothing." She slid the camera's battery cover off, exposing a tangle of white and black wires beneath. She inspected their paths, trying to recall everything she'd learned in explosives class. She wiped her forehead with the back of her hand.

"Can you do it?" Addie said.

"I don't know," Alvarez answered. "They've rigged this with two sets of wires. One to disarm it. One to cause an immediate explosion. It's going to take me longer than twenty seconds to figure out which is which."

"Please," Addie cried. "Go. Just get out of here."

"I told you, I'm not going anywhere," Alvarez said. The timer ticked down to fifteen seconds. Alvarez started muttering quickly out loud. "White or black. White or black. White or black. Oh, the hell with it . . . black." She reached her fingers toward the wires.

"No!" Addie shouted suddenly. "White. It's white."

The timer ticked down to seven seconds. "You sure?"

"Yes!"

The timer ticked down to three seconds.

Two.

There was no more time to be indecisive. Alvarez held her breath and yanked the white wire loose.

The timer hit one.

And stopped.

Alvarez's arms fell to her sides. She glanced up at Addie, eyes wide.

"Chess," Addie explained. "White always goes first."

"Holy hell," Alvarez answered. "I don't even want to know." Every bit of anxiety that had been welling up for the last hour suddenly left Alvarez's body in an enormous, inappropriate laugh. She was still laughing and shaking, tears streaming down her face, when Devers ran to the cockpit door with a handful of other agents.

"Jesus, what's so funny, Big Al?" Devers said. "Still laughing about your damn Buckeyes joke?"

Alvarez regained her composure and wiped her face with the back of her hand. "I knew you'd figure it out eventually." The entire service was aware that Devers was a die-hard Ohio State basketball fan. And even Alvarez knew they had already been knocked out of the championship. "Now give me your handcuff key," she said, "so we can get the hell out of here."

CHAPTER 63

Darrow sat on a stretcher in the back of the ambulance, watching the museum through the open back doors. A bunch of Secret Service agents had just rushed in, right before the ambulance, fire trucks, and hazmat teams arrived. Darrow craned his neck past the medic dabbing antiseptic on his wound, attempting to see what was happening.

"Hold still there, buddy," the medic said as he applied a butterfly stitch to the gash on Darrow's thigh. "You're lucky. Didn't hit any major arteries. But you've lost some blood, and we need to take you to the hospital and get you checked out by a doctor."

"Uh-huh," Darrow mumbled.

Straight ahead, Darrow spotted Alvarez. She was walking down the steps, arm around Addie's waist, flanked by Secret Service agents on either side. Darrow wobbled to his feet.

"Hey, what do you think you're doing?" the medic said. "I just said, you need to go to the hospital."

Before the guy could stop him, Darrow hobbled to the street and toward the steps. Addie spotted him immediately.

"Dare!" She broke free of Alvarez's arm and moved unsteadily down the stairs. "I was so afraid you were . . ." she began, stopping short and looking down at her hands.

"Nah. I'm not that easy to get rid of," Darrow answered. "I thought you'd have realized that by now."

Addie glanced back up at him from beneath her long lashes, a sad laugh catching in her throat. "I don't want to get rid of you," she said. "Ever."

"Good," he said.

"But listen, Dare," Addie whispered, glancing once back at Alvarez, who was a few steps away, watching. "You have to stay away from me. My life is over. He has Shi. It's too late to stop him. It doesn't matter that I'm the president's daughter. They're going to arrest me once they figure it . . ."

Darrow put a finger to her lips and the rest of her words died away. "No one's going to arrest you," he said gently. He reached into his pocket and pulled something out, pressing it into Addie's palm and closing her hand around it.

Addie stood there dumbfounded for a moment, then uncurled her fingers and glanced down. No red dot. She began to speak, but her voice caught in her throat. So Darrow did the only thing that felt right—he wrapped his arms around her, folding her into an embrace. He wouldn't let her go. Not this time. Not ever.

The moment he'd waited years for had come. His do-over.

One last chance to make his final move.

CHAPTER 64

The plane raced down the runway and, with a jolt, lifted into the night sky. They had escaped just as the APB had gone out for the immediate arrests of Karl and Michael Erlander. Fear gripped Michael's chest. At the same time, a small wave of relief washed over him. If he was a wanted man, that meant she was still alive. The bomb hadn't detonated. And Michael hadn't killed his best friend.

"Where are we going?" Michael said as he opened his computer and began loading Shi.

"Somewhere safe," his father said. "To a place whose government values the information we have at our fingertips. The president is going to regret not taking our threats seriously. If he thinks his daughter is all that matters, he needs to think again."

Michael nodded, easily logging on to the White House network. Father had created a new opening for them days earlier, just in case she had second thoughts and closed the hole she'd created. A few more keystrokes, and Shi was up and running.

But as the plane banked left and the D.C. skyline receded in the distance, Michael felt like the entire world was falling out from beneath him. His long fingers trembled as he typed. He stared at the screen, terrified to open his mouth and tell Father what he was seeing.

"What is it, son?" Karl asked.

Michael turned his dark blue eyes to the man across the table, then back to his computer, watching as Shi wormed its way through the White House network—fixing every flaw it found. How? *How?* In a rush of horror and rage, he realized: somehow in the scuffle with that boy, Michael must have grabbed the wrong program. Feeling light-headed with terror, he spoke.

"I think we have a problem, Father."

A cold silence filled the cabin. Karl unhitched his seat belt and positioned himself behind Michael, leaning over his shoulder. The warm breath on Michael's neck felt like a hand, squeezing the life right out of him. He didn't dare move.

"I see," Karl said, taking in the display on the screen. "That is unfortunate."

Michael tried to remain calm, but every nerve ending in his body was firing at once. Sweat beaded off his forehead. His tongue felt like sandpaper on the roof of his mouth. He didn't know how Father would punish him, but he knew it would be harsh. For a moment, he wished for the sting of the belt. At least pain could be managed. Pain was finite, with a beginning and an end. Michael knew whatever Father did to him now would not be. And he was completely and utterly alone, in this tin can hurtling through the sky, with no place to hide.

Karl sat back down in silence. He was still in the tattered clothing of a vagrant—torn jeans, ill-fitting T-shirt, grungy pea-green overcoat—that he'd been wearing on the Mall tonight.

His hair was wild and disheveled. Michael shuddered as his father reached into the pocket of his jacket and pulled out his phone, eyes narrowed into slits, not saying a word as he typed out a message.

Addie sat in the back of the ambulance, head resting on Darrow's shoulder. His white shirt was damp from the tears that wouldn't stop coming. She had spent so long telling herself she needed no one, and it felt good—terrifying, but good—to let Darrow hold her like this. To let herself just be human. She still couldn't believe Darrow had gotten the program away from Michael. As soon as she got home she would destroy it, make sure it could never be a threat to anyone again.

She heard the sound of sirens growing louder. Out of the corner of her eye, she could see the president's motorcade approaching at full speed. Reflexively, her entire body stiffened. Darrow stroked her hair.

"It's okay, Ad," he whispered. "It's just your mom and dad. It's over. They're here to take you home."

Addie wanted to believe him. She wanted so badly to believe that this was the end. That the good always outweighed the bad; evil never won. But Addie knew better. Even before she'd been taken—even when she was just a child, sitting in the playroom knee-to-knee with Darrow, a Connect Four grid perched between them—Addie had already understood one simple fact. The game was never over.

There was always another move.

At least now, she had something she thought she'd lost forever: hope. A deep, long-forgotten reserve of hope had inexplicably welled up in her chest. Hope that she *did* have a future—imperfect and shattered, but still hers for the taking.

The motorcade screeched to a halt at the base of the museum steps. Addie heard car doors opening and slamming shut, followed by the shouts of her parents calling her name. She knew she should go. But she stayed right where she was, letting herself enjoy the warmth of Darrow's embrace for just one moment longer. Just for tonight, she'd let herself believe in fairy-tale endings.

In the corner of the ambulance, hidden beneath Addie's seat, the screen on her phone lit up. A message flashed across, lasting exactly five seconds before burning out and disappearing again:

You have been warned.